Pieces
of **ME**

CARRIE ANN
NEW YORK TIMES BESTSELLING AUTHOR
RYAN

PIECES OF ME
SPECIAL EDITION

THE WILDER BROTHERS

CARRIE ANN RYAN

Pieces of Me

A Wilder Brothers Romance

By: Carrie Ann Ryan

© 2024 Carrie Ann Ryan

Cover Art by Sweet N Spicy Designs

All content warnings are listed on the book page for this book on my website.

PRAISE FOR CARRIE ANN RYAN

"Count on Carrie Ann Ryan for emotional, sexy, character driven stories that capture your heart!" – Carly Phillips, NY Times bestselling author

"Carrie Ann Ryan's romances are my newest addiction! The emotion in her books captures me from the very beginning. The hope and healing hold me close until the end. These love stories will simply sweep you away." ~ NYT Bestselling Author Deveny Perry

"Carrie Ann Ryan writes the perfect balance of sweet and heat ensuring every story feeds the soul." - Audrey Carlan, #1 New York Times Bestselling Author

"Carrie Ann Ryan never fails to draw readers in with passion, raw sensuality, and characters that pop off the page. Any book by Carrie Ann is an absolute treat." – New York Times Bestselling Author J. Kenner

"Carrie Ann Ryan knows how to pull your heartstrings and make your pulse pound! Her wonderful Redwood Pack series will draw you in and keep you reading long into the night. I can't wait to see what comes next with the new generation, the Talons. Keep them coming, Carrie Ann!" –Lara Adrian, New York Times bestselling author of CRAVE THE NIGHT

"With snarky humor, sizzling love scenes, and brilliant, imaginative worldbuilding, The Dante's Circle series reads as if Carrie Ann Ryan peeked at my personal wish list!" – NYT Bestselling Author, Larissa Ione

"Carrie Ann Ryan writes sexy shifters in a world full of passionate happily-ever-afters." – *New York Times* Bestselling Author Vivian Arend

"Carrie Ann's books are sexy with characters you can't help but love from page one. They are heat and heart blended to perfection." *New York Times* Bestselling Author Jayne Rylon

Carrie Ann Ryan's books are wickedly funny and deliciously hot, with plenty of twists to keep you guessing. They'll keep you up all night!" USA Today Bestselling Author Cari Quinn

"Once again, Carrie Ann Ryan knocks the Dante's Circle series out of the park. The queen of hot, sexy, enthralling paranormal romance, Carrie Ann is an author not to miss!" *New York Times* bestselling Author Marie Harte

PIECES OF ME

Gabriel Wilder.

Rock God.

Voice of an angel.

And in love with his best friend's sister.

Resisting Briar Ashford has been one of the hardest things he's ever done.

Until the one night he breaks his promise.

Only when tragedy strikes, forgiveness slips through his fingers.

Briar Ashford never let herself fall for her brother's best friend.

Until the night she did.

She wanted to live in the shadows, writing the songs for the stars who shined the brightest—not finding a way to co-parent with the man who refuses to pick up his guitar again.

The world is waiting for Gabriel Wilder to rise from the ashes. Only, first, he'll have to figure out if he's ready to finally let himself love the one woman who never knew had a claim to his heart all along.

Pieces of Me is a rockstar, best friend's little sister, accidental pregnancy romance in the Wilder Brothers series featuring Gabriel and Briar. Each one can be read as a complete standalone. A HEA is guaranteed!

DEDICATION

For the one who made me smile.
I couldn't have done this without you.

CHAPTER ONE
GABRIEL

The crowd chanted our names, their voices reverberating throughout the stadium. I closed my eyes as their shouts washed over me, and I let myself sway to the beat of the drums—a slight tempo used to invigorate the audience between songs. The guitar in my hands sang, and I strummed a few chords just to hear the people roar.

"Let me hear you scream!" Mal shouted, and the crowd answered in kind. "What should we play next?" I turned to see my best friend at his kit, sticks in hand as he played a quick beat, sweat pouring off his body.

We already knew what we would play next, the set list ingrained in our bodies, but people yelled their favorites—songs we had already played, songs we would never play, songs they wanted us to play with guests—yet we all took it in.

I never wanted this to become rote. Even as the whiskey in my system settled my nerves, everything felt new and wild. *This* is where we were supposed to be. This band. This group of people. Nothing would ever feel like this again.

"What do you say, Gabriel? Are you ready to be wicked or a good little angel?"

I flipped my best friend off, and the crowd shrieked, laughter and cheers echoing in my ears. "Well..." I said after a moment, my deep voice echoing through the mic. The crowd went impossibly louder. "What do you think, Joshua?" I asked our second guitarist and my backup singer.

Joshua pushed his shoulder-length, blond hair back from his face, sweat glistening on his brow, and shrugged. "You are the angel *and* the sinner. You choose."

"He'll never choose," Rocky added, her deep voice smooth as whiskey.

"Oh, just choose already," David snapped from the keyboards, though there was only humor in his voice.

"Well, if you want to play, David, I better pick a song you actually have something to do in." I winked as I said it, and he flipped me off, the crowd roaring again.

We didn't always need keyboards with our songs, but David filled in everywhere, a jack of all trades, and our oldest member of Wilder—the band I had begun with Mal when we'd been teenagers. Now Wilder was out on a fucking *world* tour.

It did not feel like real life.

"What about this?" I asked and strummed the first few notes of our biggest hit.

The crowd went wild, and Joshua started the second set of notes, walking slowly around the front of the stage, getting in the groove. Rocky added the bass, Mal slowly adding the drums, while David began a quick, soft melody that would grind down into the rock that we craved.

"Rain falls down and washes away," I sang as we began, "Rain On Me", each of us having our own parts to play to make it a whole.

This had started off as my dream, a dream I had never thought could truly happen, and the band held my name.

But right now, I was one of *them*—a music lover—in the stands, on the floor, in the band.

I let myself get lost in the music, in the shouts, and played to my heart's content. This was my drug of choice, sliding into my veins with purpose and power. The whiskey, now long gone from my system, sweated out through my pores as I gave everything to this song and then the next.

And by the time we were done, my shirt had been thrown out into the crowd, the sweaty mess having been caught by a fan who grinned and cried in delight.

The other band members' shirts had joined in, but Rocky kept hers, providing an obscene gesture when a couple of guys pouted that they didn't get one and wanted to see her tits anyway. Considering Rocky's wife could probably kick their asses, I wasn't quite sure why they even tried after all these years.

As we ended our final notes and said our goodbyes, we rushed off the stage. Our people sprung into action, helping us take our instruments, handing over waters, a drink or two in some cases, and a cigarette in David's. I was still riding the high, needing to breathe, and needing to do anything but think.

"Gabriel! You were amazing," a high-pitched voice shouted at me. I looked over to see three women with tiny skirts and even tinier tops practically push through security to get to me.

They had backstage passes looped around their necks, so they were allowed to be back here, but Frank, our current security guard at this venue, didn't look pleased.

"Don't worry, Frank, I've got this," I said with a grin before I slammed back the rest of my water.

The girls giggled and moved forward, each of them wrapping themselves around me. So it was just the four of us standing there when Mal came up beside me.

"Look at you, you selfish prick," my best friend said with a wink, and one of the girls left me to hold on to him.

She looked up at him with wide eyes and a pouty mouth. "It's okay, there's totally enough of us to go around."

I met Mal's gaze and figured maybe we had enough time to indulge. Then again, we had to be out soon in order to make it to our next show.

We were finishing up the U.S. leg of our tour for our most recent album, even breaking attendance records at some venues. We would never be able to break certain records though, like the ones set forth by my cousin-in-law, Lark.

But she was in a whole other realm. However, Lark was settled down and happily married off to my cousin, and I was living the single life.

Honestly, women, booze, and anything that I wanted? It wasn't too bad, considering that my brothers gave me shit for leaning into the slut boy life.

But damn it, why the fuck not?

David cleared his throat. "Boys, we need to be on the bus in ten. Unless you're bringing them with you, you've got to say goodbye."

"We can go with you," the blonde said quickly, and the brunette and redhead both agreed.

I held back a wince, knowing that David had just been joking, but now we had to get out of this situation. As much as my dick was going to be disappointed, I had other priorities.

That must have been growth, right? Not being late for my bus, so I didn't disappoint people, meaning I had to not get laid when I wanted.

Honestly, it was leaps and bounds of personal growth.

"I'm sorry ladies, but maybe next time we visit town?" I asked, as Mal already had one of the girls in his arms, his mouth busy. I rolled my eyes and looked at the two others. "But thank you for coming to the show. I hope you had a good time."

"Do you want our numbers? That way you can get ahold of us. Here, why don't you give me your phone and I'll add mine." The brunette narrowed her eyes at me, and I saw a calculating gaze there. I didn't know why she thought she needed that cunning look. And there was no way in hell I was giving away my number. I wasn't even drunk yet to be that careless.

"Why don't you leave it with Frank here? I've got to take this asshole back to the bus. We have another gig coming up. We sold out Toronto."

"And you're doing amazing. We are so proud of you," the blonde said earnestly.

I smiled at her, since she seemed like she meant it. I bumped Mal's arm. "Come on bro, we're going to be late."

"Call me," the redhead purred, and Mal wiped the lipstick off his lips, practically staggering at my side.

"Seriously?" Rocky said as she came into step with us. "Could you be any more cliche?"

"We have a girl in the band. I don't really think *that's* too cliché," I tease, wrapping my arm around her shoulders. A few paparazzi snapped photos, and I knew there'd be a new photo of the three of us walking together, Rocky in between us. There was a contingent of our fans—and some that hated us—that thought Rocky slept her way to get into our band, and we probably traded her around. While I wanted to kick ass for that, Rocky didn't care. After all, she was married to an Olympic gold medalist and world champion soccer player. And we all knew the truth.

I, however, was tired of it.

I nearly stumbled at that, wondering why I would think those words. I couldn't be tired of this. I loved this part of my job.

I thought back to the last time I'd been at my cousins' retreat in Texas, when I had had too much whiskey, and tried to drown myself in my sorrows.

Why the hell had I had been so self-absorbed?

I had women, alcohol, anything that I wanted. Fame, awards, glory. I got to go on stage with some of my best friends. There was nothing in the world that I couldn't get with a snap of my fingers. There was no reason that I had to be so fucking melancholy and in my feelings like I had been that day. It had been the drink talking, and the fact that my brothers had been moving on without me.

I was just thinking too damn hard. There was nothing wrong with what I had. I had everything that I could want.

"Hey, is that Lacey?" Mal asked, and I frowned over at him as we made our way to the buses.

"Yes, what of it?" I asked.

"I don't know, maybe I'll go to her tour bus, see what's what."

I met Rocky's gaze, and she glared at me.

Apparently, it was my turn to take care of the horn dog. I might be called a slut boy in the press, but Mal was twice as bad as me.

"She's the bassist for our opening act. You sleep with her and you're going to fuck things up."

"I am not. I don't fuck things up. She'll know the deal. She's in the business."

I squeezed Mal's shoulder and shook my head.

"You're going to ruin the tour."

"What tour?" Mal said with a roll of his eyes. "They're not coming with us to Europe. It won't screw anything up."

"Mal," Rocky grumbled, but Mal ignored us and headed over to Lacey.

The woman with a black mohawk and nose piercings grinned up at him, and he threw his arm around her shoulder.

"Well, hell," I mumbled.

"It'll be fine. He's totally not going to ruin everything."

I snorted at Rocky's oh-so-convincing tone. "Why don't I believe you?"

"Because it's a total lie, but we're used to it. I'm going to head to the dressing room here real quick to change. I hate getting changed on the bus."

"Okay, I'll see you there. Don't be late."

"We've got time. I just pulled you early so you didn't make another mistake."

I rolled my eyes, and she blew me a kiss, another photographer taking a shot. I ignored him, knowing there would be another photo all over the blogs.

Social media was amazing, wasn't it? *I loved social media.*

I stomped up the tour bus steps, realizing I was the first one there. David was on his own bus because he traveled with his wife and kids. The former drug user and man who used to play drunk more often than not was now a family man.

I was a little surprised that Joshua wasn't here yet, but he was probably making time with one of the girls he had met backstage. Surprisingly, I had been the first one to walk away. That was very unlike me, which meant I probably needed a drink.

I opened the small fridge that we had on board the bus and pulled out a beer. I quickly uncapped it and drank a big gulp before realizing that I wasn't alone.

I turned to see familiar coppery-red hair and froze.

Because that hair was not Mal's, no, that hair was his sister's.

Briar.

"I didn't know you were in town," I said softly, shocked that my voice didn't growl. It usually did when she was around.

She whirled on me and nearly fell—only at the last minute having reached out to grip one of the bunk beds. "You scared me. I didn't realize you were behind me."

"It's not like I was quiet."

I realized then that she had pulled out her headphones right before she'd spoken, and I winced. "Seriously, I didn't realize you were here. At the concert or in town."

"Mal wanted me to ride with you guys to the next

stop. He said it's because I'm not going to see him for a while."

I couldn't help the frown on my face at Mal's idea considering the man wasn't even here and had clearly forgotten his sister. "That sucks." She glared at me and I continued. "He's probably off with Lacey. So you're not going to ride with him anyway. That is, unless he's quicker than he usually is, and then he'll be on the bus in time."

The look of disgust on Briar's face would've been comical if it wasn't for the fact that my dick was once again pressing dangerously into my zipper.

It was always like that with Briar. However, this was my best friend's little sister. And there was no way that I was going to let my dick have any say. Despite the fact that it had before.

Briar finally let out a long breath before pushing her hand through that mane of hair of hers. "Oh. Well, that's just like him. Telling me to be here and then not showing up." She rolled her eyes, but then she fell silent, and the awkwardness settled in.

I was *never* awkward with people. And I hated the fact that I was awkward with Briar. But there was a reason for that. A big reason that we were never going to talk about.

"So, are we going to talk about it?" she asked, and I

cursed myself for even putting that out into the universe.

"We were drunk. We were acting on fun feelings. I was surprised I could even get it up at the time. Whiskey dick and all that," I blurted, wondering why the hell I was rambling about my dick.

We both wrote songs for a living, with Briar working behind the scenes for other artists. She'd even helped my cousin-in-law when Lark wanted help with some of her album tracks. Briar had worked on a few songs for our album, though none of them were singles as of yet.

There were no words.

"We really don't need to talk about it."

She raised a single brow, looking sexy as hell. There was seriously something wrong with me. "Maybe we do need to talk about it because it happened. However, it was a mistake. We both knew that. We were drunk, but we gave consent. And it was a mistake."

"Fine." I ran my hand over my face, annoyed at this conversation. Annoyed that I'd even thought with my dick once again and screwed everything up.

I didn't know Briar well. She didn't travel with us often, and Mal was one of seven kids. So it wasn't as if I really got to know all the Ashfords incredibly well. "Your brother's my best friend. We don't even need to go into further detail."

"Fine. As long as things go back to normal."

"Normal is all I want. We'll never talk about it again."

"Talk about what again?" Mal asked from behind me, and I whirled around, not having heard him. The sound acoustics in this tour bus were way too fuckin' weird today, apparently.

"Oh. You're back. You're done with Lacey quickly?"

He frowned, glaring between the both of us. "I forgot my bag. I'm heading back over, though I feel like a shit since Briar is here, and I clearly didn't remember. But Gabriel? What the hell, man?"

"What do you mean?"

He continued studying us before dropping the bag out of his hand and narrowing his eyes even further. "Are you fucking kidding me?" he finally snapped.

"It's not what you think," I said, holding up my hands, knowing that was the worst possible thing I could have said or done.

"Mal—" Briar began, but then I didn't move fast enough.

After all, Briar had distracted me.

At least that was the excuse I was going to give as my head slammed into the side of the bunk bed; my best friend's fist meeting my face.

"You slept with my sister?!"

And because he had a right to be angry, I let the

second punch hit my jaw, even as Briar screamed. I deserved the pain, though.

They called me the voice of an angel, but I think it's more like the voice of sin of a fallen angel.

Everything that I did these days just made me fall harder from grace.

And I didn't even want to get back up.

CHAPTER TWO
BRIAR

"Stop it. Both of you. I am not a prize. Stop fighting!" I shouted. I tried to move forward, but Mal knocked into me as he pushed his way back to Gabriel. I staggered back before catching myself.

I couldn't believe the two of them were doing this, and yet I could. Because of course best friends were going to freaking fight like this without thinking. Only it wasn't exactly that, was it? No, Gabriel hadn't hit back. Instead, he had taken two punches to the face, one to his cheekbone, the other to his jaw, and stood there, letting it happen.

Men. They were ridiculous. Stupid cavemen who didn't understand that I made my own choices. Of course, the fact that Gabriel had shouted that it wasn't what he thought, made me want to scream. Of course, it was exactly what he thought.

Damn it. I was already tired of this. "Mal. Get ahold of yourself."

"Back the fuck off, Briar. This is between me and him." And then Mal did the one thing he had never done, and shoved me out of the way. Because I had been leaning forward, I was off balance already, and fell back, hitting my head on the top of the bottom bunk.

"Okay, fuck that," Gabriel growled and stood between us.

Apparently, me nearly knocking myself out was the only thing that was going to get Gabriel out of whatever haze he was just in. I wasn't quite sure what I felt about that. Honestly, I was never sure how I felt about Gabriel Wilder. I'd spent most of the past few years *not* thinking about him in particular.

"Don't you fucking put your hands on her. You can hit me all you want, and I'll take it. Because I did the one thing that you're not supposed to do. I'm sorry. But you do not put your hands on your sister. Do you understand me, bro?" Gabriel snapped, his voice dangerously low.

I stood up, rubbing the back of my head, as Mal met my gaze. All anger washed out of him, and he shook his head. "I didn't mean to hurt you. Are you okay, Bug?"

I narrowed my gaze at him, because Mal was

younger than me but always acted as if he were older—just like all of my brothers. Whenever we were out of the house, they did their best to be their overprotective selves. There was no posturing when it came to actually being in our childhood home. Not that I was going to think about that too hard right now.

"I'm fine, Mal. Don't call me Bug."

"I'm going to call you Bug if I feel like it. Did he hurt you? You know. Before."

Gabriel muttered something under his breath and I glared at my brother, even as mortification settled in. "Are you kidding me? Of course he didn't hurt me. And you don't even know what went on. This has nothing to do with you. Gabriel and I were just having a chat, and then we were going to go on our merry way. You only have me for one more tour stop before I have to head out. You're leaving the country for a while and I won't see you. I wanted to spend some time with you. But I'm not going to if you're just going to yell at me."

"I'm not yelling at you." He turned away from me as if I didn't matter and glared at his best friend. "I'm mad at you."

Gabriel raised his bruising chin. "You should be. I fucked up."

"Did you take advantage of her?" Mal asked slowly, and I moved forward, putting my hand on Gabriel's arm to try to get him out of the way. That was the wrong thing to do though, because Gabriel stiffened, and Mal's cheeks reddened.

"You're going to want to stop touching him, sister of mine."

This had gone on long enough. "Mal. We're all friends here. You don't need to act like this."

He breathed through his nose, and then glowered at Gabriel while he spoke to me. "You think I'm an asshole when it comes to women? He's ten times worse. He's the slut of this band. Do you know how many women he's been with? Hell, he practically had a foursome on the way to the bus. It's what *we do*, Briar. You know that better than anyone, being in this business. Why the fuck would you sleep with him?"

"I'm so glad that you think so highly of me," Gabriel said, and I wasn't sure that Mal heard the hurt in his tone. But I did.

I also didn't like hearing about Gabriel or Mal's past —or *current*—exploits. "Mal. It's none of your business. I can sleep with whoever I'd like. Hell, I could have a foursome on this bus with your roadies, and it's none of your business. So do not fight with your best friend over this. Do not ruin everything."

Because I was afraid I had been the one to do that.

Mal just scowled at Gabriel before stepping forward, nose to nose. I sucked in my breath, afraid of what was going to happen next, before Mal's shoulders fell.

"Fuck you, man. You had one job. Don't fuck with my sisters. But you couldn't even do that. I can't be here. I'm going to go to the other bus."

"Mal. Don't leave," I pleaded, but he ignored me, moving off the bus as he turned his back to us. Gabriel followed, and I didn't hear what was said, but somebody shouted, and then Gabriel moved back, rubbing his hands over his face. He winced as he did so, and I immediately went to the small kitchen area to get ice.

"Your poor face."

"It's fine. I'll heal. It's not the first time I've taken a punch in the face." He flinched as he touched his jaw, and then moved it around. "It hurts like a bitch, though. Don't think he knocked any teeth loose at least."

"I can't believe he did that. Mal doesn't hit. He doesn't get in fights. Especially not after..." I cut myself off, not wanting to get into *that* family trauma. I didn't know what Gabriel knew about our family, and I wasn't about to get into it now.

I moved forward, pushing at his very rock-hard chest so he would sit down. He did so, and I knew it was only because he let me. When I put ice on his face, he cursed again.

"That's cold."

"It's ice. It's doing its job. You have another show in

two nights and how many photographers waiting to see what happened? They're going to have questions."

"They'll make up something. They always do." He let out a deep breath. "I just hope he didn't fuck up his hands."

The bus started moving then, and I rocked forward. Gabriel reached out and gripped my hips. "Be careful. Don't have your sea legs?" he quipped, but there wasn't any humor in it.

I swallowed hard, aware that he was still touching me. I didn't think about Gabriel like that. I wouldn't let myself. We were friends of a sort. In other words, I was sometimes around, and we hung out when Mal wanted to. But I didn't know Gabriel. Other than one night when we had gone too far.

"Can you hold this?" I asked, my voice stiff, and he nodded, letting the ice settle on his cheek.

"I'm sure his hands are fine. He takes care of himself." We both knew that was a lie. Because Mal drank more than Gabriel, and I knew he had tried drugs a few times. But the band was clean in that sense. Especially after David had OD'd a few years before. But now he was a family man, and Wilder was as clean as possible. Yes, they drank, but they didn't do anything else.

At least I hoped to hell they didn't.

"I can't believe you just let him hit you."

"What was I supposed to do? I fucked his sister. I deserve to be hit."

I whirled on him, my chest tightening. "Seriously? That's what you're going to go with. He didn't even know until you're the one who blurted it out. For all he knew, we could have just been fighting. Like we always do."

"We don't always fight. I don't fucking talk to you."

I let the hurt wash away at that. There was no need to allow it to sting. "Fine. But you shouldn't have let him hit you. Should have fought back."

"And hit your brother? My best friend? I already did enough to him, thanks."

"There were two of us there, you know. And it shouldn't be a problem. I don't understand the territorial wars when it comes to brothers and best friends." Though I did. Because Gabriel was Mal's.

The one person that he had had as a constant over the years when everything had turned to shit. Because Mal had left home, left us all behind, and for good reasons. Shame coated me as guilt curdled in my stomach.

I started to pace even as the bus moved. "I'm sorry. I can't have him hate me. I can't believe I did this."

"Don't blame yourself. We were drunk."

I nodded, wondering why he was comforting me when he wasn't even taking care of himself.

I had wanted one night where I could just be someone else. So I drank and leaned into pretend a little too much, and I let go. I let go for the first time in my life, and now my brother hated me and couldn't even look at me. And I had just ruined Mal's best friendship.

It shouldn't matter that he was my brother's best friend. It shouldn't. But it did.

"You're Mal's. I get that. I shouldn't have poached."

I reeled on him, before stomping forward and moving the ice to his chin.

He shuddered. "Hey, are you trying to make it worse?"

"No, but you are. I'm not someone to claim."

"I didn't say you were."

"You sure as hell did. Especially with how you're acting. Why did you sleep with me?" I blurted.

He froze, eyes widening for a moment, before shrugging. "I don't know."

"Really? That's what you're going with? Because I was there? Would you have just stuck your dick in anything?"

"Fuck no. We both were into it. And we weren't that drunk," he mumbled, and he was right.

Because if we had been that drunk, we wouldn't have done anything. We would've just passed out, and I would've had so many more regrets in the morning.

But the alcohol had just been an excuse, and I wasn't ready to face that.

"It can't happen again."

"It was never going to, Briar."

Once again, I ignore the sting. "Good. Because Mal is one of the best things in my life. And I'm so stupid."

"Well, we can be stupid together."

I shook my head. "Oh no, we can't. We'll just go back to the way things were. He has to forgive us, right?"

He met my gaze, and I couldn't read it. Couldn't read those beautiful eyes of his. "He's going to forgive you. You didn't do anything wrong."

I didn't understand men at all. "If you did, then I did. There were two of us."

"I'll fix it. I'll figure it out. For the band, at least."

"That's not a good excuse. He's your best friend. I'm sorry."

Gabriel sighed, before standing up abruptly and letting out a deep breath. "Fuck!" he shouted, before punching the fake wall. It caved in, and he cursed again.

"Oh my God Gabriel. What the hell?"

He pulled his fist out of the wall, and stretched his hands, blood coating them. "Well hell. It looks like Mal's not the only one with a fucked-up hand."

"Why did you do that?"

He looked at me then, his eyes so bleak, but didn't

say anything. Instead of getting an answer, I got another ice pack out and put it over his hand.

"You're a mess." My chest tightened, tears stinging. "I'm sorry."

"No, I'm the sorry one. I just need to fix this. And I will. As soon as we see him."

I pressed my lips together and hoped that was the case. I hoped that I hadn't just broken a friendship, or worse, broken the band.

Though I wasn't quite sure that was in the right order.

I let out a breath, finally letting go of him. Because touching Gabriel Wilder was always a mistake.

I turned, deciding to go sit up front since nobody else had made it to this particular bus, when the sound of grinding metal hit my ears.

The bus lurched to the left, and then to the right, and then Gabriel's arm was around my waist, and someone was screaming. I didn't know if it was him, or me, but he covered my body with his as we slammed down to the ground, and everything shattered.

CHAPTER THREE
BRIAR

Ear-piercing shrieks vibrated in my ears as my eyes shot open, and I realized I was the one making that terrible noise. I closed my eyes again, the bright lights above me far too harsh. There was a beeping sound, people moving all around, but I couldn't hear anything. Not really. Nothing made sense.

I had been on the bus fighting with Gabriel...and then...what happened?

I finally cracked my eyes open. This time, the lights were not so bright. Or at least, the harshness was not as debilitating. I blinked, trying to get my vision into focus and saw the odd lowered ceiling of what seemed to be a hospital room.

I groaned, my throat sore, and I realized that yes, I was in the hospital. There were people moving about, and I swallowed hard, trying to get my bearings. Only my world titled off axis.

A nurse walked in wearing pink scrubs and a gentle expression as she went to my IV stand.

"What happened?" I croaked as tears slid down my face. My side hurt, as did my arm. Everything hurt.

"You're awake, Ms. Ashford. That's good. The doctor will be in here soon to go over everything. You just settle back, okay?"

Her soothing voice grated through the sheer panic. I didn't want to be told everything was *just fine*. I wanted to know what had happened. I needed to know. *My family* was on that bus.

But I couldn't think of anything to say. Instead, I just tried to fist my hands and let out a shocked gasp.

"You severely sprained your wrist, and you have a few bruises. And you have stitches on your forehead, but you were very lucky, Ms. Ashford. You just rest there. The team will have answers and more information soon. Keep your wrist the way it is, okay? We just need to ensure that you rest."

She left me then, saying she would be back with some ice chips or something. She might've said other things, but I couldn't track anything.

I looked down at my bandaged wrist, at the splint that shouldn't be there. It must have been a bad sprain since it felt as if someone had twisted it with their bare hands.

Then images slammed into me.

The bus. The bus had crashed.

But there were *multiple* buses. Gabriel, the bus driver, and I had been the only ones on ours. But there were others.

The band.

Mal.

I knew it was stupid. I knew that I should probably lie back down, but instead I tried to sit up. Nausea washed over me, but I had to get out of here. Had to get to another room to see my family. I needed my family.

I finally sat up, ignoring the pain in my wrist, and tried to piece together my unraveled thoughts to figure out how to unhook myself from this IV. I wasn't good with hospitals, and I had no idea what I was doing. Before I could dive into my pure anxiety, somebody filled the doorway.

At the sight of him, my heart lurched as it always did with him. And yet...this time, it was for a completely different reason. I wasn't the only one making stupid decisions.

Gabriel stood there, leaning on Joshua, who didn't have a scratch on him. But Gabriel? He had taken the brunt of it. He had covered me with his body and protected me, and now there was a brace on his leg, cuts and scrapes all over his body that had nothing to do with the fight, and he looked exhausted.

"Briar. Oh, thank God, Briar." His voice, his beautiful voice, broke, and that's when tears started to sting behind my eyes.

Because Gabriel never broke.

"I told you she was here. Sit down before they get me kicked out of this fucking hospital," Joshua grumbled as he forced Gabriel into a seat, and I realized that they were dragging an IV pole behind him.

Joshua met my gaze and shook his head. He was doing a decent job of looking put out and unbothered, but I saw the panic in his eyes. "I'm glad you're awake. I couldn't get this asshole to stay put. His brothers are on the way here, even though they had to catch a flight, and I'm in charge of keeping him steady."

I knew Joshua was rambling, because he always did when he was worried, and that scared me more than anything.

I let out a breath, trying to sound my most haughty since it always got a rise out of this Wilder. "Gabriel, you should be laying down."

"You're sitting up, and I bet you're not supposed to either," he said softly as he leaned forward before cursing under his breath. His hand went to his side, and he sucked in a deep breath. "Okay, maybe a cracked rib instead of a bruised one." He winced, breathing through his teeth.

"Gabriel," I said again, tears stinging. "Where are the others? The other buses?" I asked, tears now freely falling. I hadn't even realized that Gabriel had scooted his chair forward as he wiped tears from my cheeks. Joshua cursed and moved Gabriel back so he was sitting up, before Joshua wiped the rest of my tears.

They were taking care of me, just like they always did because they acted like my brothers, and yet I couldn't think straight.

"I don't have any answers," Joshua whispered. "The buses in the back were fine—the ones with most of the crew. David, Rocky, and I were safe on ours as well." He paused, his face going pale.

Dread slid over me like ice, and I started to shake.

"Where's Mal?" I asked, but Gabriel didn't say anything. Instead, he just looked at me, and there was nothing behind those eyes, just darkness. Just a blankness that spoke volumes.

I couldn't breathe.

A harried doctor with three nurses stormed into the room and began trying to force Gabriel into a wheelchair, but he held up his hand.

"I'm going to stay here until I know she's okay."

"You need to be in bed," I muttered before looking

at the doctor. "I just need to know about my brother. Mal Ashford."

The doctor moved forward and cleared his throat. "Briar Ashford?"

I blindly reached forward, trying to grab someone's hand. I only knew it was Gabriel's because I felt the scrapes on his knuckles.

"I regret to inform you..."

I didn't know what the man said next.

Joshua was on the ground, having fallen against the wall as his legs gave out, and Gabriel sat there, not saying anything.

But I was screaming again.

Screaming, and screaming.

And then there was nothing.

CHAPTER FOUR
GABRIEL

"In breaking news, the band Wilder is facing a tremendous loss. The world mourns what could have been and the lives of nine people. The music industry is in shock as we wait to hear what will happen to the band, the families of those lost, and those left behind. As Malcom Ashford is laid to rest today, the world has one question on their mind: Is this the end of Wilder?"

I turned off the TV, but not soon enough. Honestly, it didn't matter anyway. I could still hear the damn voices in my head. No matter the person speaking, they all said the same damn thing.

It had been four days since the accident. Four days since I had lost everything with a heartless word and a callous mistake.

I hadn't broken my leg, but I'd bruised it enough

and sprained my ankle that it was a near miss. Thankfully, I was able to wear a damn boot. If I could be thankful for anything. I had nearly lost my spleen because I had been an idiot walking to Briar's room as I had. I didn't regret it, though. The need to see Briar had taken over—just like it always did when it came to her —and I hadn't thought past that moment. I couldn't remember much of the accident other than the grinding sounds and me throwing myself over her. It was the least I could have done, but it wasn't enough. She had been hurt anyway.

I had four bruised ribs and two cracked ones, but they all felt the fucking same. My hands hurt like a bitch, and even if I wanted to pick up my guitar, it wasn't going to happen anytime soon. My body was one giant bruise, and yet, we were the lucky ones.

Six of our crew were dead. Crew members that had been with us since the beginning. Who had helped load and unload, who had made sure we knew where the hell we were going. Crews that always wrote the city and state on a piece of tape on the inside of the curtain, so we knew where the hell we were. Crew that made sure that we were stacked in drinks and food and condoms. Crews that made sure we weren't making the worst mistakes of our lives.

Our crew was dead.

And so was Lacey. Because she and her band—along with Mal—had been on the front bus.

The buses that had been in the back of the line with the rest of the crew and most of the band were fine. They had been able to stop in time.

We had been on the third bus. Our bus driver had a concussion, but thanks to his quick thinking and reactions, he'd been able to stop in time and in a way that the people behind us were safe. And our bus hadn't rolled or caught on fire. Instead, we had just crunched like an accordion.

But Briar had bled.

And I wore every ounce of my bruises and shame like I should.

It hadn't been just those two, though. The second bus had been our crew. Six of eight dead. Six people that I knew and cared about were dead.

A drunk driver had gone across the median and had caused a pile-up on the curve. And it had been dark, and the buses did what they could.

The authorities said the only one at fault was the drunk driver.

And they hadn't died. Instead, they had walked away with a broken arm, and hopefully a jail sentence.

But the first bus...I swallowed hard. The first bus had the opening act. The band who would have one more show with us before we knew they would hit it big.

It had crumpled up like a piece of paper, metal and jagged shards of glass everywhere.

Most of the band were broken and bruised, needing surgeries and rehabilitation, but they would one day walk away. Lacey wouldn't. The sweet bassist, who had always had a smile for us, was dead. She wouldn't be smiling anymore.

I tried to stand up, ignoring the pain in my leg as I limped over to the fridge to get a beer.

Mal was dead.

Mal was dead, and the last things I had said to him had been in anger. And he hadn't even been able to look at me before he had walked away.

I would never be able to fix that.

"Are you ready to go?" Brooks asked as I stood there, beer in hand. "You don't need a beer now. It's not going to go well with your meds. We have to head to the cemetery, Gabe."

I stared at my big brother, wondering why he of all people would go to a cemetery. He had lost his fucking wife, and yet was somehow still standing here and wasn't running for the hills like I thought he would be. Instead, he was going to stand by my side as I said goodbye to my best friend. Like I wasn't the problem in the first place. Because if Mal had been on our bus, he would've been fine. I ignored the part of me that whispered that Mal was going to be on that first bus no matter what. Because he had wanted to be with Lacey for the night. I ignored that because if we hadn't fought, maybe he would've stayed. He *should* have stayed.

And now here I was throwing Brooks to the wolves, forcing him to face death once again because I couldn't handle it on my own.

My other brothers had wanted to come, but I had shouted and screamed and said only one. Only one because I couldn't let them see me like this.

So it was Brooks that was here, the others at home with their wives.

Because they were moving on and having a life, and I was ruining everything.

"I don't need to go. They don't want me there."

"Why wouldn't they want you there, Gabriel? You weren't the drunk driver. You weren't driving the bus. You kept Briar alive. You know that, right? The doctors even said that with the way that you huddled over her, you kept her smaller frame from being crushed. You didn't do anything wrong, Gabe."

That was a damn lie. I had done *everything*.

"Let's just get this over with. I can't believe they're burying him here."

In Ashford Creek—the home he had grown up in. The home Briar had grown up in.

My brothers and I had moved around often when we'd been kids, maybe not as much as our cousins who were former military, but we had moved around enough. Now the rest of them were all settled in South Texas, finding a home. While I drifted from place to place, finding my own way. I didn't have a house, just storage units, since I'd sold my last place when the security had been an issue.

Living the life of a rock star.

Well, what kind of living was this now?

Now we were here at a place that Mal had hated. Hated as much as he loved. All of Mal's family was here, at least the ones he had left, and I wasn't sure I could face them.

Brooks moved forward, pulling me from my thoughts. "You need to go. *Believe me.* I didn't want to be there the day I said goodbye to Amara. But I did. I said goodbye to her, because I *needed* to. And it was the second worst day of my life. So you're going to do it too. Even though you hate it, you're going to do it."

"And if I don't?" I asked, knowing I was an idiot.

"Then I'll drag you. And it'll be more of a media circus than it already is."

I rubbed my hand over my face and cursed as I realized that I was still bruised and cut up. "There's not much we can do about that. The vultures are always around."

"So are fans. They all want to pay their respects, but I don't know if it's helping."

"Nothing will help, Brooks. You know that."

My big brother sighed, and I could feel the history of that breath over me. "Then let's go. We'll have this funeral, and then we'll do the next."

I nodded, knowing that Lacey's was next, and then we'd have to figure out what came after. The crew's all had been yesterday, having decided to do a service as one before they were buried with their families. So we had said our goodbyes, and I had stood in the back, wondering what I was supposed to say.

And now we were here in Ashford, and I didn't know what else I was supposed to do.

I set down the beer, grabbed my cane, and followed Brooks. Every step felt as if my ribs were crackling like rice on a flame, but I ignored it. At least it was something I could feel.

Brooks drove us to the cemetery since our main security guy, Jeff, would be driving alongside us. I took a seat at the edge near David, Joshua, and Rocky. They were there with their families, tears falling freely down their cheeks. And I had nothing left.

Words were spoken, Joshua even going up to sing, but I didn't.

There was no need for me to play. Not when I didn't have a song in me.

I listened as Mal's family took their turns to speak. Mal's eldest brother, Callum, spoke first, his voice gruff and face pale. Mal's twin, Bodhi spoke next, and once again it was a kick in the gut to see Mal's face on the other man's body. The two had been nothing alike, and yet it felt like Mal stood there, speaking over the casket in front of him. Teagan went next, then the other two brothers. Briar was the only one who didn't speak, and I didn't blame her.

The Ashfords spoke of the boy he had been, and some of the man he had become. But they didn't know him like the band had. They hadn't been on the road with him these past years like we had. Briar knew, though. She'd been there all along by our sides. Making music and becoming an honorary Wilder. And the last words I had said to my best friend were a fight.

As the service ended, my best friend lowering into the ground, I finally stood back up and watched the dirt pile over him.

I had broken my best friend's heart by doing things I had promised I would never do.

And I couldn't fix it.

Gazes bored into me, and I was afraid it was the paparazzi, the media, fans, but no, as I looked up glaring, Briar took a step back, her eyes wide and her face so pale. I stood there and looked at her, and I couldn't feel a damn thing.

She turned and settled into Callum's side, and they took her away.

I wasn't sure what I was supposed to say to her anyway. What did I say to the woman I tried not to want? What did I say to the woman I told myself I'd never fall for? What did I say to the woman I'd lied to?

Because I remembered that night.

Every touch.

Every feeling.

And the falling that I'd waited until it was nearly too late?

For a man who wrote words for a living, I had nothing left to say.

"Come home," Brooks whispered, breaking me out of my spiraling thoughts.

"I don't have a home. *He* was my home." I pointed to the hole in the ground, my voice finally breaking.

But I would not shatter here. Not with people watching. Not when my face would be splashed over the media, as if they cared.

"*We* are your home. Come home Gabriel."

I swallowed hard, not having an answer. I didn't want to go with my family. I didn't want them to see what I had become.

They called me the voice of an angel, but now my best friend was the one dancing in the stars with them. And I had done it. It was all me.

I gave one last look in Briar's direction, but she didn't see me, didn't look back. So I turned to Brooks.

"Fine. Home."

But it wasn't home. It would never be. I didn't have one. Didn't deserve one. So I left with my brother, heading to the Wilder Retreat. And I left the cemetery. And I would leave the fame. Leave the band. And leave everything behind.

I shattered everything in my touch, leaving the pieces behind.

I would never be able to find forgiveness. Not when the one person in the world who I needed to forgive me was gone. Buried and covered with dirt.

There was no need to look back. Because nobody would be searching for me.

And that's just how it needed to be.

CHAPTER FIVE
GABRIEL

My phone buzzed on the counter, the vibrations a steady beat that thrummed in my veins. I'd ignored it, just like I had been doing for the past seven and a half months. The phone continued to buzz across the counter, before finally falling off the edge, the curved casing around it keeping it from shattering. Honestly, I wouldn't mind if it chipped away into a thousand pieces. That meant I wouldn't have to deal with the constant ringing.

I could have turned it off. Could have hidden it somewhere so I would never have to see it again. But after I had turned off my phone and tossed it somewhere in the cabin for two days and ignored calls from my family, my brothers had kicked my ass.

And while I had ignored Ridge, Wyatt, and Brooks'

growls and worried looks, I couldn't ignore Ava and Aurora.

My two sisters-in-law had just stared at me, sad and disappointed looks on their faces, and so I had showered for the first time in a week and turned on my damn phone. But I only answered family.

I ignored the band, ignored my manager, ignored everyone else who tried to get through.

I was out of it. Out of the lifestyle, out of the grind. There was no music left in me. There was nothing.

I picked up a guitar every now and then, but only to see if I could. I hadn't tossed the damn thing, and I still remembered the feel of it. But that was it.

For the first month, I hadn't left my cabin. I had ignored family dinners, ignored the patient glances, the yelling, the shouting. I ignored my cousins lifting me out of my cabin and tossing me in a watering tank outside so they could hose me down. I ignored everything. Frozen inside. It was better not to feel. It was better just to let the Texas heat and San Antonio humidity leach into my skin. I ignored the countless mosquito bites because, of course, San Antonio had every single mosquito in the fucking world right now. I ignored the hot wind on my face, the giant storms that would pop in every once in a while with their thunder and lightning and harsh winds.

I ignored everything.

That is until my niece showed up one month into my self-forced captivity.

The Wilder Retreat and Winery had become my home—or at least my temporary seclusion. It lay on a piece of land that my cousins had bought when they had each gotten out of the military. For some reason the six Wilder brothers on the other side of the family tree had decided to join the military right outside of high school. They all succeeded in what they did, although I knew that they hadn't come back whole. But when they had gotten out, with only Eli reaching his twenty years to get full retirement benefits, they had come together as a unit.

They had lived all over the world for years and had wanted to be a family again. Only their sister, my cousin Eliza, lived outside of the resort. In fact, she lived up in Colorado with her family. But she came down often— even to see my sorry ass.

When my brothers had hit their own versions of rock bottom, they had decided to come and work with my cousins. Now everybody had bought into the resort and winery, and everybody had a job. A place. They hosted parties, weddings, and events. There was an actual winery and vineyard with vines on the other side of the property.

Wyatt had ended up building a bar and distillery right on the property, so they made vodka, too. Actual

Wilder Vodka to go with Wilder Wines. Everyone knew their place and thrived in it. There was a spa, two high-end restaurants, as well as the resort restaurant. And my sisters and cousins-in-law had all pitched in.

And I had just wanted to hide. Brooks had dragged me here because I had nowhere else to go. And he had thought it would help. But it didn't. Nothing helped.

There were countless guests on the property, since the main focus was the inn. And since two of my cousins had decided to marry celebrities, there was an entire security team on the grounds, with my brother Ridge running half of it.

I had known Lark for years. And even written a song with her and won a Grammy. And she had ended up marrying East, the grumpiest of my cousins—although, according to my niece, I was trying to take that spot.

Because Faith, Wyatt's daughter, had shown up at my cabin, her little fists on her slight hips, and had just glared at me.

She looked so much like her mother at that moment; it felt like a little Ava standing there, judging.

"Uncle Gabe."

I had blinked up at her, wondering what the hell I was supposed to say. I'd never been good with kids and I wasn't about to emotionally scar children. I hadn't sunk that far, had I? "You should go see your mom."

"No, Uncle Gabe, I'm here to see *you*."

I didn't know when she had started calling me Uncle Gabe. Most people called me Gabriel because that's what I went by. They only called me Gabe when they were getting a point across—like she was doing, apparently. And technically, I was her step uncle. But I wasn't going to tell her that.

"Seriously, Faith, thank you for checking on me. I'm fine."

"You stink, and you're not supposed to stink. Mom makes me shower every day, sometimes twice, if I play in mud."

"I'll shower when you leave," I had lied.

"I don't believe you." She scrunched her little face and that dark part of my soul lit up just a little bit. I immediately doused it.

"I don't need you to believe me." I had growled at the eight-year-old in front of me. And then I'd paused, wondering if she was nine yet. Had I missed a birthday? Probably. Well, damn. I hadn't been sure if I had missed it while on tour, or now. But hell, I had probably missed *all* the birthdays. Many of my cousins had kids, although Faith was the eldest of them all.

I hadn't even known if some of my cousins were having more kids at this point. I hadn't been paying attention, I hadn't been looking.

So a month into my forced jailing, Faith had glared at me, and then her eyes had gone glassy.

"Don't use tears. Tears aren't fair."

"I don't want to cry." She had stomped her tiny foot. "I'm not going to cry, but I need you to be okay. Because I love you. And I don't like to see you hurt."

I had swallowed hard and stared at pocket-sized Faith, knowing I wasn't going to hurt her heart. "Fine, I'll shower."

"And you'll work."

Ice had stabbed into me, a blade slicing my chest open wide.

"I can't, Faith. I can't."

"You can work with Daddy. Or with Uncle East. But you can't stay here. If I have to do homework, so do you."

My lips had twitched at that, but I had shaken my head. "You should go, Faith. I'm not good company."

"I know you're not good company. And you don't need to be. You're allowed to be in a bad mood. But you're not allowed to stink. Because stinky people are gross. And I don't love gross people."

I'd stared at the tears staining my niece's cheeks and felt as if I was in the crash all over again. I was allowed to hurt myself. I was allowed to hide away from the world. But I was not allowed to hurt Faith. At least I could get that one thing through the drunken haze.

"Okay. For you, Faith. Okay."

She hadn't thrown her arms around me, hadn't

hugged me. In fact, the look of disgust on her face had been very much evident, but she had plodded away, chin held high, before Brooks had walked in, my cousin East at his side, and they had just shaken their heads.

I had held up my hands and forced myself into the shower.

That had begun my new life—working with my family. In the six or so months I'd been here, I'd played a few songs to myself, but mostly worked with my hands for them.

I twisted the pliers in my hand, considering how long I'd been hiding from the world at the Wilder Retreat. I was hiding from the world at the Wilder Retreat, and I was fine with that. More celebrity traumas and scandals had hit the news since then, and I wasn't top billing anymore. Yes, every once in a while, a news article would wonder where the mysterious Gabriel Wilder had gone, and if the band would ever come back. But I didn't care. I did my best to drown it all out.

"You're coming to dinner tonight," East said point-blank, interrupting my thought, as he handed over his spare toolbox.

He had given it to me, called it mine, but I wouldn't. That meant it would have to *be* mine, and I didn't want that.

I just wanted everything to stop hurting.

My best friend was dead. He wouldn't laugh again, wouldn't roll his eyes at me when I said something stupid. He wouldn't sit knee to knee with me as we both tried to come up with a lyric to fit the tone. I wouldn't have to tell him to stop jacking off in the corner because all he kept doing was playing a beat on his knees with his fingers.

I wouldn't wake up to the sound of him tapping his sticks against the top of his bunk while on the tour bus.

I wouldn't watch him smile at a group of women and witness their knees giving out, and all of them falling in love with him, if only for the evening.

I wouldn't have to hide my feelings for his sister like I always had.

I wouldn't watch my best friend give a thousand dollars to the roadies who helped us get out of a bind when the fans made their way in the back and we needed a distraction. I wouldn't stand beside him in a soup kitchen as both of us wore disguises so that we didn't look like ourselves. I wouldn't be able to hear him breaking down and complaining about his father or missing his mom. I wouldn't hear the stories of him growing up and all his siblings and friends from back home.

And I wouldn't be able to say I was sorry for breaking the code and doing the one thing I had promised I would never do—be with his sister.

I had forcibly not thought of Briar in these past months. Because thinking of Briar would make me think of my last conversation with my best friend.

I had given in to temptation and lost everything.

I didn't want to blame her, but sometimes it was easier than blaming myself. And that just made me even more of an asshole than I already was.

"Come on, we have to go work on the back pump. It was making a noise, according to Eli."

I shook my head and pushed myself completely out of my reverie, knowing that everybody was worried about me and I had to play along.

I nodded tightly but didn't say anything, instead following my cousin to his truck and hopping in. We put our tools behind us and made our way to the other side of the property. East was the so-called handyman of the whole company. He was so much more than that, considering he made sure that the place that housed countless employees and family members ran well. I wanted to think that I was closer to this cousin than I was to the others, mostly because he hadn't let me ignore the world, and he was married to someone I knew outside of our family.

But his wife, Lark, wasn't here, as she was on tour. East went with her often, but they also had times when they would be apart for his own job. He didn't need to work, but he did anyway because he was family and needed something of his own.

And out of everyone, East and Lark never asked how I was doing, or what I was going to do next. They just let me be, as much as I could be. We got to work, and I noticed the callouses on my hands changing. They were no longer just from the guitar, the strings' evidence that had worn their way onto my flesh.

Instead, I had scratches and cuts and little nicks from working with my hands. I had always been so careful with them. Making sure that I took care of them, and my voice, since they were my tools. And yet, I didn't care anymore. I didn't drink tea or do my vocal reps. I didn't take care of my hands the way I needed to. But it didn't matter. I wasn't going back.

It was funny, even thinking about my voice. There were so many documentaries these days about my childhood heroes and favorite artists of back in the day trying to find the voices that they lost over time. And watching them struggle to find their place in the world, to find that connection to who they were when they were doing the thing that they loved most, had terrified me. So I had done everything that I could to make sure that I took care of myself.

We worked in silence, sweat pouring down my back. I knew that East would be able to smell the liquor seeping from my pores, but he didn't say anything. He just let me be.

By the time we were done, the sun was still high in the air since the sun set so late these days, but with a grunt, my cousin glared at me, and I knew that was him asking me if I was going to go to the family dinner I was forced to go to tonight. I grunted back and went to shower.

I never showed up with dirty hair or grime on me anymore. Mostly because Faith would just stare at me with that little disappointed face, and a part of me that I ignored broke just a little bit more.

I couldn't disappoint my niece. But I could disappoint anyone, everyone else. It was what I was good at.

Pulling myself from the reverie, I showered quickly, ignoring my phone buzzing on the table once again. My manager and agent had shown up a couple of times, but they'd left soon after, not knowing how to help. I had just dived deeper into the bottle and my own self-pity. It was easier to do that.

I filled my cup with booze, not caring what bottle I grabbed, slid the lid on, and made my way over to the main building where we were having family dinner. Unless we went off property, to one of my cousin's places that they had bought, or in one case that Brooks had helped build, we ate at the inn in one of the meeting rooms. It was the only place that fit all of us. There were ten of us Wilders currently here, and most of them had spouses and kids. I knew Lark wasn't there, so that was one fewer, and I wasn't sure if Eliza and her brood were in town. I hadn't seen them, but that meant nothing these days. I didn't really like seeing Eliza, because that meant I would have to deal with her husband, who just glared at me. And, well, I knew he was a good guy, but he also didn't take any of my shit. So I didn't like him.

I slid into the chaos, finding myself a corner to drink in, and stared at the family that wouldn't let me go.

If I was smart, I would go anywhere else. I could hide at countless places around the world. My so-called talent had made me millions.

So I didn't need to sit here with my family and ignore their pointed looks. Or be forced to work side by side with East and Brooks. If I didn't, they would pull me out of the cabin and force me anyway.

I could be on my own. But then they'd find me. My family. The band. Paparazzi. They always found me.

So did the ghosts that I ignored.

Brooks gave me a weird look as I stared past him into the ghost that I knew wasn't there. But Mal just leaned against the doorway, hands in his pockets.

My best friend just shook his head at me, and as I blinked, he disappeared.

I knew he wasn't there. I didn't believe in ghosts.

Didn't believe that my best friend was seriously staring at me. Because if there was an afterlife, he had way more shit to do than look at me. At least that's what I told myself.

A plate slid in front of me, and I looked up to see Ridge staring there, a glare on his face.

"Eat up, you're getting way too thin," he whispered so no one else could hear.

Ghost Mal was gone, so I nodded and pulled up my fork.

"Okay," I whispered, my voice scratchy from disuse.

He shook his head at me, and I didn't know if it was disappointment or something different. Couldn't tell anymore.

Instead, I ate and tried to listen to what they were saying as they talked about upcoming events and family things. But I couldn't pay attention to any of it. Faith didn't look at me, and I didn't know if that was progress, or if I was sliding downhill into the abyss once again. I ate knowing that I'd probably keep losing weight, and stayed for another ten minutes after I finished. That way, they knew I was present and wasn't dying.

No, because best friends did that. I was the one that had to stay behind.

As the conversation moved to Lark's tour, chills

spread out over my body, and I stood up quickly, pushing my chair back.

"Thanks for dinner," I grumbled, my voice aching, and everyone froze for an instant, conversation ceasing. But they didn't say anything. They had all said everything that they could for the past few months. But there was nothing left.

Instead, I took my plate to the counter where the other dishes stood and left without another word.

Nobody followed me.

So that might be progress.

A light drizzle began to sprinkle along the packed earth as I made my way to my cabin, and I didn't mind it. It was fucking hot outside still, even with the sun setting, so I would take the rain.

I just wanted to go home and have another drink. Maybe drown myself in it so I wouldn't have to remember those disappointed looks.

There was a car in front of my cabin that I didn't recognize, and I stiffened, wondering who the fuck that could be. Nobody was allowed near my cabin. No cars, no staff. Every once in a while someone would come in and blitz the damn thing, but nobody was allowed here at night.

Anger coursed through me as I stomped forward.

If it was a reporter, I was going to beat the shit out of them. They weren't supposed to be here. Because last time a reporter had made it on the grounds, they had scared the shit out of my cousin's kids as they were looking for Bethany Cole, the Oscar winner who happened to be my cousin-in-law.

I wasn't about to let that happen again.

"You're trespassing," I growled, my voice hollow, and far different than it had used to be.

When the car door opened and someone struggled to get out, I nearly tripped over my feet, recognizing that hair.

That gorgeous copper hair.

Though it was dark out, she'd parked under the light pole so I could see every angle of her face. Every emotion crossing those eyes. Every curve of her body that I knew firsthand.

And then I looked down at the swollen mass of her belly, and froze.

She stood there, eyes narrowed, and didn't say a thing. And when she put her hand over her belly and glared at me...my throat went dry and I tried to do the math, but I was never good at math.

"Gabriel. You really should have answered your phone."

And with that, my eyes rolled in the back of my head, and there was nothing.

CHAPTER SIX

BRIAR

At least the man hadn't peed himself as he passed out.

Overall, this wasn't the most ideal way to see Gabriel after all these months, but honestly, it could have been worse.

I closed the rental car door behind me and did my best not to waddle toward Gabriel. My center of gravity wasn't what it once was, and frankly, I was still getting used to this whole pregnancy thing.

My back hurt, my ankles hurt, and somehow, I had heartburn that only occurred when I didn't eat. It made no sense. And after driving down from Austin to try to fix some semblance of my life, I did not want to be in that car any longer.

And while my sister Teagan had driven most of the

way because she wouldn't allow me to do it myself, it was still a long drive.

And even as all of that slid through my head in a millisecond, I was still worried that Gabriel had hurt himself. I stared at the man currently sprawled in the mud and shook my head. My hand went to the swell of my belly, the baby kicking at my palm, and I swallowed hard.

This was my reality. One I had tried to ignore even as I guided myself through it. And now, I was slapping Gabriel's reality in his face.

And I hadn't even told him exactly why I was here.

With my other hand on the small of my back, I tried to squat down to touch Gabriel's pulse, just making sure he was alive, as his eyes snapped open, and I froze, my balance a little off.

Knowing I was about to go down, I put both hands out, trying to catch my fall, and then Gabriel was there, hands on my hips.

"Briar? Are you okay? Shit. Did I hurt you?"

I just stared into those light eyes of his and swallowed hard. That was always the problem when it came to Gabriel Wilder.

I had always looked into those eyes and stood frozen. Not quite enraptured.

He had always been my brother's best friend. Completely off limits. At first, it had been because I thought Mal would murder me for even daring to look at his friend. Then it had turned into me not wanting to ruin the friendship of two of the most important men in my life. One of my brothers, and the man who let Mal's talent and dreams soar.

It didn't matter that I knew I was a lost cause when it came to Gabriel. I always had been. Yet I'd ignored my feelings because I loved Mal and his friendship with the man in front of me. The man touching me.

That familiar ache, which started out as a sharp pain before ebbing to a pulsating squeeze of my heart shocked my system once again, and I latched onto it. That pain, that worry, that unending grief was something I could at least feel rather than the terror and panic of what was coming next.

Teagan could work on her to-do list, could focus on what needed to happen to keep us whole, while I just tried to see through to the next day.

"Briar? Did I hurt you?"

Well, that was a loaded question. "I'm fine," I lied. "Are you okay? Did you hit your head when you fell?"

He shook his head, then looked as if he thought better of it as he winced. "Shit."

"Yeah."

I looked down at his hands that were still on my hips and realized that my belly was really close to his face.

Talk about true reality.

He let go of me quickly, and I was grateful that I didn't teeter over. Instead, I let out a loud sigh as I stood up and stretched my back.

"Briar. You're pregnant. How the hell...? Is it...? I have no idea what to say right now."

I had done a lot of thinking over the past seven and a half months. Even through the fog of grief and panic, I had tried to think about what this moment would be. Preferably, it would've been at least seven months ago, but no, it hadn't been. We'd both needed space to think and heal—only I hadn't realized the consequences of that night until we'd walked away from each other.

I never would've truly thought he would proclaimed his love to me and promise to take care of this baby, but maybe something other than looking like he wanted to vomit.

It wasn't like I loved Gabriel Wilder. He was just a friend. A friend that I had had one night of fun with, before we had ruined everything. And I knew I was lying to myself, but it was easier to do so when the truth of what our futures held lay between us.

I ignored the clawing agony and stared at the man who had changed my life in more ways than one.

"Yep. Pregnant. Tired. Grumpy. And completely lost. And yes, the baby is yours. I tried to call before, but you never answered." I swallowed hard, trying to push down the frustration and anger that came with that thought. "You never let me in, Gabriel."

Flashes of the last time I had seen him shot through my mind, and I wanted to push them away. I wanted to ignore them.

But instead they were in vivid and technicolor view in my mind.

Gabriel standing there, eyes vacant as we stood over my brother's grave. That one last desperate look toward each other, even though he hadn't seen me looking. I had felt his gaze on me as my sister and brothers had dragged me away. But I hadn't spoken to him since the hospital. Since we had both broken down at hearing the worst news one could ever hear.

And part of me had wanted to keep it that way. Because when I saw Gabriel, I saw Mal's face when he walked away, disgust and disappointment twining with each other.

"How...I mean, I *know* how. But holy hell, Briar. You're *really* pregnant."

I stared at him and wondered exactly why I was here. I had tried to tell Gabriel so many times over the past few months. It wasn't as if I wanted to keep this a secret. I had been panicking inside the entire time. After all, it wasn't as if I had known I was pregnant until the nausea wouldn't go away, and my body started to change. I'd had an IUD, so I never got periods. It wasn't as if I could miss one.

The IUD had clearly failed, the same with the condom. Statistics were never on my side. Then again, somehow I had survived a bus crash, and my brother hadn't. What statistics existed for that circumstance?

Gabriel had ignored my calls, my letters, and my emails. He should have gotten a letter from my reps, letting him know that he was about to be a father—at least in genetics.

But he had ignored the world, and now I wasn't going to let him ignore this.

I was going against Teagan's wishes by even being here. My elder sister didn't think Gabriel even deserved to know what was going on, considering he had repeatedly pushed me away. And while part of me agreed with that, the other part of me knew he needed to know. Or maybe it was because I was dying inside, hollowed out with nothing left other than this promise of the future that made absolutely no sense.

He needed to know because I was faced with my own existence.

And I had no earthly idea how to face the future without Mal. Without *Gabe*. I couldn't do this alone. I knew that. And I needed Gabriel to understand. Understand what? I didn't know. And that scared me.

"Now that you know, I'm going to go put my feet

up. Everything hurts and I hate being pregnant. I'm not good at it and I'm usually good at what I do." I was rambling now, but I wasn't sure what I was supposed to say. "You deserved to know about this baby. Not only because the press is going to find out somehow, and it's going to be a shitstorm. But because this baby deserves to know their father. I'm not asking you for anything. I never would have, Gabriel. You know that. We've always been friends—at least I thought so. But you pushed me away and our worlds ended. Only now I have to face the future. So take a moment to think. Because we don't have many moments left before our worlds change. Again."

He blinked at me, his mouth opening and closing like a guppy, but I turned away and got back into my car. I had left Teagan back in the room, even though I knew she had wanted to storm out here.

She was just so *angry*. And while I wanted to be too, I had to skip that part of grief. Each of my family members were facing the loss of Mal in their own ways and none if it was good. Though was there really a good way to get through the loss of our brother? I didn't think so.

I pulled back into the main parking lot, and heaved myself out of the vehicle as a golf cart came around the side of the building and parked near me.

I blinked at the two women who stared at me with

pale faces when they looked down at my stomach. Then I remembered who they were. I had never met them, but I knew their photos.

Because Gabriel had been family. And therefore he had shown us *his* family.

Gabriel Wilder's sisters-in-law got out of the golf cart and stared at me, slack jawed. I put my hand protectively over my belly, wondering exactly what the baby and I were going to do next. There were only so many weeks left and I didn't have answers.

"Briar…" one of them began as she came forward, the other woman staring at me as if she saw a ghost.

I wasn't sure quite how pale I was just then, so it could be the truth.

"Aurora, right?" I asked, surprised at how calm my voice sounded.

"Yes. And this is Ava. We were so sorry to hear about your brother." She cleared her throat even as pain slapped me in the face. She held up her hand before I could say some platitude and walk away. "I'm sorry," she continued. "I hated it when anybody came up to me out of the blue and mentioned my late husband. As if I wasn't wallowing in my own grief. But I *am* sorry."

"You're here visiting Gabriel?" Ava asked after a moment.

I cleared my throat. "I am."

"And you're pregnant," Ava said pointedly, staring at my belly.

"I am," I said again, before tears began to slide down my face. "And I really, really don't know what I'm going to do. But it's nice to meet you."

I wanted to run away, but instead Ava and Aurora came forward, arms outstretched. I hadn't even realized I was swaying to the side until their hands were keeping me steady.

"Let's go get you inside and sit down. We'll put your feet up and get you some water," Ava said. "When I was pregnant with Faith, I swear I always got dizzy spells. It sucked because your center of gravity is different, you know? Did you come here with someone? Are you staying here? Don't worry, Briar. You aren't alone."

Somehow, they were leading me into the back entrance, which had to be an employee part of the place, and then I was sitting on a plush couch, my feet up on a stool, and water in my hand. They also put a veggie tray and some form of a dessert tray in front of me, and I wasn't even sure how they moved so quickly.

I sucked in a sob and tried to calm down. These women were being so nice to me, and it felt as though I were watching everything happen rather than living it. "I'm really okay. I have a room on the other side of the inn."

"So you're staying here?" Ava asked.

I could tell they were being so careful about what they were asking, and I didn't blame them. It felt as though we all were walking on eggshells. "Yes. I figured it was time to explain to Gabriel that maybe he should answer his phone. Or open a piece of mail," I said, and heard the bite in my tone.

The two women looked at each other, before Aurora closed her eyes and mumbled something, while Ava just shook her head and cursed.

"Oh. So Faith is going to have a cousin," Ava blurted, and then pressed her lips together.

I swallowed hard, and tried to think of what to say, before I burst out laughing, and shook my head. The other two women looked at each other before giving me a confused look.

"I swear I haven't lost my mind. But you saying that is probably the best reaction that I've had in the past few months since I found out I was pregnant. My brothers were ready to fly down here and beat the shit out of Gabriel or send me to a commune or convent, even though we're not Catholic," I added.

Ava's lips twitched while Aurora just stared at me wide-eyed.

"Well, that wouldn't have been great about the whole beating up thing," Ava finally said.

I continued to laugh, tears gently rolling down my cheeks. "My sister is upstairs, and I'm afraid that if she knows exactly where Gabriel is, she'll geld him. And then she'd go to jail and then I wouldn't have my sister when I'm raising this baby. It would be a whole thing."

"That *would* be a whole thing," Ava said slowly, and again, Aurora didn't say anything.

I let out a slow breath, coming back to my point. "So you saying something about this baby having family? That's the sweetest thing anyone's ever said about this pregnancy."

"Oh Briar," Aurora whispered, and then I was in her arms, tears continuing to slide down my cheeks, as Ava moved forward to hold my hand. "I'm so sorry that we didn't know."

I leaned into Aurora as she spoke, annoyed that I was crying so easily. I had never been a crier before this, but apparently pregnancy made me one.

"Okay, we're going to figure this out. Let's just get you hydrated and fed, and then tucked into bed. And then later, we'll take this one step at a time."

Aurora's voice was so soothing, and I had known before she had mentioned her late husband that she was a widow. That she had gone through grief, and presumably had found her way through it. Even though I knew grief never ended, she had found love again. This time with Gabriel's brother.

"Don't worry, you're not alone," Ava said, and for some reason, with these two women who were strangers, and yet somehow connected to me in a way I hadn't expected, I wanted to believe them.

It's just that it hadn't exactly been how I had wanted the day to end, though in reality, I hadn't had a plan.

Yet as it was proven to me repeatedly over the past few months, plans never worked, and here I was, living proof of that.

CHAPTER SEVEN
GABRIEL

I swore I could feel the panic seeping from my pores, and I swallowed hard, trying not to throw up again. Part of me wanted to pour myself a drink, but I hadn't relied on it yet and I wasn't going to start now.

I just needed not to remember.

I needed not to think of Mal. And his face when he looked at me with disgust.

I saw that look in my dreams. Every time I closed my eyes. Every time I allowed myself a calm moment, I heard my best friend scream at me. I felt his fist against my face, and there was nothing I could do.

Every time I breathed, I heard my best friend. He walked around this cabin, waiting for me to do something with my life, and I ignored him.

Only I couldn't do that anymore.

Briar was here.

The woman who haunted my dreams right along with her brother. She was *here*, and a distant part of me knew that something big had happened.

"She's pregnant."

Because Briar was pregnant.

How the hell had that happened? I *knew* how it had happened. But just one night? I'd kept my damn hands off my best friend's sister for all of the years I knew her. I'd walked away when our glances got to be a little too much. I'd fallen into the arms of others when I needed to forget because Briar could never be for me.

But the one time I'd given in, we'd not only changed our lives with Mal and each other—we *made* a life.

Holy hell.

"Gabe."

I turned a little too quickly as I swayed and then Brooks was there holding me steady. Ridge stood behind him as Wyatt pushed his way in.

"Let's get you cleaned up, okay?" Wyatt had a first aid kit in his hands and probed at the wound. I winced, but it didn't hurt. Then Ridge moved forward to tug on my shirt.

I frowned, then looked down at myself. I was covered in mud from when I'd passed out and had cut the side of my head. I hadn't even realized I was bleeding.

"Briar's pregnant," I blurted.

"We know," Brooks whispered.

"It's my kid."

Ridge nodded. "We figured. You passed out, buddy. That's fucking scary. Are you okay?"

No. I killed my best friend.

But that wasn't what he was asking.

"I don't know. I mean...she just surprised me. I don't pass out, guys. That's not me. But...holy hell. I missed *everything*." I hadn't ever thought I'd be a dad. It didn't really cross my mind. The rest of my family was moving on, but that wasn't really me. I'd wanted to take over the world with my music. Starting a family hadn't been part of that.

Yet Briar had gone through *how* many months of her pregnancy without me? What trimester was she in? When was her due date? What was she planning? I knew *nothing*. And yet I could have known more. Instead, I'd pushed everyone away and nearly lost out on something I never knew I wanted.

This baby.

That is...if Briar let me anywhere near her.

Holy hell.

I saw my brothers exchange looks, and I frowned. "What?"

Brooks shook his head. "I can't say you're taking this well, but you are. I...I don't really know what to say, but let's get you into clean clothes. And a shower. You really need to shower."

I sniffed myself and nearly passed out again.

Brooks led me to the shower, and I stripped off my clothes, resting my palms against the tile.

"What the hell am I supposed to do, Brooks?"

"Well, you're starting it. And then you'll talk to Briar and figure it out. You're smart, Gabriel."

"I was smart enough to use a condom." I paused. "I remembered that safe sex talk you and Dad gave me."

"Things happen. Hell, you know our family. We like to do things out of order." Grief crossed his eyes, and I could have kicked myself.

"I'm sorry."

"Don't. Don't worry about it." Brooks cleared his throat. "You'll find out what happened, Gabriel. And you'll grovel and get in her good graces. And then get in her family's good graces. Because you fucked up, but she's here. That has to be something."

"I want to believe you," I whispered.

"Well, you might make more of an impression if you didn't smell as if you rolled in mud and sweat," Brooks said dryly.

Wyatt cleared his throat as he walked in, Ridge

behind him. "Seriously. Let's get you some soap. You're going to need some soap."

I looked over my shoulder at my patient brother and I had no idea what to say to any of them. He was being so calm. All of them were. My brothers had been through hell, but they were standing straight. They weren't naked in a shower trying to wash off their sins.

"What am I supposed to do with Briar?"

"That's not an answer I have for you." He paused, his gaze going distant. "There're some days that I can still hear Amara's voice. When I'm washing the dishes, or taking a walk and smelling that cedar as it slams into my face and all my allergies. And I can hear her voice. I can still hear her laugh. But I can't always see her face."

I faced my brother now, washing the soap out of my hair. Brooks never talked about his late wife. Just like Ridge rarely talked about who he had lost. And what Wyatt had gone through, too. We Wilders weren't good at talking. Our cousins were better at it. But they had been through their versions of hell as well. But perhaps Virgil had been their guide through the circles of hell, and this branch didn't have one. Where was our Virgil? Our guide?

Brooks's throat worked as he swallowed hard. "It's only been what, four years? And I couldn't think of her face a couple of days ago. And then I blinked, and it came back. Because I knew Amara. She was my everything. And I remember every fight, every bad decision, and every mistake." My brother let out a breath, his jaw tightening. "We walked through the abyss, through life, knowing that we don't have enough time. I don't know what I'm going to do when I can't hear her laugh anymore. I don't know who I am without that laugh. Without that smile. But I still talk to her. I still wish that things could've been different. That it would've been me lying in that bed wasting away. But it wasn't. And I'm forced to do the one thing she had asked me to do my entire life." He paused, and I swallowed hard, before turning off the water. "She told me to live. And I hated her for that. I hated my wife for telling me to live when we knew she wasn't. So I'm going to do something that Mal would've done for you."

I flinched at hearing his name but swallowed hard anyway.

"Live. I don't know what you're going to do, what future comes with Briar, and the fact that she's carrying your kid. I don't know why you won't let us say your best friend's name. And why you're shutting out the world. But just live, Gabe. That's all we want from you."

"Well, we could use a few other things," Wyatt muttered. Ridge handed me a towel, and I wrapped it around my waist, watching water droplets slice over my ink and piercings.

I had barely even looked at myself in the months since losing Mal. Since losing everything.

And if I had picked up the damn phone, Briar wouldn't have been standing on my porch nearly full term, leaving me passed out because I was such a damn idiot.

"I'll live. I don't have a choice. Because Briar and the baby deserve that."

I stared at Brooks, and I hoped to hell he didn't hear the lie. But then again, maybe he did. I had killed my best friend, right after I had betrayed him. But walking away from Briar now would make Mal even more ashamed of me.

So I would live. Whatever life I could breathe into the husk that lay before my future.

CHAPTER EIGHT

BRIAR

Teagan had decided to go for a walk the next morning as I tried to find the energy to move around. She was still working long distance, and I knew taking so much time off to help me through the pregnancy had to be draining on her. I hadn't wanted to go back to Ashford Creek and while she hadn't truly understood, she'd dropped everything to help me. I'd never be able to repay her.

The night before, Ava and Aurora had walked me up to my room and made sure I got room service. Soon after Teagan had opened the door, eyes narrowed at the situation, the three women had somehow bonded.

For some reason in my head Teagan would have yelled at them and been annoyed because they were Wilders, but perhaps maybe the solidarity of wanting to make sure I didn't lose my mind made them best friends. So now the three of them were on a walk on the property to go see the vines.

All because I was supposed to be sleeping after having a large breakfast.

I had a feeling that the Wilder women orchestrated this so I could have a moment alone, perhaps to collect my thoughts, and I was grateful. My sister had spent the past few months only taking care of me. And not taking care of herself in the slightest.

Teagan needed to keep busy and worried about other things, instead of thinking about Mal, and part of me had understood the feeling.

The rest of me needed to figure out what I was supposed to do about Gabriel Wilder.

Sun slid through the curtains, and I stared at the light playing on the wall. This wasn't how I'd expected the trip to go, then again, I wasn't sure I'd had any expectations at all. In fact, I'd done my best *not* to make them. And perhaps that had been a disservice to each of us.

Knowing I needed to get ready for the day, I levered myself out of bed and headed to the bathroom to shower. I'd take a walk, get some decaf tea, and over-think as usual. Maybe I'd work on the song that had been bugging me for weeks now. The music always played in my head. It might have been slightly quieter than before, but it still sung.

I knew that some artists could write through the pain and use their agony to write. Yet I hadn't been able to put the past few months into words, let alone lyrics that were supposed to soothe the soul—or tear it into pieces.

I showered quickly and dressed in one of the random comfort wear pieces I'd packed. I'd ended up packing far too much, but I hadn't known how long this was going to take or what I wanted to wear. Everything felt blah anyway.

I dried my hair only so it would last longer and I wouldn't have to wash it the next day. Then, with a touch of mascara and lip balm, I was ready for the day.

And by ready, I meant awake.

With a sigh, I headed down to the breakfast area, grateful they had a few scones out for an easy breakfast, and used the ready-made tea service to make a cup of decaf tea. I could have gone to the restaurant for a full breakfast or got room service like the others had planned, but I was too nervous to do anything more.

People milled about, getting ready for their days, and from what I overheard, there would be a wedding on the grounds later. Gabriel had always said the Wilders knew how to do weddings and one day I wanted to see that.

I knew I couldn't watch people promise forevers right now, however. Not when I didn't know what my future would be. Not with Baby Girl kicking at my ribs as she was. I'd had months to come to terms with the idea of motherhood and a new life. Yet all along, I knew I wouldn't truly be prepared for anything.

Not without Gabriel.

And that worried me more than I thought possible.

I finished my scone and tea, then used the restroom again since Baby Girl wanted to play soccer with my bladder. Then, not knowing what else to do, and not wanting to bombard Gabriel's little cabin, I figured I'd see if I could catch up with my sister on her walk.

As I made my way outside, I finally felt like I could breathe again. The Wilder Retreat honestly took my breath away. The main building was two stories tall, with a villa-like architecture. The front pavers were square and gorgeous and moved along into a path to go toward the wedding venue. There was a huge fountain in the front, though it didn't have water right now. This was Texas, after all, and they were in a drought.

But they had added lights to it to still make it look like an art piece. I knew there were other buildings on the property, a couple of restaurants, a distillery and bar, and even a whole winery that I knew that my sister was at right now.

And while a glass of wine sounded like perfection, it wasn't going to happen anytime soon.

"It's okay, Baby Girl. We're going to get through this." I patted my stomach, knowing that I probably needed to think of a name.

Only thinking of a name in this moment meant I would have to do it by myself. And that meant making a claim without Gabriel. Even though I wanted to hate him right then—and there were so many reasons for me to do so in this moment—I couldn't take that choice away until I knew what he was thinking.

We all went through grief in different ways, and while I was so damn angry with him for how he had ignored me, I couldn't blame him either. I'd wanted to ignore the world. Except Baby Girl and I couldn't ignore each other. Especially not when she was kicking at my bladder.

"Come on, I just peed. Can't you kick something else?" I muttered and let out a sigh.

"Do you think the baby can hear you?"

I froze at that deep and familiar voice, my heart doing that twisting motion it always did when he was near. I looked up into the eyes that I had done my best to forget. I had failed in that endeavor, but I had always tried.

That voice made millions. That voice drew people in like moths to a flame. It had done so to me, even though I had done my best to ignore it. And now that voice was asking about my baby.

Our baby.

"I'd like to think so. Sometimes she'll stop kicking when I ask gently."

"She."

Gabriel's voice cracked at the word, and I swallowed hard. Then I pulled my gaze away from those blue eyes that drew me in far too often before taking a good look at the man who'd changed my life. He had worn jeans, work boots, and a gray, long-sleeve shirt on. His hair was wet and pushed back from his face, but he hadn't shaved. That beard going strong.

The dark circles under his eyes matched mine, and I wanted to wrap my arms around him and try to find a way to breathe again. Yet at the same time, I wanted to scream at him for ignoring me and the world for so long.

Instead, I answered his unasked question. "Yes, it's a girl. I wasn't sure if I wanted to find out at first. Only then I realized nothing else in my life was certain and at some point, I needed to hold on to something real."

"I'm sorry, Briar. I'm so fucking sorry."

CHAPTER NINE
GABRIEL

My gaze caught Briar's, and I tried coming up with something else I could say in this moment because right then and there, nothing came to me. Yes, there was so much more to say, but 'I'm sorry' pretty much covered the beginning parts.

I swallowed hard and looked at that face I had known for as long as I had known Mal. Briar had always been in our lives ever since we had started the band. We had been in school, trying to figure out what we wanted for our degrees, and ended up dropping out and forming a band instead. And then Mal had brought in his sister, and she had clicked with us. It helped that she was a songwriter as well and had been able to write beside us as we figured out who we wanted to be. And then our band had exploded, and Briar had always been there. Yes, she tried to stay out of the limelight because that's what she liked about her job, but the media knew her as the songwriter who helped the stars, and Mal's sister.

So I knew her.

And it seemed that I had fucked up more royally than I had even imagined.

"I'm sorry for passing out. I haven't been sleeping and...I have no idea why I did that. It was shocking, I guess."

"I nearly passed out myself. I'm not really going to judge you." She winced as she said it.

A smile played on my face. "You're welcome to judge me. I passed out when I first saw you. Before you could even really say a word to me. Judge away. I'm judging myself."

"Well, it was a bit shocking to see me all watermelon size and all."

I finally forced myself to look down at her midsection, at the very large evidence of her pregnancy, and swallowed hard. "I know you said you were pregnant, and I can see it, but wow. *You're pregnant.*"

"For somebody who writes songs for a living, you aren't doing great with words."

Briar was still pissed at me, and I knew it was my

fault she'd had to wait so long to tell me. I'd pushed her away. "I'll try to find the words."

She shook her head, her hand on the swell of her belly. Her copper hair flowed around her face, her cheeks a little fuller than they had been the last time I had seen her. I couldn't see any evidence of residual scars from the accident, and for that I was grateful. It had taken a while for my hand to heal, and I no longer had to wear the boot. When I'd last seen her, Briar had a small brace on her wrist, and I pressed my lips together, trying not to throw up at the memory. She'd been hurt, and I hadn't been able to protect her. Just like I hadn't been able to protect Mal.

My vision went gray, and I tried not to stagger back, to show her my weakness.

Briar gave me a strange look. "It was a shock to me when I realized that I was pregnant. When I saw those pink lines, and then the words, because of course I had to take seven tests to actually prove to myself that I was pregnant, I didn't believe it. But Teagan kept looking through the tests to double check. And then she continued to make me pee on sticks until we went to the doctor and did a blood test."

I could imagine the two of them doing exactly that and nearly smiled. "I'm surprised Teagan didn't fly down here and kick my ass."

Briar winced, and I quickly looked around as if

Teagan was going to pop out of the bushes at any moment. I liked Teagan as she was Mal's sister after all, but Briar and I had always been closer. Apparently *too close,* as evidenced by everything in front of me.

"I didn't tell her or the rest of my family you were the father until recently. That was a point of contention, but you know, that's how my brothers are. It's *always* a point of contention."

I knew a little bit about her father, and the hell that she, Mal, and their siblings had lived through in their small town, but I didn't know everything. Mal had always been secretive about his childhood and had wanted to move on from the past. Yes, the pain in his words when he had written songs had always flowed through, but he didn't talk about it in detail.

And Briar only ever mentioned it in passing, so I'd never asked. It wasn't that I hadn't wanted to know, it was only that I knew it wasn't my place at the time. They would tell me when they needed to.

Then we'd run out of time.

"Teagan's here, by the way."

I stiffened, and once again looked around, and Briar laughed. A full-on laugh that hit me like a two by four, and I couldn't help but smile at her. I had always loved her laugh. And that was a problem.

"She's not standing behind you." I nearly turned and her eyes danced. "She's out with your sisters-in-law.

They went to check out the vines at the winery or something. Don't worry, she's not going to find you and kill you yet."

"It's that *yet* part that worries me." I slid my hands into my pockets, nearly feeling a slice of normal. I quickly squashed that thought. I didn't deserve normal.

"As I said, it took me a while to tell them who the father was, and I had waited because I was trying to get ahold of you."

I heard the accusation in her tone, and I let it hit me. Because it *was* my fault. I still wasn't ready to see the world or talk to most people, but seeing Briar like this had been like a bucket of ice water poured over my head.

I couldn't stand still in my own mourning and purgatory anymore.

Not when Briar needed me.

"I'm sorry. For ignoring you. For ignoring everyone. I don't even fucking know who I am anymore, but this isn't me. I mean, it clearly is, but I don't want it to be me." I ran my hands over my face and began to pace. "I feel like I'm waking up from a dream, and nothing really makes any sense."

"That's how I feel every day. Or at least how I've felt every day for the past seven or so months."

I turned to her again, trying to think about what I'd done over the past few months. Nothing. I'd done nothing. And she'd been *alone*. "I would say that I'm sorry you did this all alone, but as is evidenced by how you saw me, I don't know if I would've been the right person to help you at the beginning of this. Holy hell, Briar. *You're pregnant*."

She studied my face, those gorgeous gray eyes piercing. "You know what's funny? I really expected you to fight this. Or at least question if I was telling you the truth that this baby was yours. And yet, even though you look just as flabbergasted as I feel most times, you haven't at all. You believe me."

I looked at her, confusion washing over me. "Of course I believe you. You don't lie, Briar."

Tears began to spill down her cheeks, and I cursed. I moved forward without thinking, cupping her face to use my thumbs to wipe away those tears. "I'm sorry. I didn't mean to make you cry."

"I cry at the drop of the hat. It's either crying or peeing. Sometimes at the same time."

My lips twitched as I let my hands fall, and I shook my head. "So what they say is true? Pregnant women need to pee all the time?"

Her nose scrunched. "You would too if a little foot was kicking at your bladder all the time. Thankfully, it seems that she's asleep, so I'm not running to the bathroom right now. Although if I keep talking about it, I'm going to have to go."

Once again I looked down at her belly and swallowed hard. "A girl. The baby's a girl."

It felt as if I were walking through cement, slowly coming to terms with what she was saying. But it didn't feel like it was real. It felt as if I was watching this happen rather than being inside the moment. I could barely feel the warm breeze on my face or smell the cedar in the air. I could hear kids laughing in the distance, an event of some sort going on that I knew my cousins were handling. And it all came in slow motion, as I looked at my reality, and yet it didn't seem as if it were mine.

"Do you want to go back to my place? Just to talk? That way, in case there's a bathroom emergency, there's one right there."

It looked as if she wanted to laugh but couldn't through the weight of what needed to be said. "That would be good. That's why I'm here after all."

I nearly reached out and held her hand, but that wasn't my place. Hell, I didn't know what my place should or would be. Instead, I just gestured toward the path, and we made our way toward the tiny gray cabin. The Wilder Winery and Retreat had multiple cabins all over the land, as well as homes in which some of my family lived. I didn't have a place here but was using the cabin that happened to change hands through my family often. Many of my cousins-in-law and sisters-in-law had lived in this place, and now it was mine. Although I hadn't been taking very good care of it. As we walked inside and I took a good look around, I was grateful that I at least scrubbed some of the counters and visible places before I had left, but it still didn't look up to par. I was pretty sure my cousins-in-law would probably skin me alive if they saw it like this.

"I'm a slob. Sorry."

"You weren't always. Mal was the slob." Her voice cracked a bit, and I reached out without thinking to squeeze her shoulder.

"I'm sorry."

"I don't know what you're sorry about this time. But I'm trying to do better about mentioning Mal's name. I didn't at all for the first couple of months."

I paused, wondering if I'd even said my friend's name aloud. "I don't know what I'm supposed to say to that."

"Nothing. There's nothing to say about that. My brother's dead."

Cold arced through my veins, and I staggered back as she stared at me, her gray eyes glassy.

"Mal is gone. And I hate every day that he's not here. I can still hear him singing in my ears whenever I close my eyes. I can hear that laugh of his as he's telling a joke that nobody finds funny and yet they can't help but laugh along because it's just him. I can see him in a sunset, because he always liked to stay up late and rarely saw the sunrise unless he had to for work. I can see him in everything around me, whether it's when someone's wearing his favorite color, or when someone in my town looked at me and saw the girl who lost her way and lost her brother at the same time—hence why I moved back to my place in Austin."

"Briar…" I began, but she shook her head, cutting me off.

"Mal got out of Ashford Creek. And so did I. We got out and found our way. And yet I nearly went back because I had nowhere else to go. In the end, I made it back home to Austin, but it was a fight. All because Teagan and Callum and my other brothers needed to protect me. I was pregnant and I wouldn't tell them who the father was. We were all breaking inside. Bodhi can't even look at us, and yet I see Mal's face every time I look at him."

Bodhi was Mal's twin, and I swallowed hard, thinking about what that would feel like, to lose not only your brother, but the one that you shared a womb with. My mouth filled with sawdust, and I walked into the kitchen to grab something to drink. Part of me wanted to reach for booze, but I didn't. Instead, I filled two glasses with water and handed one over to her.

"It's a small town up there, and everybody wanted to know who the daddy was, and I never told them.

Because it was never their business. And my dad?" She shook her head. "Well, you can guess what he said."

"So he's back?" I asked, knowing that she and Mal's father had been in and out of their lives far too often.

"He's gone right now, but he'll come back when he needs money. It's what he always does. Before I moved back to Austin, he said a few things to me, called me a few names, but then I didn't care."

"And that's my fault."

Briar winced. "For not talking to me? Yes. But Baby Girl? No. We were safe. We used a condom, and I was on birth control. And yet your super sperm did their thing."

My lips twitched, even as that fire that I loved about her danced in her eyes. "That's one way to put it."

"I yell at your super sperm often whenever I'm pissed off that I'm in this situation."

Again, I nearly laughed. I wasn't sure the last time I'd laughed. "Well, that's good to know."

Briar sobered, her shoulders falling. "I came here because you never answered my calls. You didn't answer the band's calls. Or your agent's. You never opened that letter from my lawyer."

I froze, then looked at the stack of unopened mail that my family had sent over and swallowed hard. "Your lawyer," I echoed, my voice hollow.

"I don't want or need anything from you, Gabriel. I

know you're mourning. I know you're hurting, and we didn't ask for this. I wasn't even sure I was going to keep the baby, and then I realized that I wanted it. Wanted her. Maybe I was grieving so hard that I wanted to cling onto something that had to do with life, but I did. And I'm going to keep this baby girl, and I'm going to raise her, and she's going to have tons of uncles and Aunt Teagan to take care of her. So I don't need you. You deserved to know. But that's all." She met my gaze, as my world crashed down around me, and I tried to figure out what I was going to say. And yet there wasn't anything.

She had done all of this alone for months because I had had my head up my ass and had ignored everything.

Nothing was rational about my thoughts or the situation.

"You're acting so calmly right now. It's scaring me, Gabriel. I was honestly expecting the fiery Wilder with a temper."

"I'm not calm. My best friend is dead, and the one time I fuck his sister, I get her pregnant," I blurted, and both of us stared at each other.

I hadn't meant to say that. Holy hell.

"Well, I fucked you right back, and yet I'm the one holding this baby. I'm the one with swollen ankles and mood swings and food cravings that make no fucking sense. I'm the one that really has to pee right now, so you're going to have to stay here and sit in your own feelings while I do that."

She made her way back, and I swallowed hard, my mind going blank as I tried to figure out what the hell had just happened. I heard her washing her hands before she came out, and she continued to glare at me.

"You don't need me. I mean…I'm an asshole. I know that. I missed so much and left everyone. But I don't want to walk away and pretend I had nothing to do with this."

I wasn't even sure *what* I wanted, but the sane part of me screamed deep inside. If Briar left right now, I'd regret it for the rest of my life. I didn't know what I wanted. But I knew I didn't want her to go.

I'd never wanted her to go. That had always been a problem when it came to Briar Ashford. And the baby? I didn't know if I wanted to be a father, but now I didn't have a voice. And while I'd run away from my life for months, I couldn't run away from this.

I might be the Wilder failure, but I couldn't fail at this.

"I don't need anything from you. My lawyer sent something in case you wanted to sign over your rights because you clearly didn't respond to anything else I sent. So you don't need to be part of this. However, your sisters-in-law know that I'm pregnant and know that it's yours. And Ava mentioned that Faith has a cousin now, and well, I don't know what I'm supposed to do." Briar burst into tears, and I cursed under my breath before moving forward, wrapping her in my arms. She sank into me, her belly pressing against mine as I froze, realizing that there was a little foot kicking at me.

I rested my forehead on hers as she put her arms around my waist, and that little foot continued to kick at me.

I pulled back, wide-eyed, as I looked down at her stomach.

"Did she kick me?"

Briar wiped her face vigorously and nodded. "She does that. Apparently, she's awake."

My hand moved down before I thought better of it and froze right above her stomach.

"May I?"

"At least you asked. Nobody in Ashford asked," she mumbled, and I met her gaze before slowly pressing my hand to her stomach. It felt weird—I had never touched a pregnant person before. It wasn't as if there were many in my life, and yet, when a little tap pressed against my palm, I quickly let go.

"Oh my God."

"She can't hurt you right now. She can only hurt my organs. And my spine," Briar said dryly, and that kick of humor reminded me so much of Mal, it felt as if the world were falling out from beneath our feet once again.

But instead of panicking, I put my hand back on her stomach, and felt the baby move.

"How could you do this by yourself for so long?"

"I wasn't by myself. I had my family. What's left of it." Her voice broke, and I cursed. "I tried. I tried to call you, but you didn't answer. So I don't need you. I can do this."

I looked up at her then, as the baby continued to kick, and something twisted inside, some yearning I didn't realize was there.

"I should have answered my phone."

"Yes. You should have. The band misses you. The world misses you. I miss you," she said, tears falling again. "But I don't need you. I can do this."

"You can do anything you put your mind to, Briar. But before this, I never walked away from my responsibilities. And I don't want to do that now." I'd regret it for the rest of my life.

"I don't know what to do, but I don't want you to do this alone. And I know you have a family that loves you, but this baby is half me. I'll do what I have to in order to figure out how to be human again, but along the way, I'll be here too. I promise. Not that my promises are worth a damn right now. But I'm going to try."

I met her gaze again, and she nodded, light shining

in her eyes. "There's the Gabriel I remember," she whispered. "Mal would totally come back as a ghost and kick your ass if you signed over your rights and never talked to me again. I'm just saying."

I didn't realize I was crying with her until she reached forward and used her thumb to brush a tear from my cheek.

"I miss my brother, Gabriel. But I also missed *you*. We're about to be parents, and while I've had a few months to deal with that, you're brand new to this, so you're welcome to panic a bit. But you don't have much time to continue to do so."

Such the practical Briar. It almost felt like old times.

"I feel like I'm walking in quicksand right now."

"You don't walk in quicksand, you sink. So let's not sink, okay?"

I swallowed hard, feeling four steps behind. "How are you so rational right now?"

"Because if I'm not, I'll break down and I don't have time for that. This baby needs me to be strong. So if you could be strong as well, that would be great. Especially because I'm pretty sure I hear Teagan coming over, and she's probably ready to kick your ass."

Before I could say anything to that, or let the fear crawl over me, the door opened, and Teagan walked through, looking just like her sister, yet a bit taller and a little more slender.

"So, Gabriel. You *do* know how to answer a door at least. There's that."

"Hey, Teagan," I said, before I stepped toward her and opened my arms. "I'm so fucking sorry about Mal."

And with that, Teagan let the tears fall and glared at me. "Fuck you," she growled, before wrapping her arms around my waist and crying. I moved to pull Briar into the hug, and suddenly my arms were full of Ashford women, both of them crying into me. I was so far out of my depth, it wasn't even funny. We stood there for a few moments and once again, this felt like an odd dream I couldn't wake up from.

"Okay, there's enough of that," Teagan said as she moved back, wiping her face. Briar did the same and gave me a watery smile.

"You know, I never cried like this before."

"I just cried in front of you, too, you know, so we can just call it hormones."

"Hormones aren't contagious, jackass," Teagan muttered, and I smiled over at Mal and Briar's sister.

I had been so deep into my own darkness, I hadn't thought about anyone else. And while I was still to blame for what had happened, I needed to stop hurting everyone else. I knew that, but I knew it was only words at this point.

"I don't want to sign away my rights," I repeated.

Teagan stared at me, but I only had eyes for Briar,

the girl that I had never let myself see. The girl that I had never wanted more of because if I did, I knew I would cross a line.

The woman that I had crossed a line with.

And the woman that was apparently having my baby.

"Just don't go back to ignoring us. You can't. Because if you do, you'll hurt more than me. More than your family. More than yourself. And I'm already panicking enough for the both of us."

I rubbed the back of my neck and knew that my life was never going to be the same. Then again, it hadn't been since the accident, hadn't been every day since. And while I knew I would probably fuck this up like I had done everything else, I knew I could never hurt Mal's sister again. Or walk away from the consequences of my decisions.

As much as I wanted to hide away again, as much as I wanted to drown in that darkness, I wouldn't.

Briar needed me.

And for once, maybe I wouldn't mess everything up.

It didn't seem likely.

CHAPTER TEN
BRIAR

It had been two days since I'd shown up at the Wilder Retreat, not knowing exactly what I was supposed to be doing. And in those two days, my emotions had gone all over the place. It was hard to keep focused on anything other than what was growing in my womb, and yet the worries of what would come next haunted me.

"Okay, you've had your vitamins, you're hydrated, and you've already had your protein for the morning. We're doing great."

I smiled over at Teagan's familiar refrain. My sister had her phone in her hand, most likely going through the checklist for the morning. If we had been at home, she probably would have had her paper planner out, but that planner only stayed at her desk. I wasn't quite sure why there was a difference, but that was why she was Teagan, and I was Briar.

We were the two girls in a family full of men. And when we had lost our mother, we had banded together trying to be the feminine space in the house. Though we both had been far too young to even understand what that meant at the time.

And frankly, in the house we had grown up in, there would never have been a time for that anyway. Not with the yelling. Not with the fighting. Not with the constant berating.

I ran my hands over my belly, and pressed my lips together, hoping that I wouldn't cry. I cried at the drop of a hat these days, and I really didn't want to do that again.

"What's wrong?" Teagan asked.

I looked up to see my sister had moved closer to me, worry on her face. "I was just thinking about Ashford."

Understanding filled her gaze, and she knew I wasn't merely talking about the small town we had grown up in. No, it was about exactly *who* we had grown up with. The fact that we bore the same name as the town didn't have quite the history some might have thought.

My sister pressed her lips together before letting out a breath. "We are going to take care of this baby. This baby's going to be loved and cherished and healthy."

"Meaning this baby's never going to meet Dad," I said pointedly.

"You don't have any reason to worry about that."

Teagan had pulled up her chestnut hair from her face, determination clear. I knew her lovely hair probably wouldn't stay chestnut for long. My sister was constantly changing her hair color just because she could. I had a feeling at first it was because it annoyed our dad, and then because she couldn't pick a color. I wasn't even sure what her natural color was anymore, and I was fine with that. I loved the ever-changing Teagan.

It was such a dichotomy, considering everything else in her life had to be structured, while I was the one who went with the flow. I was the one who had traveled with Mal more often than not. I wrote songs for a living, able to work wherever I needed to as long as I had my notebook and pen. If I could have a guitar or piano? Even better, but I could make do with the notes in my head.

I was the so-called free spirit, and yet in that moment I needed a plan.

Only I did not have one.

"We won't let him ruin this," Teagan reassured me.

I nodded. "Thank you for traveling with me. I realize that you didn't want to come all the way down to Texas."

"No, it really wasn't first on my list of desires, but we have a plan."

I raised my brows. "You have a plan? Because there's no *we* about this. I sort of just got in the car and decided I was going to see Gabriel in person. Because he deserved to know."

Teagan narrowed her gaze. "We can decide later if he deserved to know anything."

"Teagan. He lost Mal too."

Teagan's eyes went stony and I wish I hadn't said our brother's name. None of my family members were taking Mal's death healthily. If anything, I was the steady one here, and it was only because I had my future slammed right into my face.

I didn't have time to grieve and to wallow when I had to take care of this baby girl.

"We have a plan for the baby. A birth plan, and I've already made sure that we have the easiest routes to the hospital just in case you go in labor while we're here."

I let out a breath, knowing that I hadn't been thinking clearly when we'd made the drive to the Wilders. "I love you so much for everything you've done. I promise I'm putting this baby first by being here. I needed to see Gabriel. I realize that I'm in a baby fog and I'm making irrational decisions, but I needed to see him."

My sister's face softened. "I know that you did. I

just kind of wish you would have figured this out a couple of months ago, rather than when you're so close to term."

That made us both let out a nervous laugh. "And we will make it back, my doctor will help me deliver this baby, and I will raise this baby in love and light and a slight panic."

"I like that you're adding the panic, because we're both in the middle of that," Teagan said with a shake of her head.

"I realize that this is not the most opportune moment of this pregnancy, but I couldn't do this without him knowing." I began to pace, rubbing the small of my back. "I thought I *could*. I thought I could wallow in my own anger that he wasn't contacting me and pretend that he wasn't part of this. That this was all *me*. But I can't. I wouldn't be able to walk away without trying if he was some stranger, and I sure as hell can't do that to Gabriel."

"You would have been in your right to do that," a deep voice said from the doorway, and I whirled, nearly falling before I caught myself. I hadn't realized that Teagan had left the screen door open, but there he was.

Gabriel.

"Hey Teagan," the rock god said as he lifted his chin at my sister. He looked better than he had before, and way better than he had the first time I had seen him.

He'd pulled his hair back from his face with a slight ponytail and it made his cheekbones pop out even more. He had on dark jeans and a black shirt that stretched across his chest. Somehow, the man had gotten even more muscular since the accident, and I wasn't quite sure how that was possible. Gabriel had always been more built than any of the other band members. But now it looked as if he had been pumping iron or doing some form of outdoor activity in order to gain all that muscle.

And I really needed to stop ogling the man.

"Gabriel. You're here." Apparently stating the obvious was the only thing I could do these days.

"Can I come in?" he asked as he slid his hands into his pockets.

Teagan looked at me, and I realized that it was my turn to answer. So I swallowed hard and nodded. "Yes. Come on in. We need to talk anyway."

"Gabriel," Teagan's voice sounded icy as ever, but then she did the one thing I knew she probably would, despite her anger and bluster. She opened her arms to bring Gabriel into a hug. He looked surprised as hell, and frankly, he shouldn't have been. Because Gabriel had always been one of us. He was Mal's best friend, and even though we were all hurting, and even though we were all angry, we all needed to stick together. Something we hadn't been doing at all.

He finally hugged her back, before each took a step away from each other.

"I realize that I should have said something to you at the funeral. But I wasn't in my right mind," Teagan said after a moment. And then she looked between us and gave me a tight nod. "I'll leave you two to talk. I'm going to go make more plans just in case she decides to give birth here instead of back home."

Gabriel's eyes widened, his face paling.

I glared at my sister. "Stop scaring him."

"You *should* scare him. You are how close to your due date? A lot of things are about to change." And with that she left the cabin, and Gabriel and I stood in the small living room, the awkwardness settling in.

"Are you really going to have the baby here?" he asked, his gaze on my stomach.

Feeling self-conscious, I ran my hands over my belly and shook my head. "My goal is to be back up in Austin and be with the obstetrician I've been working with. But Teagan apparently has a plan in case I decide to stay here."

"Oh." He ran his hands over his beard before growling just a tad.

I had always liked that growl. And it annoyed me that I was even thinking that in this moment.

"I have no idea what I'm supposed to say."

"Same. That's why I'm standing here awkward when I probably should be sitting down with my feet up."

That seemed to have pushed him into action, because suddenly his hands were on my shoulders and I was being set down on the couch, with my feet on the ottoman.

"Do you need more water?"

I pointed to my emotional support water bottle. "I'm good."

"Do you need something to eat? Pickles?"

Despite myself, I burst out laughing. "Pickles aren't my craving."

"What are your cravings? What else did I miss?"

And there it was. The not-so-quiet reason things were so awkward.

He had missed everything up until now, but yet again, I had been in such a tremendous amount of grief, it felt as if I had missed living through it as well.

And that was a problem.

"Honestly, I've been craving popcorn. Which isn't great for me because my stomach has never done well with popcorn."

"I remember," he said, his lips quirking into a smile. "But you always ate my popcorn at the movies."

"Because popcorn's amazing. And I've wanted every flavor out there. Except for the fact that I haven't been able to have every flavor out there recently. I've been trying things with salt that make me feel like it's popcorn, but then salt's not really great because you retain it."

His lips quirked into a smile, and I had no idea what the man was thinking. "Can I get you something that's *like* popcorn?"

"I'm really okay."

Gabriel took a seat on the coffee table in front of me, our knees brushing. He stared at me so intently I felt as if I were being studied. Perhaps that was the case, though.

"Is there something on my face?" I asked, trying to break the tension.

"I miss Mal every single day," he said after a moment.

I swallowed hard, not knowing where this would go.

"I miss him every single day," he repeated, "and all I can do is think about the fact that the last things that we said to each other were in anger."

My stomach clenched, even as the baby kicked. I reached out and gripped his hand, surprising the both of us. "The last time that I saw my brother, I was yelling, too. And you guys were fighting, and I was so angry that he would get into our business."

"Well, I broke the code."

"Fuck the code."

His eyes widened for a moment before his shoulders fell. "I'm never going to be able to apologize. To make it right. And that's why I didn't answer the phone. That's why I buried myself. That's why part of me wants to do it again. To hide from the world. But *you* didn't. You didn't have a choice." He looked pointedly at my stomach.

I swallowed hard. "You're right. I don't get to hide from it because this baby needs me."

"Exactly. You've always been so much stronger than us. You never fell into what we did as the band. You were always better."

"Don't idolize me or put me on a pedestal. I was with you guys. I partied. And then I would go to my little house in Austin and write music until I couldn't think anymore, and then go back out on tour with whoever needed me. I liked my job. I liked my life. And it's completely different now. It would have been completely different even if I didn't get pregnant. Because Mal's not here and neither one of us can say we're sorry. But I don't want to be sorry." Gabriel's eyes widened. "If I'm sorry, then this *baby* is what I'm sorry about. And I cannot start this new life like that. I grew up in a family where we were told we were all mistakes. Constantly. I'm not going to have this baby live that too."

"Well shit," Gabriel said after a moment.

I raised a brow. "That's all you have to say?" I asked, and I hadn't realized that I was crying until he reached forward to wipe my tears.

"No, I just keep thinking that you're so much better at this than me."

"I've had more time to go through each one of my spirals."

"How are you so calm?" he asked.

"I'm not. I'm screaming inside. Sometimes I feel like I'm a little hamster on that wheel, but the wheel's going too fast and I keep knocking into the sides."

His lips twitched. "I hate the fact that I can imagine that."

"I know, right?" I smiled along with him.

"What else have I missed?"

"The list is far too long." He flinched, and I cursed. "I mean far too long to sit here and talk about it right now."

"Will you tell me? Because I don't know what I'm supposed to do."

"I'm going to be a mom, Gabriel. And you need to figure out if you're going to be a dad." His eyes widened. "I'm not saying that you have to be. But you're Mal's best friend. And you're *my* friend." I swallowed hard. "So you need to figure out what you want.

And I'm giving you that option because the baby deserves it. We don't. I should have tried harder, and you should have tried in the first place. So we don't deserve those chances. But this baby does."

"I'm not going to abandon you." The conviction in his tone stopped me in my tracks.

"What?" I asked, surprised at the tension holding me in its grasp at those words.

"I won't abandon you. I'm going to be this baby's father. Whatever you need me to do. If that's showing up on weekends, if that's staying every single day and rocking that baby to sleep, if that's paying for things and then staying out of your life because you can't stand to look at me, we'll figure it out. But I'm here. Whatever you need me to do, I'm here. Because I have fucked up so much. I fucked up with Mal." He paused. "He was on that bus because I fucked up."

"He wasn't," I said quickly, my eyes filling with tears. "He was going to get on that bus no matter what."

"He might have stayed. Because he remembered that you were there. If he hadn't fought with us, he might have stayed."

I froze, my heart feeling as if it had frozen in my chest. I had never thought about that. The fact that Mal might have stayed on the bus if we hadn't fought. If

Gabriel and I hadn't slept together. He might have realized that he'd invited me on the tour and should probably hang out with me. Mal did that all the time. Blew off plans with others to spend time with his family. He might have done that.

A sharp sound escaped from my mouth, and I realized that sharp cry was nearly a wail.

Gabriel cursed under his breath and cupped my cheeks. "I'm sorry. It's my fault. My fault."

I let out a shaky breath. "There were two of us in that bed. And there were two of us on that bus. And we can't change it. So don't blame yourself. Because if you blame yourself, then you have to blame me, and I need to be strong for this baby. Okay? Can you just stop blaming yourself?"

"I don't know if I can do that."

"At least you're honest."

He reached out and continued to wipe my tears as I let my thoughts wander, trying to compose myself.

"Who else knows that I'm the father?" he asked softly.

"Nobody knows that you're the father other than Teagan. And I suppose your family now." I paused, letting that settle in. "My brothers, of course, know that I'm pregnant. But they don't know it's yours. And the band knows I'm pregnant, but not that it's yours. All of Wilder knows." He stiffened, and I shook my head. "They were my friends too. So they know I'm pregnant. Rocky's been sending me all these baby blog links of things that I need to know for birth and after. It's actually quite frightening."

"I haven't answered their calls either," he said, his voice hoarse.

"I know. And you should. They're not out on tour. They're all in their relatives' homes, resting. Figuring things out. But they're waiting for you. Giving you space just like I did. But I couldn't do it anymore, so you should talk to them."

"And when I do, tell them the baby is mine?"

"Yes, we should. Eventually."

Gabriel brushed my hair from my face and I tried not to lean into that touch. It wouldn't lead to anything good. "Will you tell me everything else that I missed? Every single doctor's appointment? I'm sure Teagan has it written down in some planner of hers," he teased.

I smiled then, feeling like this was the Gabriel that I remembered. Even if it was just a sliver of him.

"Yes. I'll tell you everything. And then we can call the band. Because I really hated lying to them about who the dad was. Even if it was just a lie of omission."

He squeezed my hand so tightly it shocked me for a moment before he let go.

"Okay. Just tell me what I missed."

And so I told the father of my baby everything that

he'd missed when he had been lost in grief. And I saw the pain and sadness slice into him over and over again. Just like it did me.

And I knew this wasn't over. And I was afraid it never would be.

CHAPTER ELEVEN
BRIAR

After the dust settled, I went back to Austin. Honestly, it was the only decision to make. I needed to nest in my own home, complete the nursery that I had been working on for months, and be near my doctors. It wasn't that far of a drive, but I needed to be home.

Teagan, of course, came with me. She stayed in the guest room, mothering me in a way that I knew would annoy us in any other situation. But neither one of us really knew how to be a mother because we didn't have one. Thankfully, we had the baby books to guide the way.

As well as the Wilder women.

Once Gabriel and I had spoken in that cabin, it

seemed to open the floodgates for everybody who had been holding back.

Because every single Wilder woman, yes Gabriel's sisters-in-law, but his cousins-in-law as well, had come over. They all had advice, baby books, different websites to use, and I had ended up with a car full of baby things. Some passed down, some new. And they all had said that they would be there for me no matter what, and would be annoying me with offers to babysit, to help out during the first few months, and to send over food and meal trains and cleaning services. I had been overwhelmed, but Teagan had taken to it like a moth to a flame with her planner. I had a feeling I would not be dealing with meals or cleaning for as long as the Wilder women wanted to help.

The band hadn't been an obstacle when we'd told them that Gabriel was the father. It turned out they had all known before we could tell them. Apparently, we hadn't been as circumspect as possible. I didn't know what they had said to Gabriel, or if they had even talked about the band itself, however. It wasn't my place. And I knew they were all still hurting, just like I was. There was a hollow place within me that I would never be able to step out of, but perhaps one day I would. Perhaps one day I would have to.

The band knew and was ready to invade my home with help and love. Although only one of them were parents, they were all ready to step in and be the best aunts and uncles ever.

Tears threatened just thinking about it, and I knew that I would always have a connection to them. Because of Mal, and now Gabriel. I had no idea what was in store for Wilder, but for the Wilder currently growing inside me, that was what was the most important part.

Gabriel's parents had even called me, and while I had known them somewhat, I didn't know them very well.

Carlos and Rebecca Wilder were loud and enthusiastic, and so excited to once again be grandparents. Although technically Faith wasn't Wyatt Wilder's birth daughter, as Ava had married Wyatt as a single mother, Faith was one-hundred-percent their grandkid. And now they would be having another.

That wasn't overwhelming at all.

But the fact that this baby would have a grandmother at all? Yes, it made me cry. The fact that this baby had a grandfather who actually *wanted* to be one. And was a good human rather than the dark abyss that mine was? I had no words for that.

So now I was at home, my Bohemian nursery all set up, waiting for my due date.

Which was *tomorrow*. But the baby kept kicking, and I was ready for this new phase to begin.

"Come on, Baby. You can do this," I said, rubbing my stomach.

"Are you asking her to come out now?" Gabriel asked, and I smiled over at him. He sat in the rocking chair, phone in his hand, and baby book on his lap. He was researching and dealing with everything that he had ignored for so long. I was pretty sure he wasn't sleeping, but it wasn't as if we slept in the same room.

No, Gabriel and I would just be co-parents. We would figure out exactly how that would work, considering our jobs later, but *co-parents*. Not lovers, just friends. Who happened to sleep together once.

There were no extra feelings, no worrying about falling for each other. We were friends. There wasn't time for love or emotions that got a little too mushy. Complicated would be the basic word for what this was if it went further than just friendship.

So I would never fall for Gabriel Wilder.

All the crushes that I might've had before this were firmly stowed away and would never come back.

"I feel like a blimp, and my ankles are swollen, and my cheeks are swollen, and I just want to be finished. I'm really scared about everything that comes after this, even though Teagan has planned so much of it. I don't know. I just want it to be there."

"She really has planned so much, hasn't she?

"Do you know that part in Father of the Bride 2 when the dad is going a little crazy and has that clock with the map?" I asked, using my hands to try to explain.

"As you made me watch that movie like ten times, yes. I know." He paused. "Were we even alive when that movie came out?"

"No. But it's a classic for a reason."

"True true. And don't worry, Teagan can handle everything. I am behind on my studies," he said, holding up the book.

"Well, we did throw you in the deep end."

"Just a little."

His phone buzzed again, and he winced. "Sorry. I have to answer this."

"Hey, answer your phone. Seriously," I said dryly, and he grinned at me, and I ignored the little twinge.

It had to be gas. It wasn't any emotion toward Gabriel Wilder.

"Hey Joshua. Yeah," he said, his voice deep as he stood up and left the nursery.

I began to pace, knowing that this time that we had left where things were on a precipice, yet feeling slightly calm at the same time, was going to end soon.

I wanted to trust that Gabriel would stay. That he would be all in. And the Gabriel that I had known before would. But this Gabriel? The ones with shadows in his eyes? I didn't know. And that worried me, but it wasn't like I had a choice right then.

Because we both deserved a second chance. Gabriel wasn't staying here. It really was only an hour away on I-35. Two hours during traffic. Which was most of the time these days. And if he took the tollway around Austin and came up from the north, he could bypass time.

And he was doing it. Nearly every day.

I knew that things were going to get more complicated when the baby was here. And that was an understatement.

And the press was going to find out. That worried me. Because the press had been hounding us during the first few months after the accident. They had wanted to know what would happen with the band, and why I was on the bus at all. They just wanted answers. The rest of the band and management had done their best to stem the tide, but they wanted to see Gabriel Wilder. And they hadn't been able to. And for now, Gabriel had been able to wear ball caps and hoodies in order to hide his face as he came into my house.

But at the hospital? I didn't know if he would be able to hide. And then there would be questions. So many questions.

I might be a Grammy winner, but that was for song-writing, and I didn't ever make the live shows. Gabriel was the star.

And now we would have to navigate that set of trials and tribulations.

"Sorry about that. Joshua just had a question about one of the companies that we used."

"Are you guys looking for a drummer?" I asked and could have kicked myself. Because Gabriel's face whitened, completely draining of color, and I shook my head. "I'm sorry. Pretend I didn't ask that." Honestly, the idea that my brother could be replaced at all made me want to throw up, but my brain wasn't thinking all that clearly at the moment.

He finally swallowed hard. "No. You should. And I don't know. We're talking about what happened and what they've been up to. But all of us have been pointedly not talking about finding a drummer. Or if we're going back on tour. But the thing is, they said the tour was *delayed*, not canceled, over in Europe. And there's a bunch of legal stuff that I've been ignoring."

"I can only imagine."

"I fucked up so royally. My friends have been so good. And now I need to clean up the messes."

He kept saying those words, and I wanted to believe it. But there was that hollowness in his gaze. He blamed himself. And he would always blame himself unless he talked through it. And I didn't think he would.

"Gabriel," I began, wanting to step over that crevice, to try to see if he was truly in the moment, or just taking the steps he thought he needed to. But I didn't have a chance to finish that sentence. Instead, my back tightened, and liquid gushed from between my legs.

"Holy shit," Gabriel said.

I looked up at him then, and then down at the small puddle on my beautiful rug that I had searched forever for when I had been in one of my pregnancy hormonal time periods.

"I just ruined that rug."

"Did your water just break?"

"Did I hear the words 'breaking water'?" Teagan asked as she ran through the doorway and pushed Gabriel out of the way. It was so comical that I laughed, ignoring the next wave of pain in my back and stomach.

"I ruined the rug." I didn't know why I was so fixated on that.

"It's a washable rug." Teagan winced. "Although I don't know if that type of fluid is meant to get out of that fabric, but let's not think about it. Okay, it is 4:00 PM, and we are going with plan C. Let's go."

"You weren't kidding about Father of the Bride," Gabriel said with a laugh, and I shook my head, excitement, nervousness, and a little bit of nausea running through me.

Teagan grabbed a couple of things and ran out toward the car, figuring we would follow. But instead I just stared at Gabriel, not knowing what to do.

"The baby's coming."

"Yeah." He swallowed hard and moved forward, hands outstretched. I nodded in answer, as he put his hands on my stomach, and smiled down.

"Okay Baby Girl. Let's meet you. What do you say?"

Tears once again slid down my cheeks because he had said the right thing. The *exact* right thing. And I really hoped to hell that this wasn't the beginning of the end.

Leaving Teagan out in the car, I found another set of clothes to change into, as Gabriel threw the rug and my ruined clothes in the washing machine. Soon we were in the car and heading toward the hospital.

"I texted my brother that your water broke, and they are on their way in shifts."

"We have a plan," Teagan said as she drove cautiously, and yet like a bat out of hell at the same time through Austin traffic in order to get to the hospital.

"One of them is going to stop by the house and make sure everything's set up and the dishes and clothes are washed. You know, *that* rug," he said, trying to make me laugh.

It didn't work as another wave of pain slammed into me, and Gabriel reached forward to grip my hand.

"You've got this, breathe."

"Excuse me, I'm the birth partner here," Teagan said with a laugh, though her eyes were on the road.

"You're both allowed in the room, but Gabriel, just know, it's going to get scary," I put in.

"I saw the photos in the book. I can't say that I'm ready because nobody can be ready, but I'll be there." I looked over my shoulder as he squeezed my hand back. "I'll be there. I want to be."

I looked forward again, rubbing my stomach. "Okay. Let's do this."

ACCORDING TO THE DOCTORS, I HAD BEEN IN labor for most of the day. Those back pains weren't just pains from standing or sitting for too long. No, those had been contractions.

But now the contractions had moved from my back to everywhere else.

The nurses and staff had pulled me into my private room right away. Gabriel and his team had worked with the hospital to get in through another door, so nobody noticed *the* Gabriel Wilder was in their midst.

They were going to eventually. They always did. But hopefully we had this moment of privacy.

A couple of nurses' eyes widened as they saw him, but nobody pulled out their phones and everybody acted professional. I had to hope that would stay the case.

I knew the waiting room was going to be full of Wilders soon, each of them taking shifts. Considering that a lot of them had children of their own, and I didn't know everybody well enough for them to be in the room, I was grateful that they had that covered.

"Are the boys on their way?" I asked, speaking of our brothers and holding Teagan's hand.

"Yes. But there's a problem."

"A problem?" I asked. Gabriel let out a hiss. I quickly let go of his hand. "Probably shouldn't break the hand that you know does the whole guitar thing," I said quickly.

"No, it's fine. Two years of rehabilitation surgery and I'll be tip-top. Do you want an ice chip?" he asked.

I shook my head, grateful for his humor when we were both freaking the fuck out. "What problem? Teagan?"

"There's a blizzard. And DIA is shut down."

I blinked. "It's Denver. They don't shut down for snow."

"Well they did, but the guys are getting out of there. They're driving up to Cheyenne and flying out of there and having to do a layover."

"Okay. But they'll all be here?" I asked, considering I had more than a few brothers.

"They will be. Dad will not," she said pointedly.

"Good," Gabriel growled, and there wasn't much to say after that.

It took another three hours, which apparently wasn't too long. However, it felt like the longest moments of my life. Considering I had been in labor for most of the day, the pain just kept hitting me, but I breathed through it.

I held Gabriel's and Teagan's hands. When it was time to push, they each held my thighs, and Gabriel pressed his forehead to the side of my head.

"You've got this, Briar. I believe in you. You've got this."

"Okay, remember the plan," Teagan said, and I couldn't help but smile at the two of them—even through the pain and stress.

And when our daughter was finally born, her first cries hitting my ears, everything changed.

Everything changed.

I looked up at Gabriel, who stared forward, his eyes

wide, and a giant smile covering his face. I had never seen that expression on him before, and I would remember it until the end of my days.

Teagan was sobbing happy tears next to me, and I finally looked forward as the doctor moved away to take her for whatever they needed to do. I would remember that later, of course, as I'd read all the books, but everything moved far too quickly for me to remember. They'd taken care of the rest of the birth while we caught our breaths and I tried to calm down.

Then the nurse placed our baby girl on my chest.

All sense of modesty was out the window since I was practically naked in front of everybody, but I didn't care. Childbirth was something that I was never prepared for and wasn't sure that I ever wanted to do again.

But in that moment, I didn't care.

Because my baby girl was on my chest.

Gabriel hadn't asked about names, but I had been thinking about one forever.

A name that made me smile because it was the name that Mal would have had if he had been the girl that my parents thought he would have been. When he had been born, he had surprised everybody, including the doctors, by being a boy. So he had been born Malcolm Ashford.

And so I held my daughter for the first time and

then the second time after they cleaned her up, as Teagan left the room to update everyone.

Gabriel wiped my forehead, and then kissed me softly on the mouth. "Congratulations, Mommy."

Tears pricked, and I smiled. "You're a daddy."

He paused for a moment, awe on his face, before he grinned. "You know I would have a joke there, and so would Mal," he teased.

I started crying harder, the baby so quiet and calm in my arms. "Do you want to hold your daughter?" I asked, so many emotions sliding through me that I couldn't hold on to them. They slid through my grasp, and it was all I could do just to breathe in that moment.

Gabriel leaned forward again and kissed me once more. This time, a little more poignant. I couldn't tell what he meant and couldn't tell what I wanted from it. But in this moment, it didn't matter.

He pulled away and nodded. "I'm really fucking scared."

"I would say language, but I curse as much as you."

One of the nurses laughed, and I handed over our baby, a little rocky at first. We had never done this before, after all. But he held her so close and so carefully, as if she were his whole world.

And she was.

Just like she was mine.

"Hello Baby Girl," he whispered, that voice such a croon. That true voice of an angel.

"Do you want to know her name?" I asked.

He looked over at me, a smile playing on his face.

"I was waiting for you to tell me."

"Gabriel? Meet Maisie Wilder Ashford."

He froze, the baby lifting her little arms toward her daddy. And I would remember that image for the rest of my life.

"*Maisie*. Well Briar. You know exactly how to kick a guy in the gut."

"It's okay that Wilder's in the middle, right? I mean, I would say it's for the band, but we both know it's for you."

"I'm honored. You did good, Mommy."

"And you look really good holding that baby, Daddy," I teased, and then he handed over Maisie again, and Gabriel leaned toward me, both of us enraptured in our daughter.

After this moment, nothing would ever be the same.

And I was finally okay with that.

CHAPTER TWELVE

BRIAR

No matter how many books I had read, how many online resources, and people I could speak to at birthing class and in my OB's waiting room, nothing could have prepared me for the first month of motherhood.

Maisie screamed in my arms, her little face scrunched up, her eyes closed, her little mouth moving in sucking motions, though she wasn't hungry. She fisted her little hands and screamed and screamed and nothing I was doing was helping.

I had a feeling that all of the residents of the Wilder Retreat could hear my baby's cries.

Exhaustion weighed on me, and it didn't matter that I had resources, people to lean on, and I hadn't actually had to cook a meal since I had been back—I had never felt this drained in my life.

I might not be wearing a diaper anymore, but my baby was, and she was not happy about it. The rash had finally gone away, but she still cried and cried.

At one month, she was supposed to cuddle and sleep and feed and that was all that was supposed to really matter. The doctors and books said that most of what my little girl did right now was reflexes. And her brain was growing, and she was learning just by being in our arms.

And yet this crying did not feel like a reflex. It felt as if I were failing, and she was making sure I knew it was me.

Everything I was doing was not enough for my daughter.

I had no idea what I was supposed to do next, but all I wanted to do was make my baby stop crying so she would be happy.

And I had no idea how to do that.

"Okay, Maisie baby. You've just nursed, and you threw up, and then you nursed again, and you've now been changed twice, and are in new jammies because wow, I have never actually seen a blowout like that before in my life. You are all clean and spick-and-span and adorable. I just need to know what's wrong, Baby

Girl. You need to tell me. Mommy's really worried that I'm not doing this right."

Maisie continued to cry.

I put her on her shoulder, trying to rock her the way that had worked the night before, and was no longer doing so.

Over the past month, everything had changed so dramatically, it felt as if I were running to catch up. Maisie could raise her head ever so slightly when she was on her stomach for tummy time and turn her face to the side. And she could focus on me. Watching her focus on me was one of the most stunning moments of my life.

Of course, however, she had all eyes for her daddy.

"I don't blame you, Kid," I muttered as Maisie quieted for a moment.

For a moment my heart stopped, and I didn't breathe, hoping that she would stop crying so I could put her to sleep, and maybe get a shower for myself. I still smelled like vomit, and that blowout, and I didn't want to think about it. But it didn't matter. As long as my baby girl was healthy, that was all that mattered.

But she wouldn't stop crying.

I set her back down in my arms to rock her, and she reached forward to grip my hair. She had just started doing that little grasping motion. It had been when

Gabriel had reached for her, his finger out. And she had gripped it with such a hard strength, that Gabriel and I had met gazes, and I had started crying.

Hormones seriously never ceased to amaze me, and I needed to stop crying in front of Gabriel Wilder. I still didn't know why I was here. No, not holding my baby as she cried and cried. But at the *Wilders'*.

I had a home in Austin, but right now, it wasn't safe for me to be there. We'd only spent two nights at my home in Austin. Two nights in the beautiful nursery that I had set up. And then on the third night, the paparazzi had found us.

I closed my eyes, still listening to my baby girl's cries as I thought of that night.

Somebody from the hospital had taken photos of Gabriel. He couldn't hide that bright smile of his, even with the dark circles under his eyes.

And now the news stories weren't about the long-lost Wilder in seclusion. No, now they had a false narrative of *why* he had been in hiding.

Because he was going to be a father. With his best friend's sister's baby.

The headlines on those so-called articles and social media accounts made my stomach roll. But they hadn't gotten a photo of Maisie.

Gabriel's family owned the security company that

worked for the retreat and winery, as well for the three celebrities that they had in the family. Considering Gabriel's cousins had married an Oscar-winning actress, as well as a Grammy award-winning pop star, they had countless hours of practice in keeping their team safe and making diversions.

While there were no photos of me looking like the bedraggled mess that I was, and no photos of our daughter, I couldn't stay in my cute little bungalow with my beautiful nursery that my sister and I had spent so much time working on.

Teagan had to go back home because she couldn't take any more time off work, but had stayed for three weeks. And my brothers had been here for as long as they could, but now the Ashfords were back north in Colorado, and I hadn't gone with them.

I tried not to think about the fight that had occurred with that, but I hadn't been able to go.

And it wasn't just because of Gabriel.

It was because of the little girl in my arms. And the fact that I would find a way to get back into *my* home. I would find a way to make this not so insane.

I hadn't read any of the articles and I hadn't had time to find out any more than the initial headlines. So I had no idea what they were saying about me. What they were saying about Mal or Gabriel. Only that I was in hiding on this retreat in this little gray cabin because there was nowhere else for me to go and still feel a connection to my home.

Because Ashford Creek wasn't home. Not anymore.

Ava and Aurora had somehow created a beautiful nursery in the spare room of this cabin. It really wasn't a cabin and more like a house. They had brought over not only some of my things, but some of the other Wilder items.

So Maisie had a beautiful nursery in a place that wasn't my own, but was safe.

But my baby girl still cried.

The door opened, and I whirled with my little girl in my arms as Gabriel walked in, a frown on his face.

"My girls are up late," he said, and my heart twisted a bit at that.

Because he lost that frown that he tried to hide from me and smiled. But it didn't reach his eyes fully. No, his eyes only brightened when he looked at Maisie.

I knew that he couldn't do a 180 from what he had been hiding for the past eight months. He was still the man who had passed out after seeing me pregnant. Still the man that ignored phone calls for months on end. But he was also the man that was trying.

I couldn't get a read on him. And considering I had no idea what I was feeling or thinking, I didn't blame him for hiding. I had no idea what I was doing, or what would happen after this, but for now, I just needed

Maisie to stop crying. And I had to stop thinking about the fact that he called us *his girls*.

I hadn't always been good at pretending I didn't have feelings for Gabriel Wilder, but I'd found a routine. I'd work with the band and see my brother...and see Gabriel in the process. Then we'd hang out, laugh, and I'd tell myself I didn't want to continue to fall in love with him. We'd both move on to other people and I would try to keep the longing gazes to a minimum.

Then I'd let myself fall into his arms...and fall for him.

We were just playing family at this point, to figure out our next step because of who Gabriel was and the life he lived. Only I was too tired to think beyond that.

"Okay, I'm here. Daddy's here."

I wanted to resent him for that, but as soon as he lifted Maisie into his arms, the little traitor stopped crying.

He rocked her quietly, and I stood back, ignoring the way that I was afraid my breasts were going to start leaking milk soon as they *always* did. Because I was a disgusting mess and all I wanted to do was shower.

"How are your brothers?" I asked, trying to keep my voice somewhat calm. And yet I felt nothing like calm.

"They're good. They had a bunch of paperwork to sign since I own part of the property. The Wilders wanted to go all in, you know?" He paused and his throat worked as he swallowed hard. "I wanted to thank you."

He continued to rock Maisie, and the little girl didn't even peep. I wanted to feel a lot more resentful for that, and yet I couldn't. Not when the two of them were a sight to see. I would take a photo of this moment, but I already had enough photos of him holding our little girl while he wore tight jeans and a button-up collared shirt that was made out of cotton. He just looked like the Gabriel I knew. Holding our child.

I wasn't quite sure when I had slipped into this timeline, but I wasn't sure how I was going to get out of it.

"Thank me for what?" I asked, my voice soft.

"For being so nice to my parents."

I had picked up a cloth to wipe at a stain on my shirt and frowned at him. "Why wouldn't I be nice to your parents?" I asked.

"Because they were a lot, but they were excited to meet their granddaughter."

They had come last week, giving us two weeks to deal with the media, security, as well as my family, and the Wilders that lived here. They had been so sweet and caring to both Maisie and me. And while I had met them a few times before this, it had been awkward nonetheless.

It wasn't as if Gabriel and I were a couple. Nearly everybody in our life knew that this had been a one-night stand and our connection was Mal.

Only nobody talked about it. We sure as hell didn't talk about it. And now everybody walked on eggshells, purposely not mentioning it because they had Maisie in their arms and that was all that mattered.

And for now, while the world shook and shattered around me, I was just going to focus on that.

"I love your parents. I loved them when they went on tour and your mom and I would scream in the stands along with all of your fan girls just to get a rise out of you."

"I remember that. Wasn't my mom the one who threw her bra?" he asked and shuddered. Maisie burbled a little, but didn't start crying again.

The memory brought a smile to my face. "It was a sports bra that she bought at the store on our way there. Mostly just to annoy you."

"That sounds like Mom. Mal picked it up and said he was going to keep it. And then I had to beat him up. It was a thing."

Gabriel froze for a moment, and I realized that he had said Mal's name again. That stone on clear water that neither one of us knew what to do with.

The baby started to suckle at Gabe, and he winced.

"Okay, sorry, Little Girl. That's your momma's job. I'm not equipped."

As soon as Maisie let out a cry, my breasts ached, and I went to sit down in the rocking chair that they had brought over from one of Gabe's cousin's houses.

It wasn't my rocker. Not the one I had chosen. But it was so close enough to it that it brought warmth to my heart. I would make memories in my own nursery soon. As soon as the news story died down and the team finished with the extra security measures for the neighborhood—something my neighbors loved, I'm sure. For now, I'd use the rocker that had been loved by others and sat in the living room as it was too big for the nursery.

Gabriel handed Maisie over, and I unbuttoned my top, immediately letting Maisie latch on. Modesty was still all out the window at this point, and yet sometimes it felt awkward in front of Gabriel. Because it *didn't* feel awkward.

Gabriel kneeled down in front of me and ran his finger along Maisie's cheek as she drank.

The fact that it was so close to me made me swallow hard.

"Did you eat?" he asked, his voice that low rumble.

"Yes. Although I'm sure that at one point we're going to have to cook for ourselves," I teased.

"Are you kidding me? My cousin-in-law is a world-

enowned chef. She owns two restaurants on this prop-
rty alone. I'm never cooking again."

I rolled my eyes and rocked as Maisie continued to
at. "You know I just fed her," I said with a laugh.

"Well, it's second breakfast." He paused. "Or second
linner? It is getting pretty late."

"True."

That awkwardness settled in once again, and I didn't
know why it felt like he was a stranger. It shouldn't. I
knew Gabriel. Intimately.

And yet it felt as if I didn't know him. I wasn't sure
this was the *real* Gabriel.

"So did you also talk to David?" I asked after a
moment, and Gabriel froze. Just for an instant, but I
saw it. That flinch.

The true Gabe.

He cleared his throat. "I did. They'll be here in a
couple of days. Lark has a studio at her place on the
other side of the property. So we're going to be working
there. Just to figure some things out. And so they can
kick my ass."

"Oh. Good. Not about the ass kicking part. But
they've been wanting to see the baby."

"And the thousands of photos that we've sent probably aren't enough."

"It never is," I said inelegantly.

Maisie finished feeding then, a little milk drunk, and

I was grateful when Gabriel stood up to give me som space to get situated again.

I rubbed Maisie's little back, and then she starte screaming. And I wanted to tell myself it was jus because we were tired, but no, it was because her dadd wasn't near her anymore.

So Gabriel moved forward, and took the baby from me, helping her get out all her little worries and gas. A soon as he situated her afterward, she immediately fel asleep on his shoulder.

Anger coursed through me. Stupid anger that had nothing to do with Gabriel, or maybe everything to do with him. It had no place here.

Everything that I was doing didn't feel like enough. I was covered in dry milk and vomit and God knows what else. I felt as if I had been run over by a truck, and everything still ached, and my baby loved her daddy more than me.

It was irrational, and yet it was totally true.

Gabriel gave me a weird look, and I realized that I had my hands fisted in my lap, as a tear fell down my cheek.

"I'm going to go tuck her in. Be right back."

"Okay. She'd like that probably." I wasn't a fan of the bitterness in my tone.

Again, he gave me a weird look and moved toward the nursery. The baby monitor was on, so I'd heard him singing a sweet lullaby, that croon of a voice echoing through the room.

He was so damn talented. The reason why Wilder took off. Oh yes, the rest of the band was brilliant, my brother included. But Gabriel had that spark. He was the one that lit up to the point that the band was able to circle him.

And now he sang to our baby.

Gabriel came back out while I was still sitting in the rocking chair. A frown covered his face, and I stiffened. "Let's get you in the shower."

I raised a brow. "Oh?"

"Come on. You're stuck with me for a little bit."

He reached forward and grabbed my hand, and I snatched it back.

"I'm fine. It's just been a long night."

"And you should take a shower, Briar."

I shook my head. "Maybe you need to take a shower."

Okay, now who is the petulant baby that couldn't stop crying? In answer, Gabriel rolled his eyes, and then lifted me into his arms. I let out a cry and wrapped my arms around his neck as he carried me into the bathroom.

"Gabriel Wilder put me down."

"If I do that, I'm going to drop you. And I don't actually want to hurt you, Briar. Although sometimes wondering what the hell is going on in that mind of yours makes me want to shake you. But I won't do that."

I had no idea what he was going to do next, but then he walked into the huge shower that took up most of the bathroom and set me down on my feet.

"Gabriel, what are you doing?" I asked.

In answer, he turned on the water.

I spluttered, pushing my hair from my face.

"Are you kidding me right now?"

"Not really. Come on, let's get you all clean. I gave you tonight alone so that way you could have some time without me hovering, but clearly that was a bad idea."

"Gabriel Wilder. You're not my mother. You're not my nanny. And now I'm soaking wet."

"Well, ladies are usually soaking wet around me."

I shoved at him. "Are you serious right now? That's the line you're going with?"

"I'm a rock god. That's what I do."

He was saying the words and yet it was still a little off. Not quite the old Gabriel. But he wasn't going to be. I wasn't the old Briar. He was hiding something and playing a part. Maybe that's what he needed to do. Then again, I was doing the same.

Gabriel started tugging on my shirt, and I pulled it back down.

"Really?"

"I've already seen everything anyway," he said, with a roll of his eyes, and then I was helpless to do anything but stand there as he pulled off my clothes, and I finally let the hot water slide over me.

Gabriel undid his shirt, and I raised a brow.

"Oh?"

"I'll keep the wet jeans on. Although these are going to be a bitch to get off later."

"We really need to work on your cussing around Maisie."

"True. But I think I'll wait around like three months for that."

"If her first word is fuck, I'm going to blame you."

I was arguing with him about curse words while I was completely naked in front of him, and I hadn't even realized it.

I wanted to cover myself, knowing that I didn't look like I had the first time he had seen me naked, but I was too tired to care. Instead, I just closed my eyes and let him wash my hair, trying not to think about what was going to happen next. Or what should happen next.

His hands were so careful, and yet sure in his movements.

His fingers had always been talented, and I blushed at that, because I had been thinking about his guitar

159

skills, but yes, his fingers were talented at other things, too.

But that wasn't this.

This was just him being kind.

And I had no idea what the hell I was doing.

He rinsed my hair, and then he used the loofah on me. I opened my eyes, and I realized that I was leaning on him as he washed me slowly. I didn't feel beautiful. I didn't feel anything really. Yet he continued to run the loofah over me, taking his time as both of us caught our breaths.

When he moved me fully under the stream to wash away the soap, I reached up and pushed his wet hair from his face.

"She always stops crying in your arms," I whispered.

"Because she's a baby and sometimes they do that. She sleeps in your arms too, Briar. It's just a bad night."

I shook my head, and leaned against him, skin to skin. "It doesn't feel like that."

He kissed the top of my head, and I let out a breath. "It's okay Briar. I have no idea what the hell I'm doing either."

I looked up at him then, and I didn't know if he meant in this moment, or with Maisie, but then he leaned down, and I couldn't think at all.

His lips brushed mine, just a simple caress, and then a deeper one, his tongue brushing along mine. I wanted to kiss him back, wanted to wrap my arms around him. I wanted to push him away.

But before I could do anything, before I could make a decision, he took a step back.

"Shit."

"Yeah, shit."

I ran my hands over my face, and then realized the water was still on.

And I was completely naked in front of him.

I turned off the water and reached for a towel.

Gabriel sighed. "I'm sorry. I shouldn't have kissed you."

"I was kissing you back," I said, holding the towel to myself.

"This would be a mistake. For Maisie."

Just like before had been a mistake for Mal. Only I didn't say that.

"I know. We're just tired."

But I was still standing in front of him. Both of us still looking at one another, and I swallowed hard again. And then Gabriel moved forward and brushed his lips once more against mine. And I once more kissed him back.

"A total mistake," he whispered.

"You're right. It would be." But I still leaned against him, this time in my towel, and him in his wet jeans, and I just let myself breathe for the first time in far too long.

Because what scared me wasn't merely the kiss; it wasn't everything churning inside that made no sense. What scared me was that other than the times he looked at Maisie, the look he had given me before he kissed me was the first time I had seen true emotion in his eyes in far too long.

And I had no idea what to do with that.

CHAPTER THIRTEEN
GABRIEL

Guilt swamped me as nausea continued to threaten, but I swallowed hard, staring at the people who had been in my life for so long. They were family. Family that I had taken for granted and ignored.

Joshua stood at the studio desk, randomly touching buttons and knobs that would probably have to be fixed later. He wasn't looking at me, and I didn't blame him. After all, he had been the one to take his time to answer me back when I had finally called.

Rocky leaned against the wall, phone in hand as she texted her wife.

While David sat in front of me, notebook in hand.

It had been a week since the band had come back. A week since they had met Briar and Maisie and had fallen in love. They hadn't said a damn word about us having a kid. Everybody was ignoring the giant elephant in the room.

We had suddenly fallen into domestic bliss that was anything but blissful, and awkward as hell. But everybody was ignoring that, too.

And I was just fine with that, as I didn't want to have to deal with the big emotions. I had to deal with the shit show that was happening today.

"We can stop this, you know," David said, ever the patient one. At least he was now. "Walk away and tell everyone we changed our mind. It's our prerogative."

"No, we should do this. Max already put out the word, and people are heading to the property now. We should do this." I cleared my throat, staring at my band again.

"I want to do this too, you know," Rocky said as she slid her phone into her back pocket. "It took me a while to get out of my own head, and then Mandy's dad died, and well, life sucks. But I was going to come down here and kick your ass. I was just afraid once I did, you'd tell me to leave and then the band would be over. I don't want it to be over."

"I thought it was," Joshua said, staring off into the distance.

"I'm sorry. For ignoring all of you." I ran a hand over my sternum, remembering the initial months of recovery when my ribs had ached and my leg had been in the boot. I didn't have a scar on me, but that was only surface deep.

"Mal was your best friend. I get it." Joshua sighed. "You were injured too."

"And now here we are, doing auditions for a fucking drummer." My rhythmic guitarist finally looked at me, his eyes glassy.

"I hate this." I looked between all of them and realized we all hated it...yet needed it. Music was in our blood. This was our livelihood and something we loved. And though I'd hidden from it for months, I needed to do something that Maisie could be proud of. That Briar could be proud of. "Are we ready?" I asked.

David finally cleared his throat. "No. And we're never going to be ready. But us sitting in a room and talking about all the mistakes we've made and pretending that we're okay when we're clearly not isn't going to help anything. So we're going to do what we normally do and jump in headfirst to make a lot of fucking mistakes. We have fifteen drummers that we are going to audition today. Some people we know. Some newbies that want a chance."

"And they already signed the NDAs?" I asked, my voice low.

The media was still harping on trying to get more images of my kid. I hated the paparazzi. I despised the flashes that stained underneath my lids, so they were always there no matter what I did. They kept writing stories about Rocky and put Mal on a pedestal, as if he had done nothing wrong in his life. The angel where I was now the devil.

And it was damn ironic because they always called Mal the force to be reckoned with. The one who bulldozed his way through life and was constantly in the news for something he did wrong. Even if he wasn't the one doing it. But they talked shit about him, made up lies, and now erased it all to talk about how heroic he was.

And now the media wanted to know if Wilder was going to come back. If the band was going to make it.

So in the past two days, when news of auditions had begun to spread like wildfire, the media had shown up.

Thankfully, we were borrowing Lark's studio on the property, so nobody was allowed on set but us. My brother was handling most of it, and I had already apologized to him more than once for it. But they dealt with this often, so I was going to lean into their expertise.

"You're right. We really do dive in headfirst and say fuck the consequences," I said, blowing a bubble with my gum.

"Well that doesn't sound too bad." Rocky shook her head. "I know that we have skipped over a lot of the formalities. But we do have an album to finish, one that we're already on contract for. And we have to decide if we go back to the old tour, redo those dates. Then deal with everything else that we are on the line for. I know Max said he can get us out of it, and a lot of the promotions have been decent about it, but they're starting to growl. And the execs aren't going to be so kind soon."

"I don't want us to break up. We already lost Mal. I don't want to lose us either." Joshua wiped his tears, before blowing a raspberry. "Okay fuck all these emotions. We can put it in lyrics, or we can bury it deep inside and deal with it later. Let's just find a drummer."

"Yeah. We need a drummer." My stomach rolled, but I knew if we didn't do this, we'd regret it. And Mal would kick my ass.

My phone buzzed, and I looked down at it, a photo of Briar and Maisie filling the screen.

Aurora and Ava had taken the duo out for a day trip, and I was seriously stressed out. They'd had their six-week visit a little bit ago, and now Maisie was allowed to be out in the real world. But she was so tiny. I just wanted to wrap her in cotton wool and hide her from the world.

I knew that doing that would probably just make everything worse.

I wasn't with them for a multitude of reasons. Namely, because every time I left the property, people took photos. They wanted answers. And I didn't say anything. But they were one day going to get a photo of Briar, me, and Maisie and I wasn't sure what I was going to do.

And not just because I could still feel Briar against me, that spark that had always been there that we had done our best to ignore.

There was a reason the two of us had fallen into bed together that night. Even if we did our best to ignore it.

"Earth to Gabriel," Joshua said, and I looked up, shaking my head.

"Sorry. Briar just sent a photo of Maisie." I turned it so they could see. My friends smiled at me, even as an odd tension filled the room.

"That's so fucking weird," Rocky blurted, before closing her mouth.

"I know. I'm a dad. How the hell did that happen?" I asked, an odd spark filling me. Because I was a dad. Maisie was half of my DNA, and every ounce of tethered bonds that I could imagine.

She was my kid. And she looked just like Briar. Though Briar said she looked like me. We could agree to disagree.

"So we have two dads in the band now. We might even have a third soon if we hire one of these drummers," Joshua put in.

I pulled my phone back to text Briar and nodded. "A

tour with diaper bags and bottles that don't have liquor in them. Going to be a little weird," I muttered.

> ME:
>
> Where are you guys? I missed those chubby cheeks.

> BRIAR:
>
> Did you just call my cheeks chubby?

I winced and typed quickly.

> ME:
>
> You know I was talking about our girl. I like your cheeks. Both sets.

> BRIAR:
>
> That is a ridiculous line. You used to be good at this. You're out of practice.

> ME:
>
> No shit. You guys having fun?

> BRIAR:
>
> Yes. But I already miss the little cabin. Is that wrong?

My heart warmed, and I didn't know why.

> ME:
>
> I miss you guys too. Stop by the studio when you're done?

BRIAR:

It depends on nap time. But sure. I
want to see the band. And you know
that they love holding Baby Girl.

ME:

I miss you.

It took a while for Briar to type back, and I could not
believe I had typed those words. What the hell was
wrong with me?

BRIAR:

I miss you too. We're ridiculous.

ME:

Somehow, I got baby hormones too.

BRIAR:

Eye roll emoji.

"Hey, let's get started," David said, and I put my
phone away, trying not to feel the warmth sliding
through me that had nothing to do with picking out a
drummer. However, that heat slowly settled down the
nerves that were threatening to make me throw up. So
maybe that was a good sign.

The first drummer walked in, complete in leather
pants and a leather vest with nothing underneath. He
held one drumstick in his left hand, and the other in his
back pocket. I had never heard of this guy, and he
wasn't in any band that I knew, but we were going to

give him a chance. They did introductions and I stood there with my arms crossed over my chest.

"I just want to say I love you guys. Wilder has always been one of my top bands. And, well, thanks for giving me this chance."

We all nodded, and David thankfully took charge. "No problem. Let's hear you play. And maybe we'll see what happens."

Before this would've been my job. The lead singer, and the lead. But I wasn't sure what I was supposed to say. Why was I even here?

I pushed that thought from my head, as Samuel grinned. "And I'm sorry about Malcolm. He was a good drummer. My idol. Hell, all of my idols are drummers, and they keep dying. What's up with that?"

I stiffened, as Rocky's eyes narrowed, and I knew that no matter what kind of talent this kid had, he wasn't going to gel with us. We let him do his audition, and I didn't say a damn word as he walked out, David finishing the interview.

"Well, he somewhat kept the beat," I drawled.

Joshua shook his head. "I really don't have a good feeling about this."

And the man wasn't wrong.

The next drummer didn't like our kit and proceeded to move everything around away from Mal's preferred liking. And while I wanted to rip this guy's head off for doing so, I knew that we were replacing a drummer. And somehow, I was supposed to make this work. This shouldn't be happening.

I tried to ignore the shadow of Mal behind the kit, staring at me. I wasn't drunk, but I was apparently seeing things.

The second drummer finished his audition, and I had no idea what he had played.

The third and fourth drummers were fine, but there was no spark.

We ignored the fifth drummer because all they wanted to do was talk about Mal.

"And Gabriel man. Where'd you go? I mean, we saw the rest of you, but we didn't see you. I hear you're a dad now. Cool right? Mal as an uncle would've been really great. Too bad he's gone, right?"

I hadn't even realized I was standing up, my forearm against the guy's throat until Joshua was pulling me back, but it wasn't as if he was really pulling that hard.

"Okay, we're done," David said, and pushed the other guy out as Rocky and Joshua kept me calm.

"Well, we're going to go with a no on that," Rocky said dryly. "And Gabriel, maybe we don't beat up the drummers."

"I'm making no promises."

It kept going like that, one shitty audition after another.

We hadn't given much notice, and somehow getting the band Wilder to rise out of the ashes was going to be hell on Earth, but I wasn't sure what else we were supposed to do.

Rocky finally stood up after the last audition and shot her fist in the air. "Yes."

We stared at her like she had lost her mind.

"Did you just like that drummer? He didn't even know what a snare drum was called," I snapped.

"Oh no, he was terrible, but I was really hoping that my friend would show up."

"You have a friend?" Joshua asked, and Rocky flipped him off.

"I have a few. But she's been doing band gigs up in Hollywood for movie scores and shit. However, she's wanted to try out a few things that aren't so regiment-ed." Rocky raised a pierced brow. "You're going to be okay with two women in the band?"

"You're saying that she's so good that she's just going to get the spot?" I asked, wondering why I had never heard of this friend.

Rocky shook her head. "I'm not saying that at all. Let her audition, and let's see what happens. We all know that it's going to be a probationary period anyway."

I nodded. "Because if they don't gel, we're not going to be a band."

And that was the scariest thing of all. We had no idea if this was going to work. It probably wasn't. And this was probably the end.

Maybe that was fine.

Maybe I'd just find a cabin in the woods and learn to whittle. And then Briar could show up every once in a while with Maisie, and I wouldn't be too much of a deadbeat dad.

Ghost Mal just shook his head in disappointment.

"Knock knock."

I looked up to see a woman with platinum blonde hair, a septum piercing, and gorgeous curves, wearing a sundress.

"Kiera, you're here." Rocky moved forward and wrapped her arms around the other woman. Kiera laughed and hugged Rocky right back.

"Sorry it took me so long to get here. I-35 is a mess." Kiera looked at all of us and smiled. "I know this sucks, you guys. And I am sorry that you even have to have auditions and sit through this awkward interview. But hi, I'm Kiera. I play drums."

"In a dress?" Joshua asked, and then ducked Rocky's slap.

"Really?"

"Actually, I was wondering how you play in a dress, considering I don't play, but I know how Mal moves. Moved," I corrected and continued before anyone could comment. "However, now that I'm thinking about it, there are some drummers that wear kilts." I stood up and held out my hand. "Gabriel."

"I know who you are. It's nice to meet you all." Kiera let out a breath and shook out her arms.

"Okay, I'm seriously nervous. Mostly because I love you guys. I love your music. And I realized that even if you find me the new goddess of percussion, you could hate me. But just give me a chance, okay? And I'm wearing a dress because my flight got in late and I didn't have time to change. Long story."

I looked at David, who had an odd smile on his face, but the other man hadn't said anything.

"Well let's see what you got," I said, and again, David didn't say anything.

Apparently, I was leading this, and I wasn't quite sure I liked that.

Ghost Mal didn't say anything. Obviously.

Kiera set up, and then we sat back and watched her play.

Mal had always had a frantic energy to him. His whole body moved with the flow, but sometimes it was a little jagged. He would laugh maniacally and sing along when needed. He was the crazy ball of energy behind us, pushing us.

Kiera was different.

I wasn't quite sure how to explain it.

Yeah, she had energy, but her body moved a little more gracefully. I wasn't sure if that was rock band material, but she could play.

She started with a Taylor Hawkins song, and moved into a few other bands that we knew, and then, picked up Rain on Me.

I froze but realized that we needed to hear how she sounded with our most popular song.

Part of me wanted to grab my guitar, lay my fingers on the fret, and play along, and then, in that moment, I realized that I hadn't played since the accident. I felt like maybe I was the one that's going to need that audition. I quickly pushed those thoughts from my mind, as Kiera finished up and wiped sweat from her brow.

"Whew. Thanks for letting me play. I always loved that song. Mal really knew what he was doing. He was the best. And I'm sorry that he's gone. And I will stop saying his name if you want. I don't know how to deal with grief."

"I don't think we know what we're doing either," Rocky whispered.

Before I could add anything in, Briar walked in, Maisie in her arms.

"Ridge said that you should be done soon. I'm sorry, am I interrupting?"

I immediately moved forward and took Maisie from arms. "Hey Little Girl."

"I'm sorry, I *am* interrupting." Briar cleared her throat and smiled softly over at Kiera. "Hi. I'm Briar."

I moved to the side, and without thinking, put my arm around Briar so she was facing the center of the circle with the rest of us. Only the rest of the band caught the motion, and they froze, and I did as well.

I had no idea what the hell I was doing, but it just felt like I should. I had our kid in my arms, and I wanted Briar to feel comfortable. But I needed to stop touching her.

I let my arm fall as Kiera smiled back.

"It's nice to meet you. I should go and let you guys talk. And even if this doesn't work out, it was an honor to play for you guys."

"I'll walk you out." Rocky gave us a look, but I didn't say anything. "We're not making any decisions today."

Kiera just smiled. "No problem. Honestly, I just needed to get out of classical music."

"I have so many questions," Joshua said and followed the two of them out.

David looked between Briar and me, confusion on his face. "Well. It's still fucking awkward to see the two of you holding a baby like that."

"We really need to do better with that language," Briar said as she rolled her eyes.

David leaned forward and pat Maisie's belly. "She

179

can't understand anything yet. I mean, I'm a dad. I know things."

"I'm not quite sure that's true," I said with a laugh, as Maisie woke up, burbling that little baby noise of hers.

She immediately wanted Briar and her breasts, and frankly, I didn't blame the kid. And as we shifted Maisie into Briar's arms, David kept watching the routine we had found, but I ignored him.

And the feeling that this was right. I had no idea what was going to happen with the band. I had no idea what the hell I wanted. But right then and there, this felt like something I could do.

Making sure Briar felt safe and keeping Maisie happy.

Even if I had nothing else, I could do that.

And I ignored Ghost Mal along the way.

CHAPTER FOURTEEN
GABRIEL

I hadn't realized how quickly babies grew.

Two months old and Maisie stared up at me with wide eyes.

"I'm headed back out to practice. This one is in front of other people. I'm sorry that you can't come and see me play. But one day. Your mom and I got you little headphones. But I feel like they're too big for your little ears."

Maisie, of course, didn't say anything, just continued to stare at me with those beautiful eyes that were starting to lose their baby blue and brighten into the Wilder blue.

I stood in Briar's kitchen, rocking Maisie back and forth. Briar was in her office, guitar in hand, trying to get work done before her next deadline. We had come back to her home in Austin once my brother had put in decent security. She was in a gated community, but everybody who ran services, deliveries, or friends had been able to get their own code to get in.

Somehow Ridge and Trace had worked with the HOA to get tighter security, and the neighborhood felt a little safer. In fact, the neighbors were grateful because now they didn't get a single solicitor at their house. It also meant there weren't any photographers sneaking around the area.

It had helped that we had spent most of our time on the Wilder property, hiding from the masses. However, the news had broken that we had officially added Kiera to the band on a temporary basis for at least this first album. I wasn't sure what was going to happen, if we were really going to meld, but in the past month, we had done our best.

It felt as if I were walking through quicksand, or perhaps even watching my life happen as an observer, rather than living it. Sometimes it didn't even feel like I was here, holding my daughter, a daughter I had never expected.

"I'm never going to let them hurt you," I whispered, rocking her to sleep.

I had the exhaust vent over the stove going because Maisie liked that sound for some reason, but as soon as I turned it off when she fell asleep, I could finally hear the strum of a guitar and Briar's soft voice.

I froze, realizing how much I had missed that.

When Mal and I had been on tour the first time, our band playing in ridiculously small venues, and David shooting up in the bathrooms, Briar had shown up as well. She had been there to make sure that Mal wasn't getting in any scrapes, but of course we all were.

And she had partied with us and played her own music. And I'd done my best to ignore my dick every time she was around.

She never wanted the spotlight. No, she wanted to write the songs from her heart. As well as songs from other artists' hearts, as sometimes those artists couldn't get it out in the way that they wanted, and so Briar would come around and help.

Right now she was writing a song for a popular male artist that had just finished a two-year-long tour around the world. The guy wrote some of his own music, but really liked working with a variety of different song-writers.

He had won two Grammys using Briar's songs, so I knew that they had a good working relationship.

My stomach churned at that, remembering the rumors that the two had dated. I wasn't sure if that had been true, considering there were hundreds of rumors about people I had dated in the past. But with the easy camaraderie that they had, even through video chats recently, I had a feeling that maybe that rumor was true.

But I had no right to be jealous.

Except that I was.

"Back off, Gabriel. She's not yours."

I ignored the feeling that Mal was watching me once again. I knew he wasn't in the room. I knew that his ghost wasn't haunting me. Those didn't exist.

And yet, I could still feel him. Judging.

My best friend was dead, and I was the one here. I had touched Mal's sister, and now our lives were forever entwined because of the precious soul in my arms. Mal had never been able to be an uncle to this baby girl because I had ruined everything. And no matter how much time passed, no matter how hard I tried to pretend, I wasn't okay.

Maisie shifted in my arms, and I moved to the office door, continuing to listen to Briar sing.

She had such a good voice, an alto that had a vibrato that just stuck with you. She could belt if she wanted to, but she was better in the lower register. If she had wanted to be a full-time singer with a career that lasted ages, I figured she could do it. But she liked what she did, and I wasn't going to push her.

The fact that I was still staying at her house while neither one of us spoke about the consequences or logistics of it, meant that we weren't good at talking about anything.

We were just living day by day, taking turns at her house and then my little cabin. I didn't have a house near here, and Maisie didn't have a nursery at the cabin. She would, though. A home of her own, once I figured out what I wanted. The problem was that I had no idea what I wanted.

However, that wasn't only just about Maisie.

When Briar stopped singing, I knocked gently on the door, hoping it didn't wake up Maisie.

"Come in," Briar said softly, and I twisted the door-knob, making my way inside. She sat on the ground with her legs crossed and her guitar on her lap. She had three notebooks spread around her and various colored pens. Her hair flowed down her back and her eyes were bright with the creativity that pounded through her veins like it did mine.

"Hey. I need to head out. But Maisie's down for the count."

"Did the exhaust fan work?" Briar asked as she put her guitar away and came forward, arms outstretched.

She was so damn gorgeous. It was hard for me to think sometimes. Hence why we had been together that one night anyway. It had nothing to do with the drinks. I had lied to myself far too many times, and I needed to stop doing that. But no good could come from me giving in to temptation. It would just hurt Mal once again, and Maisie needed to stay safe and not stuck in the middle of whatever the hell was going on between us.

"You know it," I said as I gently placed Maisie in Briar's arms.

"You guys have that major practice today, right?"

I nodded, pulling my gaze from hers to look down at Maisie in her arms. "Yes. It's probably going to go to like shit because we're not ready, but the execs want to see us try. They're not happy with Kiera."

"Because she's a woman?" Briar asked, a brow raised.

I winced. "Yeah. Apparently, it was okay if we had one woman in the band because we could be a little quirky. But two? Way too much of an estrogen fest."

"So you're going to kick their asses, aren't you?" Briar asked, a smile playing on her face.

"I'd like to think we would. But we're not ready." I frowned, annoyed that we weren't the best. We'd never be what we once were, but each of us was off. Kiera couldn't blend with us if we weren't sure who we were in the first place.

"You're trying. That's something." She bit her lip, worry in her gaze.

I nodded, my throat going tight. "Yeah. Guitar in hand and everything. I'm a little rusty, though."

"It's always been a part of you, Gabriel. You can do this."

"Not today we can't." I cleared my throat. "Anyway. I know you wanted to interview a few nannies tomorrow, but I don't know if I'm going to be able to make it. It depends on how today goes. The ad execs want more meetings that I wasn't prepared for." I should have planned for that, since they tended to try to take over any schedule we made.

Briar recoiled. "Okay. But I won't make any decisions without you." She let out a breath. "I just hate the fact that we have to hire a nanny."

It wasn't my favorite thing, but it wasn't out of the norm for what we did for a living. "It's not like the two of us work in a place that has a daycare center. Or even the idea of us dropping off Maisie at a place? No, I can't do that."

"I know. And I realize that we are both very privileged in the fact that we can afford it. But you're going to go out on tour someday soon. And I don't know what I'm going to do. I can't have Maisie strapped to me twenty-four hours a day when I'm trying to work as well."

I leaned forward and ran my finger over Maisie's cheek, and then did the same to Briar without thinking. She stiffened but didn't pull away.

I needed to stop touching her. "You're allowed to

have a life, you know. While part of me wants to just lock Maisie up on the Wilder compound and keep her safe from the world, I also want to make sure that someone's always with her when we're out of the house, you know?"

"Exactly. But I'm going to have mom guilt."

"My mom says that mom guilt never goes away, but you learn to live with it. I already have dad guilt though."

"Your mom has been so great."

"She's the best." The two of them had really gotten to know each other over the past month. Though she didn't live here, she video chatted often, and always had answers for all of Briar's questions. Hell, she had answers for me as well. The Wilder women had helped tremendously, and while Briar and I were exhausted and still finding our footing, we were never alone. I still felt lost, not having any time to prepare for this, but then again, Briar said she felt lost as well.

We hadn't asked for this. Hadn't known what we were doing, but we were doing it. And I was doing my damn best not to ruin it by putting my hands on Briar once again.

"I'll check on you soon. I don't know how long we'll be."

"Go kick ass. You're good at this. You've always been good at this. Don't forget that."

I leaned forward and brushed my lips against hers. I couldn't help it. I just needed to at that moment. "For luck," I whispered, and she studied my face, and I had a feeling she knew that was a lie.

"For luck. But you're *the* Gabriel Wilder. And you can show the world whenever you're ready."

"You have way too much faith."

"I think Maisie's the only reason that I can pretend to do so."

And with that, I ran my hand over Maisie's head, and then through Briar's hair, before heading out to the studio.

We weren't using Lark's for this major practice session, as it felt weird to have all of those people on the Wilder land. I didn't mind the label. They had been good to us in the past. But I knew that they were straining at the wait.

They wanted us back on tour, and they wanted to use the tragedy to push our next album. In a publicity sense, I guess it made sense. But all I wanted to do was shove it down and never think about it again. So now I stood in a studio that was not my own, with people that I had abandoned, wondering what the hell I was doing.

"You ready for this?" Joshua asked as he tapped his fingers on his thigh. He looked just as nervous as I did.

"You've at least been playing in the past few months."

"Yeah, but not for anyone else. You know me, I put my life through music."

I sighed, looking down at my hands. "I used to. It's weird that the guitar in my hand doesn't feel like mine anymore."

I hadn't meant to say that out loud, but Joshua gave me a knowing look.

"I know how you feel. But we'll figure it out. I mean, I don't know what else we're going to do."

I heard the desperation in that, and I understood it. Because what would we do if this was the end?

We got into position as Kiera took her seat behind her kit. She wasn't wearing a sundress this time, but instead jeans and a tank top. She had pulled her hair into a ponytail and had a look of grim determination on her face. She was damned good at what she did, and while she was friends with Rocky, she had finally started to get to know the others in the band.

I had been avoiding her.

I knew I was being an asshole, but deep down in my gut, I knew it should be Mal sitting behind that kit.

While I knew that it was irrational, and that I shouldn't be a bastard to her, I didn't want to see her there. So I didn't turn around. Didn't meet her gaze.

Instead, I tilted my head at David, who spoke in the mic to the crowd.

"We're just practicing here. It is not a full show."

"That's fine," Max said with a slight smile. Our agent looked just as nervous as I felt.

I hadn't felt nerves like this since our first show. It made no fucking sense. But here I was, pretending I knew what I was doing.

Kiera started the beat, and I swallowed hard, noticing the difference.

It wasn't Mal. It didn't feel right. But we had been at this for a month now. It was never going to feel right. But music played in my bones. This is what I loved. And I had to remember that.

I played the first note, letting it wash over me, but as I sang, my voice a growl, I didn't feel it.

I'd been using the past month to take care of my voice. To use the vocal techniques I'd been taught, and to not end up like an aging rockstar who couldn't sing anymore. I didn't want to lose my voice in the next few decades, so I had to take better care of it.

Nothing felt right.

With each passing song, I felt the tension rising. Those in the crowd were kind at first, understanding in their eyes, but the few fans that we had there, the studio members, and label execs started to lose their shine. They were nice, kind, until they weren't.

I saw the worry there. The anger.

Jacob missed a note, and then Kiera started the wrong verse.

Rocky had tears sliding down her face, and turned away so the others couldn't see. But that meant I was the one who had to face it.

And I continued to sing, but I didn't hear a single ounce of emotion in it.

David kept going, but I knew it was out of desperation.

And by the end of it, there hadn't been a single moment where we'd clicked. The vibes weren't there and it pushed down any sense of talent we might have.

I slid my guitar off and handed it to one of the new crew members. Someone to replace one of our fallen and walked out.

"Gabriel!" David called, but I held up my hand.

"I need some air. I'll be back tomorrow."

"Damn it," the other man growled, but then the sound of running feet came from behind, and I turned to see Rocky coming toward me.

"I don't want to talk about it."

Her face red and blotchy, she shook her head. "I don't either. I'm just going to my car. I didn't mean to cry."

I cursed under my breath, and then pulled Rocky in for a hug. At that moment, I realized that I hadn't hugged her in all this time. She stiffened for a moment, before wrapping her arms around my waist.

"This fucking sucks. That wasn't good, Gabe."

"No. It was worse than a garage band of dads trying to relive their youth."

She snorted into my shoulder. "They would at least have rhythm. And wouldn't be crying like a girl."

"You *are* a girl."

"Fuck you."

We stood there for a moment, before I finally let her go. "I'm going to go see Maisie. She seems to be the only thing that I'm doing right right now."

"And Briar?" she asked.

I shook my head. "Don't go there."

"Maybe you should. I've seen the way you two are with each other. You're so careful about not talking about anything. You should probably talk about something."

"No. If I do that, I'll fuck it up."

"How do you know that? You two were always flames around each other, long before the accident."

"I don't want to talk about it, Rocky," I snapped.

"Fine. Don't talk about it with me. But figure out what you want. Because one day Maisie's going to grow older and wonder why her parents are hanging out all the time, but don't know what they are to each other."

"I don't want to hear it. We just played for shit out there. They're going to drop us from the label, and I don't even know if I care. What does that make me? The asshole that's going to ruin everything once again?"

"You weren't the drunk driver, Gabriel."

I paused, then held up my hand. "No. I'm done."

Before Rocky could say anything, I ran to my car and got in. I wasn't going to talk about it. Wasn't going to think about it. Because if I was going to bare my soul to anyone, it wasn't going to be her.

It was going to be the woman that I wasn't allowed to think about.

I ignored my phone that continued to buzz in the cup holder and drove on autopilot toward Briar's home. I got through the gate, putting in my security code that was specialized to each person and had additional security behind it. By the time I pulled into the garage, I was shaking.

I didn't have it anymore. That urge to sing—to feel music. It just wasn't there.

What the hell was I going to do if I wasn't Gabriel Wilder?

I turned off the car and got out, pushing those thoughts from my mind. I couldn't think about that. Couldn't think about anything. Because I was still fucking wired even through that shit of a practice.

Briar was in the kitchen, humming along to music as I walked in. She looked up, confusion on her face.

"You're here early. I was just making dinner. I figured if you got home and wanted to eat it later, you could heat it up." She turned off her music and stared at me. "What happened?"

"We were shit."

She wiped her hands on her kitchen towel and came forward. "I'm sorry."

"How the hell are we going to make this work? I have no idea what I'm doing."

"I don't think any of us do. I wish I'd been there."

"I'm glad you weren't." A stricken look covered her face, and I cursed. "So you couldn't see my shame."

"It couldn't have been that bad."

"I don't know." I shrugged and kept staring at her. She had piled her hair on the top of her head and wore an apron that covered her jeans and a T-shirt. Because she was so short, she constantly had to lean over her kitchen counters and ended up with stains everywhere. Hence the apron for even minimal cooking.

I didn't know why that was so sexy.

"You can have another practice. I mean, you haven't been back at it for that long."

"I don't want to talk about practice anymore," I growled.

She studied my face. "Okay. What do you want to do? Dinner?"

"Not that either."

And then, without thinking, I cupped her face and

pressed my mouth to hers. She froze for just an instant, before she leaned into me, hands on my waist.

This was idiotic.

I should not be kissing her. I should not have my hands on her. But I'd been telling myself that for far too long. And I couldn't help but want more.

"What are you doing?" she asked as I pulled away, both of us breathing in pants.

"I have no idea," I whispered, finally telling the truth.

"Okay." She studied my face and nodded tightly. I was ready for her to walk away, but instead she tugged on the belt loop of my jeans and pulled me closer.

I tugged on the string of her apron, drawing it forward. She moved away, both of us breathing heavily as I tugged the apron off completely, and then picked her up, cradling her in my arms.

"This is so stupid," she whispered.

"I've been doing stupid things all day. So I don't think that it's anything new."

A small smile covered her face, and her teeth bit into her lip. "That works for me."

I carried her into the bedroom, the same bedroom that I had been carefully keeping away from. I hadn't been sleeping next to her this whole time. I had been trying to give us space. And yet I didn't want any space right then.

I lowered her to the floor in front of the bed and undid the clip on the top of her hair. It fell in copper waves, and I groaned. "I've always loved your hair." I tugged on it slightly, and she groaned.

"I always thought you hated it. You always called me weird redheaded names."

"It's copper. Like a penny under the sun. Plus, it was easier to make fun of you than tell you that I wanted you."

Her eyes widened, but realizing I had said too much, I leaned forward and took her mouth again. She pulled on my shirt, and I stepped back to let her strip it off, and she sucked in a breath.

"I always forget."

I tilted my head, running my hand up her shirt to cup her breast. She arched into me, her nipple pebbling into my palm. "You always forget what?"

"The fact that you're so built. It's a little intimidating."

"I'm in love with your curves, Briar. You have nothing to be intimidated about."

She licked her lips and leaned forward, pressing a kiss to the ink over my chest. "You've seen me naked more times than I can count recently, and yet I have only seen you shirtless."

"So let's change that."

I crushed my mouth to hers, our movements a little

jerky, unpracticed. But then I was pulling off her shirt and undoing her bra. Her breasts were fuller than they had been before, and I cupped them gently.

"Just let me know what's too much. I don't want to hurt you." I paused. "I don't think I've ever slept with a nursing mother before," I muttered.

"Don't talk about other women when your hands are on my breasts." She grinned up at me.

"Deal," I said, my lips quirking into a smile.

"And I have no idea what hurts or not. So just touch me, and we'll figure it out."

My dick hardened impossibly more. "Sounds like a plan."

And then my mouth was on her nipple, sucking it gently into my mouth. She stiffened, and I immediately took a step back.

"Did I hurt you?"

"No, I'm oddly sensitive there."

I shook my head, and gently ran my knuckle over her nipples. "Well, then I should take better care of you." I laid her down on the bed, and paid extra attention to her breasts, ensuring that I wasn't too hard, and that they had their proper attention.

She squirmed beneath me, rocking her core against my jean-clad cock. "Gabriel," she panted.

"I've got you."

I moved back, undoing her jeans as I tugged them over her hips. She lifted her ass since her curves were so bitable that it took a little bit of effort to get her jeans off. And since I was already there, I shoved her panties off as well.

Then she was naked in front of me, and I licked my lips. "You're like a fucking goddess."

She slid her hand between her legs, covering herself even as she blushed all over. "Gabriel."

"What? I'm going to fuck you soon, but let me eye-fuck you first." She laughed then, and I tugged her hand away before kneeling between her legs.

I spread her folds before me, watching the way they glistened underneath the bedroom light.

"You're already so wet for me," I whispered.

"It's always a problem when I'm with you. Always has been."

I looked up at her then, grinning. "Really?"

"Don't look so conceited about it. You know you're hot."

"Well, but now that I know that you're always wet around me, it's going to be hard to walk with a hard-on."

Briar laughed then, before gasping as I pressed my mouth over her. She tasted sweet, tart, and I licked at her clit. She writhed around me, wrapping one leg around my shoulders. I pinned her down, wrapping my arm around her thigh so I could use my thumb on her clit.

She shivered in my hold as I continued to taste and touch. I explored her, spreading her with one finger, then two. She was so damn tight, and I was afraid I was going to hurt her. And I remembered that the first time we had been together, I had stretched her, and both of us had needed a moment to breathe.

I remembered every moment of that first time, even though I had lied and said I didn't. Because that first time had been exactly what I had craved all these years. And now she would know exactly how much I wanted her.

I continued to lick at her, before curling my fingers to find that bundle of nerves deep inside her. When she came, my name on her lips, I nearly exploded in my pants. But instead I lapped up her orgasm, sucking and licking before finally pulling away.

Meeting her gaze, I licked her wetness off my fingers, and her eyes darkened. "Dear God."

"You taste fucking good."

She sat up then and undid my belt. I helped her, standing up so I could pull off my pants. When she raised a brow, I shrugged.

"I need to do laundry. I forgot enough underwear."

She shook her head and gripped the base of my cock.

Groaning, I slid my hands through her hair. "Next time. Next time, I want to shove my cock down that pretty throat of yours. But if we do it now, I'm not going to be able to slide into that tight cunt of yours. And that's going to be a crime."

"I forgot that you talked so fucking dirty."

"Well, you're just going to have to remember."

And then I kissed her again, knowing she could taste herself on my tongue. Then I pushed at her shoulders, forcing her back on the bed, and lifted one of her legs. With her ankle on my shoulder, I positioned myself at her entrance, and slid home.

We both groaned, her pussy tightening around my dick. I had to count to ten, trying not to come right then and there. And then I was moving in and out of her, one stroke, then another. She was so damn flexible that I was able to lean forward, her knee at her shoulder as I pounded into her. And then, knowing I was too close, I pulled out of her and turned her over on her stomach.

Before she could say anything, I lifted her hips and pushed into her again. She met me thrust for thrust, both of us not thinking, both of us breathing and feeling.

And when I knew I was ready to go again, I pulled out of her once more, ignoring the way that she moaned, her body quaking. Then I was over her, sliding into her once again, but this time face to face, perfectly between her legs.

I tangled my fingers with hers, kissing her softly, as I moved in and out of her, loving the way that she finally arched beneath me, clamping around my cock as she came. And I followed her, my orgasm long and hard.

Then I was kissing tears from her cheeks, both of us still entwined, my cock deep inside her, and I just held her, knowing that I had fucked up. Once again.

In this moment, with her wrapped around me, it was the first time I had felt peace in nearly a year. And finally, after we cleaned each other up, I slept. With the woman that I knew I had loved for far too long in my arms. The woman that I was never going to have.

CHAPTER FIFTEEN
BRIAR

I would have liked to say that I had slept all night in the arms of someone that I truly cared about. That I trusted. Sadly, that wasn't the case.

We were up every half hour since Maisie didn't sleep through the night and I'd left the makings of dinner on the counter. I'd ended up throwing some of the ingredients away and ordering in.

Gabriel had slept for a good two hours, and I was honestly surprised. I knew he didn't sleep well most nights, even if he didn't sleep next to me. He would toss and turn on my guest bed, and then I'd hear him quietly strumming his guitar, trying to find whatever he thought he had lost.

Sometimes he'd even let me sleep if Maisie was awake and wanted to be held but wasn't hungry.

Although that was a rarity since Baby Girl wa~~ways~~ hungry. She was a growing girl after all.

With Gabriel still in bed, I finished nursing an Maisie in my arms, rocking back and forth in parental way that must be inherent.

I wore cotton shorts and a tank top that I cou easily move the neck down so I could breastfeed. I wasn't the most glamorous outfit, and I had to shower again, but it wasn't as if I really knew what I was doing.

This was my life now. A mom.

Honestly, I wasn't sure I had ever thought about the future like this.

Yes, I was nearly thirty, and the idea of family and being a mom was always on the periphery, but I thought I'd had time. I'd had a few boyfriends over the years, but nobody truly serious. My work consisted of a lot of traveling. Yes, I had my little bungalow and home here, the nest that I had made, but before I'd gotten pregnant, before the crash, I was out visiting other artists, creating. I wasn't just Briar Ashford, Mal's little sister. I wasn't Briar Ashford, Gabriel Wilder's secret.

Because that's what they called me.

His secret.

Everybody wanted to know how long we had been together. If we were still together. If I knew that he was with Rocky and now Kiera.

And to be fair, he could be with anybody he wanted.

It wasn't as if we were exclusive. My heart ached, and I rocked Maisie back to sleep.

"It's okay. It's okay."

Only I wasn't talking to her. I wanted to believe that I knew what I was doing, but it truly didn't feel that way most of the time. I set Maisie down in her crib, and then looked at the mirror above the changing table, shaking my head.

"You need to wake up."

I looked over my shoulder, realizing that I had said that aloud. I really hoped Maisie didn't wake up. I took my phone and walked into the kitchen. Since I had just breastfed, I was going to have my one cup of coffee for the day. I couldn't wait to indulge in pure caffeine. Maybe injected straight into my veins.

This whole mom side of me was very out of character, and I really had no idea what I was doing. And Gabe and I were just playing house. I knew that.

And when had I started calling him Gabe?

He was always Gabriel. Of course he was always Gabriel Wilder to me as well. But the man sleeping in my bed right then, felt like Gabe. The man behind the fame and screaming adoring fans. The man who wasn't always being clutched at by women.

I rubbed my hand over my chest as my coffee brewed. I had no right to feel jealous.

He wasn't mine.

I couldn't even claim Gabe, let alone Gabriel.

My phone buzzed, and I picked it up, answering the video call. "Hey there," I whispered.

Teagan raised a brow at me and shook her head.

"I love you sister mine. But when did you shower last?"

I thought of the shower after we had had sex, both of us cleaning each other up, and blushed. "Last night. But I went to sleep with my hair wet, and I just finished feeding Maisie. I'll shower soon. Probably once Gabe gets up."

"Gabe is he?"

Of course my sister would catch that.

"I think I'm too tired to even finish saying his full name," I lied. I set my phone down on the counter and propped it up, while I doctored up my coffee.

"So what's the flavor today?" Teagan asked.

I loved our morning coffee chats. Part of me wished I still lived in Ashford Creek, but the rest of me knew I never wanted to go back. I was long past the girl I had been when I had lived there. The screaming and the shouting. The fact that Callum had always tried to protect me. Teagan had done the same, but my father had bowled right through her as well.

Mal had been the one that took the most beatings

for me. At least, that's what I remembered. Maybe all of my brothers had tried to do the same. Even their friends had tried. Because my father had never hidden who he was.

I shuddered before finally answering my sister. "We're going with sugar-free hazelnut. I have an oat milk creamer next."

"Oh, which brand?"

"I actually made this one," I teased.

Teagan let out a long sigh. "You really do scare me. I don't know when you became such a homemaker."

"You say that as if it's a bad thing?"

"I say that as someone who doesn't know how to do that. Considering you and I have no experience."

"It's funny that you mention that. I was just thinking about our childhood."

"I haven't eaten yet, so my stomach kind of hurts. Let's not talk about that at all." Once again, I heard the teasing tone.

There was something going on with my sister. I knew there was, but she wasn't ready to talk about it. When she was, I would be there.

After all, she had been with me throughout this entire pregnancy.

And I really wish she was here.

"You look different," Teagan said after a moment.

I frowned and brought my phone to the small kitchen table.

"I don't know what you mean." I sipped my coffee, and Teagan studied my face.

"You didn't."

I blinked. "What? I didn't what?"

"Are you sure that's wise?"

"I have no idea what you're talking about."

I did, but she had to be the one to say it. Because if this was just her fishing, she was doing a really good job with it.

"Did you sleep with Gabriel?" she asked, her voice a harsh whisper.

I looked over my phone and all around the kitchen to make sure nobody was around. Although it was just the three of us in the house, Gabriel walked far too quietly.

"No," I lied.

"You did. And that's why you have sex hair."

"I washed my sex hair, thank you very much," I snapped in a decent whisper.

"Okay. Okay." She blinked at me and my stomach clenched once again.

"What is going on in that head of yours?"

"I could ask you the same thing. I don't know how I feel about this. And it's not like I really get a say. We joke, but I don't get an opinion."

"Maybe you should give one because I don't know what I'm doing, Teagan."

My sister let out a long sigh. "I've always noticed the way you two were around each other. Even though Mal did his best not to."

I swallowed hard. "What? It wasn't like that before."

"Because both of you were very good about not showing it. Only every time that Gabriel hung out with us, or we went out on tour with Mal, you two orbited around each other. You couldn't help it. And while I had hoped it would always just stay friendship because you know how Mal always was with us, part of me hoped maybe it would be more."

I let my coffee grow cold as I stared at her, honestly confused. "It wasn't like that. I mean, we wouldn't have let it."

"Have you two actually talked about what you want?"

"That would require me knowing what I wanted," I answered honestly.

"Touché. Okay. Maybe you should have a conversation with him."

"And say what? It was a mistake?" Why did that make everything hurt inside?

"Do you feel it was a mistake?"

I scowled. "Why are you answering all of my questions with a question?"

"Because I don't have any answers. I like Gabriel. Even though I really wanted to hurt him for leaving you in that position."

"He didn't leave me in that position. I didn't tell him." When had I started defending him over what had made me so angry before?

"Because he wouldn't *let* you."

"I could have shown up at his house sooner."

"Maybe. But could you have really? Do you remember how we were right after the funeral?"

I wiped away another tear and nodded. "We were a mess."

"We all are. And the two of us coming back to your house in Austin was really what saved me. And how selfish is that?"

"It's not selfish. I don't know how you can stay in Ashford Creek."

Teagan gave me a small smile that didn't quite meet her eyes. "Because it's home. Even though I hate parts of it, it's home. But you're right, every time I go around a corner, I see Mal. And I miss him so much."

"I hate that he's gone. I hate the fact that the last time I spoke to him we were fighting. And he didn't even blame me. He only blamed Gabriel."

"Have you two talked about it?"

"Not enough. And I hate it. Because I want to know what he's thinking about. I want him to know it wasn't his fault. But that's what he feels. So what am I supposed to do? Needle him until he finally breaks down?"

"You do need to talk to him. For his sake. And yours. Because you can't move on or move to whatever step you need to for Maisie, and you, without it. There was a reason he blocked himself off. And maybe he's not doing it physically anymore, but he's still doing it."

"I should be worried that you can put my thoughts into words so well."

Teagan ran her hand through her hair, the new pink streaks subtle. "Because I'm on the outside looking in. I miss Mal with every breath. But I wasn't there. And I'm not sitting next to Gabriel every day. Living in a house with him. Raising a child together. So figure out what you want, Baby Sister. And I'm always here for you. I promise."

"I'm always here for you, too. I love you. And I don't have any answers."

"And that's okay for now. But you deserve them."

We said a few other things, before she finally hung up, and I heated up my coffee, hating that I'd let it go cold. With Maisie still asleep, and Gabriel seemingly the same, I walked into my small office and pulled out my guitar. I was working on a song that sounded decent. But I couldn't figure out who it was for.

"You said you'd never leave. You promised you'd stay." I

strummed the guitar again, frowning. *"But now I'm standing here all alone in the pouring rain."*

"I haven't heard that one."

I turned to see Gabriel standing there in gray sweatpants, leaning on the doorjamb.

He had his arms folded over his chest, so my gaze couldn't help but drop to stare at his forearms and I had to swallow hard. And his sweatpants did not hide much, and *everything* about him was a little too much.

Pulling my attention back to him and not his gray sweatpants that left little to the imagination, I cleared my throat. "I'm just starting it. I don't know who it's for."

"I didn't mean to interrupt you. But your door was open."

I flushed. "There are a few times I forget that I'm not alone in the house. Which is weird because it's not like this is new."

"Sometimes everything feels new."

There was a cry from the nursery, and Gabriel cleared his throat. "I'll go get her."

"Thank you."

I put my guitar away, knowing that I couldn't write that particular song with him around. Because that would mean he would see far too much. I had just stood up when Gabriel walked in, Maisie in his arms.

My ovaries practically exploded at the sight.

And then Maisie decided to throw up on his naked chest, and as he winced, pulling her back, her diaper exploded in his hands. Both of us looked at the mess covering him and the floor, before we burst out laughing.

"If only the masses could see me now." He shook his head, humor still in his eyes, and I reached for her.

"Oh my God, let me get her."

"No, no. I'll start with the bath. If she were a little older, I'd say we'd get in the shower so we could hose off, but I don't want to drown her."

"Okay, you just go stand on some tile or something." The original rug from the nursery, sadly, had been a lost cause.

"I'm glad that you don't have carpet in this house," he said with a shudder, and we laughed as he worked to clean up Maisie and stripped off his gray sweatpants in the process.

It took every morsel of strength within me not to look down and stare at him. There was a naked, tattooed, and pierced Gabriel Wilder in my bathroom.

And I'd licked nearly every inch of him.

My face ablaze, I had handed over a wet towel, as Maisie lay on her back, looking happy and far too proud of herself.

"Go wash and cover yourself, Mister."

He looked down at his new hard-on. "Sorry. I would say it's morning wood, but you're here."

"Gabriel," I warned.

He waved me off, and then went to shower. *Thank God.*

I looked down at Maisie and clucked my tongue. "You are a mess, you know that." She just smiled up at me, and I knew it was just gas. "Okay, let's feed you again so you can make more of a mess."

By the time that Gabriel came back to the nursery, he had my secondly-reheated coffee, and a mug for him.

"I am all clean. Do you want to go shower?"

"Are you calling me dirty?" I asked, wondering why I was teasing him.

"I'm not even going to go there. But I do like when you say dirty things to me." His lips crooked into a smile, and I saw light in his eyes. Just a glimpse of it, but it was like the old Gabriel.

Not the one hiding things.

"What are we doing?" I blurted, before taking a seat in the closest chair.

He swallowed hard and set both coffees down on the side table. I rocked Maisie in my arms, hoping she wouldn't throw up at the moment. When he kneeled down between my legs, I let out a shaky breath.

"I don't know, Briar. I want to figure it out. We have

four weeks until our real show. And I need to do better. I need to figure this shit out. The band's going to come stay at the Wilders', and we're going to use Lark's studio. That means I need to be there."

My heart sank, and I nodded. "That makes sense."

"I know you're settled here, but I want you there too. And not just because I want to see Maisie."

There was so much in his gaze I couldn't read, even as my heart swelled once again. "Gabriel."

"I know you need to work. I know we need to figure out the nanny thing, and I know that I want you."

With that last volley, I froze, swallowing hard. "Okay. Okay."

"This is where you say you want me too," he whispered.

I smiled then, rocking Maisie as she nuzzled into me. "And are we going to stay in the same place so we can pretend that we know what we're doing?"

"Like always." He stood up then, and kissed me softly, and then a little more deeply.

"And then we're going to keep doing that?" I asked, my voice breathy.

He rested his forehead on mine. "Am I a bad person if I say yes?"

"Then I'm just as bad as you."

He kissed me again, and before I could do anything

more, Maisie woke up crying. And so he plucked her out of my arms, and once again the baby calmed.

I wanted to hate that. Wanted to be so frustrated. And yet, my heart felt as if it were finally settling. Because Gabriel was a piece of me, just like Maisie. And that's what worried me. As once shattered, I might not be able to put those pieces back together again.

CHAPTER SIXTEEN
GABRIEL

The final chord drifted into silence, and I cleared my throat before setting my guitar to the side.

"Well, that didn't suck completely," Joshua grumbled. He ran his hands over his face and gave me a look.

I shook my head, unsure of what I was supposed to say. I used to be good at this. And yet right now I didn't feel like I knew anything. "It was better. I just...I don't know."

"When I come in from the second verse, I feel like sometimes I am stepping into a place I shouldn't."

I turned at Kiera's voice and frowned. "What do you mean?"

Kiera bit her lip before finally letting out a breath. "Right now, I find myself trying to mimic Mal's style versus using my own. And I realize that maybe that's what I should be doing to keep others happy, but that's not why you have me here." She paused. "Or maybe that's exactly why you have me here and I'm really not a good fit."

I frowned at her, then looked over at David, who scrunched his nose. Rocky moved forward, but I was the one who spoke up. I'd told Briar that I wanted to come out here to try to make this work—the band and whatever the hell the two of us had going on. It was past time that I started trying.

"I don't know what we want. But if you're saying that you need to use your style, then show us. If you're stepping over my lines, when you're trying to do what Mal could do? Then it's not going to work. If you think you can do better, do it." I heard the snap in my voice, and the way that Kiera didn't back down. She just continued to look at me, and I wasn't sure if I was supposed to feel bad about it, or move on.

My best friend was dead. We were never going to have our band back. Mal could read my mind when it came to our music. I didn't have to ask him to do anything, he just did it and it made sense.

I didn't know Kiera. I didn't want to play with her. I wanted my best friend back.

If Mal was back, he would still be kicking my ass for sleeping with Briar. Again.

I would do anything for Mal to be back.

Just like I would do anything to have Briar again.

No wonder I didn't know what the fuck I was doing.

"Gabriel—" Rocky began.

I held up my hand. "Let's just try it your way. It's not working the other way. Clearly."

Keira met my gaze before rolling her shoulders back. "I'm not changing the song, Gabriel. I promise. You don't want that. The fans truly don't want that. But I'm a good foot shorter than Mal was and because of that, I'm going to play slightly different. I don't want to feel like I'm trying to run a sprint during a marathon." She shook her head. "I know that doesn't make any sense."

"You're a percussion. It makes complete sense," David put in.

I glared at the other man, before realizing I was the only one on this side of the battle line.

Rocky and Kiera had been friends long before this, so there was already that connection. David was doing his dad routine where he just wanted everyone to get along. And Joshua, well Joshua I couldn't read. He either seemed so enamored with Kiera that he was fucking up his notes, or he was just trying to pretend that we were all okay.

And we weren't.

I was pretty sure that if we didn't finish this album and do the shows that we had promised, this would be it. We'd all walk away. Once again, I ignored Ghost Mal in the corner, because I knew he wasn't really there. I felt that judgment. And not just judging me for being with Briar.

"Let's just do it."

Kiera nodded. "Okay. You start the count, and I'll be here."

I frowned and realized that that was wrong. Mal had been the one to start the count. He was the fucking drummer. It's what he did. But Kiera had let me do it because everybody was walking on fucking eggshells around me. Even Briar. We were so good at not discussing anything important. The only person that I seemed to be doing anything right with was Maisie, and I knew at any moment I would fuck that up, too.

"No, you do it."

Kiera's eyes widened, and out of the corner of my eye I saw Rocky's shoulders finally relax. Had they always been that tense? Why the hell wasn't I noticing anything? Not only was I being a shitty leader of this band, but I was also a shitty friend. I didn't know what I was supposed to say. So I just lifted my chin, and then turned back to the mic.

Kiera counted us in, and we began the song that had started it all. Our rise to fame, before we all fell.

And part of me hated the fact that Kiera had been right. When we hit the second verse, we weren't stepping on each other. With each passing note, it started to flow.

And the ghost of Mal faded just that much more.

I REALLY LIKED MY COUSIN ELI'S PLACE. ALL MY cousins other than Eliza had lived on the property when they had first bought the property. The original retreat had been an inn with a huge barn that had been retrofitted to be an event center, with over a dozen cabins and small homes scattered along the land. In the years since, they had added multiple businesses, additional cabins, and done everything to increase what they offered, but at the same time, tried not to impact the environment too much. Their main goal was to make sure that whatever they did didn't increase erosion or change the way the floodplains worked. Considering it was South Texas, flash flooding was a problem.

I oddly liked to sit back and listen to Brooks and East talk about what they were doing. East hadn't started out in this business. Hell, none of my cousins had. But now he called himself the resident handyman of the company. Even though he did far more than that. Before Brooks had come along, he had practically built and rebuilt most of everything around. Including the winery itself. The winery had been part of the Wilder retreat before the Wilders had even thought of going into this business. My cousins who ran that had increased it tenfold, and it was a little scary to know that Wilder Wines was all over the U.S. at this point. Even my brother Wyatt was taking his distillery outside of South Texas.

Everybody was moving on, and growing, and figuring out what they wanted. And now Brooks and East were in the corner of Eli's living room discussing what they were going to do for the next update.

After a storm had taken out part of the buildings, and nearly killed my cousin in the process, Brooks had come on to help rebuild. And then he had never left. That had brought Ridge and Wyatt along with him, and though I didn't live here technically, I had followed suit.

In reality, I had been here nearly a year now. My stomach tightened at that, thinking about what the anniversary would mean.

I wasn't sure when I was going to leave. Or if I even should.

Hell, I felt as if I were practically living with Briar. Not that we were talking about that.

Speaking of Briar, I looked over to see the woman that I couldn't stop thinking about standing in the corner talking with Ava and Aurora. The three had become fast friends, and I wasn't quite sure how I felt about that.

It wasn't any of my business, but my sisters-in-law had gravitated toward her the first moment they had met, and they were never letting her go. No matter what happened between Briar and me, I didn't think those three would ever walk away from each other. Another woman stood with them, Ava's friend. I couldn't think of her name just then, but it was maybe Rory? Rachel? It was something with an R, and she came around often because she was best friends with Ava, and Faith's godmother.

The Wilders took everybody in, including me. It didn't matter that I had the name, or it was the name stamped all over my band...I still felt out of place. I knew part of me wanted to go get a drink and pretend it was all a farce. But I wouldn't. I kept my soda in hand, and watched as Ridge paced the dining room with Maisie in his arms.

And then, before Ridge could continue his track, Elliot plucked my baby girl out of his arms and moved into the kitchen. Thankfully, I could see most of what was going on, because I wasn't about to let Maisie out of my sight.

That was odd to think. After all this time of being out on the road and trying not to have any responsibilities other than to myself and to my band, I was a dad.

How the hell had that happened?

"You okay?"

I nearly jumped out of my skin at Brooks's voice. "I didn't realize that you were here. Hell. Don't sneak up on a man."

"I was sitting here for a good minute before I said anything, and you didn't notice me. You watching Maisie? You know no one's going to hurt her."

I nodded as one of my cousins-in-law took my baby girl from Elliot and rocked her against her shoulder. "I don't think Maisie's ever going to be laying down in her bassinet upstairs, is she?" I asked.

"No, not at all. Elijah's over there with his baby girl, and the older kids are all running around with Eli. I'm pretty sure someone else is out there with them, but we really have too many cousins with E names."

I snorted and took a sip of my soda. "I'm really glad that our parents didn't decide to go that route."

"Damn, I don't think there were any E names left for us."

My lips twitched, and my gaze met Briar's again. She smiled at me, a little awkwardly, before she turned away to go back to her conversation.

"You got it bad, you know."

I shook my head. "I don't know what you're talking about."

"You do. But well, you don't have to talk about it right now if you don't want to."

I looked over at Brooks, but he wasn't looking at me.

I followed his gaze, and for a moment I thought he was staring at Briar with that odd distant look in his eyes. But no, he was staring at Rory. That was her name. Rory.

I almost said something, but since Brooks was giving me my time to wallow, I let him do the same. But it was interesting that Rory was doing her best not to look over here, even though her shoulders tensed.

Then again, Briar's shoulders were just as tense.

"You want to go for a walk?" I asked softly.

Brooks cleared his throat. "Yeah. You should tell Briar though."

"She's not my keeper," I snapped, before Brooks just gave me a look.

I hated that raised eyebrow, so I sighed and moved my way over to the group of women. "Brooks and I are going for a walk. Maddie has Maisie."

She smiled at me, and I tried to tamp down the need to brush my lips against hers. "Enjoy your walk. And I can see that Maisie's being tossed around like a hot potato. But so are the other babies around here. It's nice."

"Yeah. It is." We stood there, awkwardly, before Ava leaned forward and squeezed my forearm.

"Take Wyatt with you? He's been antsy all day. We're waiting on a bid from another company for a project of ours, and he's crawling up the walls."

I nodded at my sister-in-law, before letting out a breath. "Got it. Should I take Ridge too?" I asked Aurora.

She smiled over at me. "Go for it. We'll take care of the kids."

"Yeah. Because there's more than one of them now. Hell."

"Crazy, isn't it?" Ava asked, looking between Briar and me.

I didn't say anything, and neither did she. I just tilted my soda toward them, before leaving to go get my other brothers. Soon, the four of us were on a small walk around the property, but not too far away.

"So, you want to tell me what's going on between you and Briar?" Wyatt asked.

Of course it would be Wyatt who asked. Because he was always the one who spoke up. Ridge may be the most dangerous, Brooks the quietest, but Wyatt was the one who didn't hide his feelings or thoughts.

I, on the other hand, did my best to pretend. "We're taking it one day at a time. For Maisie's sake."

"I notice you guys are spending your time together no matter which house you're at," Ridge put in.

I shrugged, staring off into the distance as we walked. "It's easier with the two of us, as we are still trying to find a nanny. I mean, we both have to go back to work someday. And it's not like we have a stable life, you know?"

And that was the problem. I was either in the studio or on tour, and I used to be out partying. But that wouldn't happen anymore. And not just because of Maisie. It wouldn't be the same without Mal.

Hell, it wouldn't be the same without Briar. But I wasn't going to think about that.

"What do you want?" Wyatt asked softly.

"I don't fucking know," I said, finally feeling honest. "I can't hurt her. And I can't hurt Maisie. But I don't know what I want. And I sure as fuck don't know what Briar wants."

"I'm going to say you should talk to her, but we all know that it's easier said than done." Ridge squeezed my shoulder but didn't say anything else.

Brooks didn't say a damn word, and he was quieter than usual. Again, that worried me. But I didn't know how to start that conversation. I didn't even know how to finish this one.

Wyatt nudged my arm. "You should talk to her, though. You guys have a kid together. Communication is sort of the thing."

I gave Wyatt an incredulous look, but my brother just shrugged. "If I talk to her, she'll leave. And I don't know what I want, let alone what I don't want to lose."

"You don't know that she'll leave, so figure it out. You're running out of days before things burst. Before she has to go back to work to work on an album, and you have to do the same. You're not going to be able to stay hiding on the Wilder compound for too much longer." Ridge didn't look at me as he spoke, but I understood.

"I want to yell at you and tell you that I'm not hiding, but I sure as fuck am. I've been hiding ever since Brooks took me back from Ashford Creek. But what the hell am I supposed to do? The media wants to know more about me and Briar. They want to know about the band. They want to know everything. And I don't have the answers. I don't know what questions to ask."

"Briar might."

I glared at Wyatt. "And what if her answers include walking away and not being in my life? And I don't even know if I want her in my life like that. She's Mal's sister."

"She was Mal's sister when you got her pregnant. She was Mal's sister when you covered her body with yours to save her life. She was Mal's sister when you had Maisie. And she was Mal's sister when you slept with her again."

I nearly tripped over my own feet at Ridge's words, then stiffened. "How did you know we slept together again?"

"We didn't until you just said so," Brooks whispered. "But we see the two of you together. You always know. Things change. Even if it's just quiet and nearly unreadable. Things change. So figure out what you want to do, Gabriel. We'll be here no matter what. I'm so damn sorry for what happened. But maybe it's time to take a breath. Step into that sunlight. Because you might not be in the darkness anymore, but you're covered in shadows."

I swallowed hard at Brooks's words, wondering why I was the one who wrote songs when Brooks was the one who could speak poetry. A lyric hit my mind, and I wanted to write it out, to follow that thread. But before we could do that, we were at Eli's front porch. And Briar stood there, Maisie in her arms.

"What's wrong?" I asked, alarm spreading through me. I took two steps at a time up to where she stood, and she shook her head at me.

"Nothing's wrong. Maisie's just getting a little fussy. And frankly, I'm tired. I was up too late working on a song that finally hit. You know how that is."

I leaned forward, running my knuckle over Maisie's cheek, then doing the same to Briar without thinking. She braced but didn't pull away. "I know exactly how that is. Do you have your bag?" I asked, even though I could clearly see it on her shoulder.

"Yes. I have everything. Do you want to go say goodbye?"

"We'll do that for him. You guys head out. You know the Wilders, saying goodbye takes a good thirty minutes." Ridge kissed the top of Briar's head, and I glared at him, before my brothers walked inside, leaving the three of us on the porch.

The three of us. As if we were a family. Why did this feel so normal and abnormal at the same time?

"That makes things a little bit easier. Let's head back to the cabin."

"Is it weird that I really like that cabin? It's supposed to be temporary, but it's comfortable." Briar walked softly beside me, and once again, it felt right.

"I've been living in it for nearly a year now, so it's a little weird, but I feel the same."

Briar gave me a soft smile, before we clipped Maisie into her car seat, and made our way back to the retreat. I knew that Ridge and the others on the security team had amped up security not just for us, but for the rest of the family, and I liked being behind these barriers. I just wasn't sure how I was supposed to raise a kid and live life in this kind of world.

After Maisie ate and we changed and took care of her nighttime routine, the baby was sleeping in her crib. And now the one barrier between Briar and me was asleep. And no longer that line of demarcation.

"I'm going to go shower. Is that okay?" Briar asked.

I frowned. "You don't have to ask, Briar."

"I don't even know why I asked. I just feel all weird. I think the hormones are finally getting to me."

"Finally?" I teased.

She shoved at my shoulder, her eyes sparkling. "Shut up. I'm going to go use the main bedroom shower, though. Is that okay? Because I love those showerheads more."

"You use that shower every time we're here. Just stop asking. This is your place, too."

We both froze, because once again we weren't talking about the real things, and I pushed her hair back from her face. Then I continued to run my hands through her hair, and then down her shoulders.

"You go take that shower." I cleared my throat, my dick hardening at the sight of her. Hell, it had started hardening as soon as I thought of her in the shower. I wasn't going to do anything about that. We were just playing house. We weren't living it. If I kept telling myself that, it would totally make sense.

Briar made her way into the main bedroom, while I checked on Maisie one more time, and then went to the kitchen to get some ice water.

Just thinking of Briar in the shower right then made it difficult to breathe.

Imagining water sluicing over those bare breasts,

down her stomach, to the V of her thighs. She was so damn beautiful on any given day. But watching the way that she moved with those curves of hers? She was a damn goddess.

I looked down at my cock pushing at my jeans and groaned.

It would be a very, very bad thing if I went back there and did something about it. And yet, I couldn't help but want more.

I hadn't even realized that I was walking toward the bathroom until I stood in the doorway, the sound of the shower and water hitting tile filling my ears. I leaned against the wood as I stared at Briar. She had her face in the shower stream, sliding her hands over her body.

I held back a groan as she cupped her breasts and slid her hand between her thighs.

Well, hell. This wasn't exactly what I was imagining. Or then again, maybe it was exactly what I was imagining.

Water slid over her face as she leaned into the stream, one hand on her breasts, the other between her legs. I groaned as she arched into her hand. "Gabe," she whispered.

I nearly dropped the water bottle. However, a cry did eventually escape my lips.

Briar froze, and then turned toward me, not

lowering her hands. "How long have you been standing there?" she asked, her voice breathy.

"Long enough to watch you nearly get off while saying my name. Are you thinking about me? With my hands between your legs? Or my mouth on your cunt?"

"Oh. Um."

"Say my name. But do so when you're riding my face."

I set down the water bottle and prowled toward her. She moved her hand from her breasts, pushing her wet hair from her eyes.

"I couldn't help it. You were all growly in the kitchen. Fuck, all day. And those jeans? They do something for me."

I smiled then and was grateful for the way that the shower was built, so there was no door. I kicked off my shoes but kept the rest of my clothes on as I pulled her into my arms.

"You're so fucking sexy. It's hard for me to breathe. Do you know how long I've been hard? Do you know how difficult it is to walk around with an erection?"

"How about walking around when the seam of your jeans keeps pressing into your clit?"

"I love when you talk dirty to me." And then my hand was fisted in her hair, tugging her head back, and I was crushing my mouth to hers.

She groaned into me, and then I couldn't think, water soaking my shirt and jeans.

I pressed her hand back to her pussy, rocking herself over her hand.

"That's it, continue to get yourself off. But I'm in charge."

"I was almost there before. Even without you."

"Well then, maybe you should remember exactly who's getting you off."

I guided her fingers into herself, and the feeling of all four of our fingers inside her nearly had me coming with her.

Her eyes widened as I worked us in and out of her, and I swallowed hard.

"That's it. Stretch yourself for me. Because you know that my cock is bigger than this."

"Bragger," she teased, and then I moved faster, grinding the palm of my hand into her clit. She came in an instant, her eyes darkening as her knees nearly went weak. I immediately went to my knees and lapped at her pussy. She staggered, and I gripped her hips to keep her steady as I licked and sucked and kissed. I sucked on her clit, and then spread her for me, needing more. She tasted sweet, even as the shower beat down on us. She put one hand on the shower wall, and the other on my head as she pushed me toward her, guiding me. I smiled against her pussy, and continued to suck and lick and tease. And when she came again she screamed, "Gabe!"

I stood up, my wet jeans a problem, as she pulled on my shirt.

"I need you inside me."

"Damn straight. Face the wall."

Her eyes widened. "Oh? So bossy."

I reached around and smacked her ass. She let out a shocked gasp, but her eyes still deepened.

"Oh, you like that, do you?"

"Don't even think about it."

In this moment, we were playing, kissing, touching. And there were no worries. Nothing else.

Yes, there is a baby monitor on the counter so we'd be able to hear Maisie when she woke, and yes, the world would crash down on us soon, but for now it didn't matter. For now, it was just this moment.

We pulled off my wet shirt, laughing as it stuck over my head for an instant. And then I turned her toward the shower wall, pressing her breasts against the tile, and I ground into her ass.

"That's it. Do you want to take me? In that pussy? Or maybe in your ass?"

"Don't even think about it. Just my pussy, thank you very much."

"I love that word falling off your lips. You always stumble over it."

"Well, maybe I wouldn't stumble over it if you were actually fucking it."

I laughed, and then undid my jeans. I could only lower them slightly since they were wet, but it didn't matter. In one quick thrust, I was inside her, both of us moaning.

"Oh my God," she gasped.

"That's it. Take all of me."

It was hard, fast, wet. I kept her steady so she wouldn't fall, as I pounded into her, both of us meeting thrust for thrust. And when she came again, her body going lax, I caught her, thrusting once, twice, and then following her. The shower had drawn cold, but as I filled her, we both heated. I kept kissing her, tilting her head so it was easier for me to capture her lips.

In this moment, we could pretend. In this moment, we could have everything. As we stood there, still joined, I held her and never wanted to let her go. Even though I knew I would have to soon if we didn't figure out what we wanted most.

CHAPTER SEVENTEEN
BRIAR

"Why is she still so tiny?"

I pressed my lips together as Callum held Briar in his hands as if she were a bomb ready to go off. Considering she had just been changed because her diaper had exploded, it wasn't that far off. But still, seeing my big brother with his large hands, grumpy face, and broad shoulders holding Briar as if he could break her at any moment just made me smile.

"You don't have to carry her like you're going to drop her at any moment."

"But also, carry her like you could drop her at any moment," Teagan put in, wringing her hands in front of her.

I smiled at my two siblings, knowing that they were

here for me as much as they were for Maisie. The one-
year anniversary of losing Mal was coming up, and
while they wouldn't be here for that day, they were here
now. And I was so grateful to them, even though
Callum looked as if he were ready to run away as
quickly as he could.

"Here, you're supporting her head, and she's
looking up at you with happiness in her eyes."

"Teagan said it was just gas," Callum rumbled.

"It is just gas," my sister said with a sigh.

Callum and Teagan were both older than me, while I
was third in line.

We had a decently large family, or at least I had
thought I'd had until I met the Wilders.

I knew that they missed Mal in their own ways and
were dealing with it in their own ways. However, having
Maisie in our lives seems to have at least healed some
of the hurt.

I didn't know how all of my brothers felt. Mostly
because they did their normal Ashford guy thing and
hid their feelings and only spoke in grunts if I could
even get them on the phone. Perhaps if I had moved
back up to Ashford Creek like many of them were
doing, things would be different. But I had no plans to
do so.

I was going to stay in Austin. Or San Antonio. And
I was going to travel the U.S. and the world with

Maisie in my arms, and doing what I loved best. Writing songs for people who knew how to truly feel the lyrics.

And maybe along the way I would figure out what the hell I was doing with Gabriel. Not that I was going to talk about that right then. Because Teagan would be nosy and want to fix everything for me. And Callum would want to beat the shit out of him, just because he dared touch his little sister.

Then again, maybe he wouldn't. Maybe he would be glad that Gabriel and I were actually doing something about whatever the hell we were in the middle of. Not that I knew what we were doing. And frankly, Mal had already taken care of the beating part.

I held back a sigh, nearly shuddering when I remembered our last moments.

I didn't want to think about that, or what had become of that night.

I wanted to pretend we had all moved past it, but Gabriel had pointedly not talked about it at all. We moved on in our lives as if nothing had happened, and we weren't worrying about the bad things. Even though I knew that that was exactly the opposite.

"You have everything in the bag?" Teagan asked as she took the diaper bag from me and began to rummage through it.

I rolled my eyes. "Of course I do. And it's organized

in terms of efficiency. Please don't reorganize. I'm the one who had the baby."

"Excuse me, Baby Sister, but I taught you this organizational skill, thank you very much."

"Are you sure one of you doesn't want to take the baby? I figured I could just drive the girls around and then make sure that they were fed. And then bring them home. Without actually having to hold Maisie."

Callum kept saying those things, but he didn't tear his gaze off her.

I quickly snapped a photo, as Teagan gave me a thumbs up behind Callum's back.

That was going to go in a frame somewhere.

"You guys will be fine." I bit my lip, trying not to freak out that I was letting two of my siblings take my baby away from me, even for the afternoon.

"Of course we'll be fine. We're the best aunt and uncle out there."

"Don't say that around the Wilders, or you're going to have to fight," I teased, even though worry continued to slide over me at the thought of not having Maisie in my arms the entire day. "Maybe we can just stay here in the cabin and you guys don't have to leave it all."

Callum and Teagan gave each other looks before Teagan finally stared at me.

"You need a break. We need to be the fun aunt and uncle. But you need a break. The media doesn't know what Callum and I look like. So cameras aren't going to be following us around, and Maisie's all caught up on her shots. So we can go out in public. And you can get some work done because I know you have a song right at your fingertips and you've been antsy. Hence why you called us. And you have to go through the applications for your nanny. And you have a girls' lunch with the Wilder women. So enjoy your afternoon."

"But I could still do that with Maisie," I said quickly as I moved forward, pulling Maisie into my arms. Callum looked bereft for a moment, and if I wasn't so stressed out about the afternoon, I would smile at the thought. Considering the man was so afraid of holding a baby, here he was, not wanting to let go.

"Give that baby back, Briar Ashford. I love you with all of my heart, but you need to take a moment and just breathe. You're allowed to do that."

"I know that. But it's just so weird. I like her in my sight at all times."

"Hence why you're going to do the big girl thing and let us have her for a couple of hours. I know this sucks, but you're the one who said you had a lot to do, and this gives us time with our niece."

"Okay fine. But we're going to go over the list one more time."

"That's fine with me," Teagan said quickly as I finally let go of Maisie and put her back into Callum's arms. He looked nervous again, but I was grateful as he moved over to the car seat to buckle her in.

"Watch her head," Teagan and I said at the same time, and Callum growled.

"I've done this before. She might be small and I'm afraid to break her, but I'm not actually going to do it."

"So grumpy," Teagan teased.

"Okay, the list."

And we went over it one more time, and I watched the Ashfords take my baby off the Wilder property and out for an afternoon.

Away from me.

I was a terrible mother.

But I knew this was important as soon as I would have to travel for an agent meeting, and a session in the studio. And right after that, Gabriel and the band had a gig. Meaning all of us would be traveling with him. I didn't know exactly how that had come about, but I'd be going with them. As Maisie's mother, and maybe just with Gabriel. I wasn't sure where we stood, because that would mean we would actually have to talk to each other. And that was something that we were very good at not doing.

It frustrated me to no end that neither one of us could actually bring up Mal. Or what we wanted. It didn't help that the awkwardness always settled in when we were together, and then that would turn into heat, and there would be no speaking.

I could be myself with him when we were in bed. I could growl right back and tell him exactly what I wanted. And I could let him take control in those instances because it made sense in those moments.

But as soon as the orgasms faded, and we had to act like adults, we were too polite to each other. I didn't know who we were to each other, even though the feelings that I had been hiding from myself for so long were coming to the forefront.

I had loved Gabriel Wilder in some fashion since I had first gotten to know him. And I had pushed those feelings away because it would just complicate life.

Gabriel had been a playboy, going out into the world with Mal and sleeping with way too many women. And I had tried to pretend that I didn't have any feelings.

And then I had given in one night.

And now I kept giving in.

Lyrics began to slide through my mind at that moment, and I went into the small office that really wasn't an office and pulled out my guitar. It looked odd sitting next to Gabriel's, as if they were a perfect pair, and this was something that we did all the time.

But it wasn't.

Once again we were playing house. I sat cross-legged on the floor, notebook in front of me, and let the first verse slide through me.

Can you stay for me?

I continued to write, singing softly as the words began to flow. And then the hairs on the back of my neck stood on end as I turned to see I wasn't alone. "Oh. I didn't know you were there."

"I didn't want to interrupt. But you're fucking amazing."

"Oh yeah?" I asked, a blush staining my cheeks.

"I love hearing you work. I love the sound of your voice. It's just so damn good. I mean, you have two Grammys. You know you're the shit."

I rolled my eyes, tapping my pencil on the paper. "Hmm? You have more."

"And you'll get more through your writing. I know you will." He paused, before taking a step into the room. When I didn't say anything, he sat down next to me. He leaned against the desk, crossing his legs at the ankle in front of him.

"Who's that song for?"

I shook my head. "I don't know yet. I'm not a singer, not really," I corrected as he raised a brow. "I know I have a good voice. And I'm not ashamed of that, but I don't want to go out there into the limelight. I like writing. It's what I'm good at. Chris Stapleton did that for years before he got his breakout hit. And I don't want that breakout hit. I just want to write. And I make good money doing it. Somehow."

"Because you're damn talented. And I want the song."

I froze, blinking up at him. "What?"

"The one you're working on? I want it."

My lips twitched. "You can't just claim it, you know."

"Maybe not, but I'll fight for it." His eyes darkened, and I tried to ignore the warmth spreading through me.

"So you're really going to make sure Wilder stays together?" I asked, knowing that the question was as if I threw a rock into a quiet pond.

He picked at lint on his jeans, before giving me a tight nod.

"I don't know what else I would do. I think I need it."

"Okay. But you're going to have to prove that you earned the song. And technically, I'm working on two songs at once."

His eyes brightened. "Can I hear?"

"Only if you help me with this bridge."

"Damn straight. I'm here to help." He scooted forward, and I set the guitar on my lap, letting a few notes play through me. "This is good," he said, looking at the words, and then he began to sing, that growl of a voice soothing somehow. It went straight through me, just like it always did. He was so damn sexy when he sang, and yet it was more than that. It was the emotion of everything slamming into me, and I knew he felt the words. And when he got to the part that I didn't have lyrics for, he continued, as if he knew exactly what I wanted to say, even though I hadn't known it at all.

"What do you think?" he asked, frowning down at the lyrics.

"I think you finally figured it out," I said, a little annoyed. "How did you do that so quickly?"

"Because you had everything right there. But what about this note? I think it needs to go one octave lower."

I frowned, before nodding. "You need a harmony there."

"Yeah, Joshua could probably do it, but maybe Rocky?"

I shook my head. "No, I don't know if her voice would work. What about Kiera?"

He stiffened, and I realized I might've stepped into it again. "I don't know how her voice sounds. Isn't that a bullshit answer?"

"You guys are still getting to know one another."

"You don't have to placate me. I know I'm an asshole to her."

I sighed and set down my guitar. "You *are* an asshole to her. And I get why you're angry."

"Mal should be there."

I froze, and knew that he rarely brought up Mal. I needed him to. Desperately. But every time that I did in the past, he'd just stop the conversation.

"But he's not, Gabriel. And I hate it just as much as you."

"I don't know if Kiera can do it."

"Then maybe we could work it so it's just your voice. Or you can ask her."

He was quiet for so long that I was afraid I'd gone too far. "The only voice I hear with mine is yours."

I shook my head even though his answer did something to me I didn't want to think about. "I don't sing. If you want this song, we have to make it yours."

"It's ours, Briar. Maybe that's the problem."

And he continued to work as I stared down at him, wondering what the hell we were doing.

I was damn good at what I did. I had power behind the scenes in certain aspects, power that I knew could slip through my fingers if I didn't keep on it. But now I needed to figure out if I could do this as a mom with Gabriel. Because I could work anywhere, and I had when I had been on tour with Mal and Wilder.

Later that day we had to interview nannies, and that would be one step into figuring out what this phase of our lives would be. In the end, we would have to talk about Mal. The one thing that we never truly did. Beyond a casual slipup.

"It should really be your voice," Gabe repeated.

"You'll find a way to make it work. Because it's your song, you know. I think I was always writing it for Wilder."

He met my gaze and leaned forward, brushing his lips on mine. "Thank you. You're so fucking talented."

"You're not too bad yourself."

And then we went back to work, before my alarm buzzed, and we had to start the next phase of the day. Picking out someone who would take care of our child. And once again, we moved to the next step as if it were a sure thing. As if Gabriel would always be there, and I wouldn't get my heart broken. I would give him this moment, give him these few weeks. And then, for Maisie's sake, and for mine, things would have to change.

As he kissed me again, I let the bubble stay where it was.

I could burst it later and fall through the pieces I knew that remained.

CHAPTER EIGHTEEN
BRIAR

Six days later I woke up in Gabriel's arms. I had slept in his bed every night since the evening of the shower. There was no more wondering if someone should sleep on the couch or in the guest room. We had fallen into each other, clinging to one another.

He was who I wanted, except I didn't know which Gabriel I was going to get. The caring one who gave all and was always there. Or the one so lost in his thoughts he forgot what he wanted.

And if I didn't start standing up for myself, I was going to get walked on far more than I ever planned.

Gabriel groaned behind me, his hard cock pressing into my back. I wanted to press back into him, to wake up like we had every morning, but then reality settled in.

I knew exactly what today was. And why I couldn't be in his arms until I spoke to him about what today meant.

I carefully slid out of bed, grateful when he clung to the pillow in my stead.

I nearly rolled my eyes at the moment, wondering if maybe he just liked cuddling, and I happened to be just as fine as a pillow.

But nothing truly felt funny today.

I ran my hand over my heart, aware that Gabriel's T-shirt was thin and worn enough that he would be able to see every curve.

I couldn't hear Maisie on the baby monitor, so I walked into her nursery, and rested my hand on her little chest.

She slept with her mouth pouting, and I knew she would wake up soon and want to be fed. And we would begin our day.

Today of all days.

Knowing I didn't have much time until she woke up, I made my way to the guest restroom, so I wouldn't wake up Gabriel. He rarely slept these days. Between the band, his family, and me and Maisie, he didn't have time to sleep. And when he did, it was a restless kind of sleep.

I would love to know what he was thinking, but the damn man never told me.

I leaned against the bathroom counter and stared at the woman in the reflection.

My breasts were fuller than they had been, my face a little softer, my hips slightly wider. But I still looked like the Briar from a year ago.

My wrist ached every once in a while, and sometimes I woke up to the sounds of screaming.

But today was the day that I never wanted to come.

Because today was one year since my brother had died.

It felt like so much more time had passed since then. I was a completely different person from that moment in time.

I could barely even remember the Briar I had been when I had walked onto that tour bus, knowing that I would see Gabriel.

I had been nervous, even though I had pretended I was nonchalant and totally over it.

There was no getting over Gabriel Wilder. I'd even lied to myself in my own thoughts, and yet I had been there, waiting for him just as much as I'd been waiting for Mal.

It honestly hadn't surprised me that Mal had forgotten I would be there. That he had found a way to hook up with someone. What had surprised me was that Gabriel hadn't. Part of me had hoped to hell he hadn't brought a fan onto the tour bus with him. That wouldn't have been awkward at all.

But I wouldn't have done anything else with him. I wouldn't have pushed at him or wanted more.

Because it would've been awkward. Because I never knew what he was thinking. And Mal would never have been okay with it.

I didn't understand the jealousy, or rather the over-protectiveness. But then again, I didn't really have a best friend that would date one of my brothers. I had friends in the business, and I was truly friendly with Lark but that was as close as it had ever been even before she married my cousin. But Lark was on tour, so I didn't get to see her often. And Teagan was my best friend.

How pathetic was that?

I had somehow closed myself off from my past, from all the connections that I had had before Maisie, and I felt as though I were an island. With my only connection to the real world, Gabriel.

And yet I wasn't even sure what we had was real.

Something needed to change.

I let out a breath and wiped the tears from my face.

"I miss you Mal. I hate it. I hate that you're not here."

Maisie's cries echoed at that moment, and I swallowed hard and splashed water on my face.

I walked into the nursery and stared down at the person that was now the center of my life.

"Hello Baby Girl. Good morning."

Her little face scrunched, and I leaned down to pick her up.

"You've got to be hungry, aren't you? You know, one day you're going to be a morning person. And not so grumpy in the morning."

She wailed even harder.

I settled myself into the borrowed nursery chair and made sure that Maisie got her breakfast.

Gabriel walked out at that moment, shirtless, in a pair of gray sweatpants.

The way he was tenting them told me that he hadn't done anything about that erection from when I had woken up. But it didn't matter at that moment.

Not with the lost look on his face, and the way that he rubbed at his eye, trying to push away sleep.

"Morning."

I stared at him, letting that gruff voice wash over me.

"Morning. She was grumpy this morning."

"I could hear that. I can get her ready for the day if you want. You said you were going out, right?"

So domestic. And I had no idea what to call him. He

wasn't my boyfriend. It was way too complicated for that.

But was this a relationship? I would ask those questions. Just not today.

Not today of all days.

"I promised Callum that I would pick up that signed book for him. The author rarely goes out, but he pre-ordered from a little bookshop. And since they don't ship, I get to go in and get it."

He studied my face, and I tried not to blush. Why did he always do that to me? "I remember him talking about that. I always liked that he collected books that way. It was easy to get him birthday gifts when we were on the road. Are you going to do anything else when you're out?"

I didn't think he realized what day it was yet. He wasn't quite awake. I wasn't sure I wanted to be here when he did. Though the additional connections in our past—the fact that he'd always been there—wrapped around me like a comfort. Maybe we didn't need labels since we'd found this odd peace.

Or maybe I was fooling myself.

"Maisie and I are planning on meeting Aurora for lunch, since she'll already be in the area." And so I wouldn't be alone today. Aurora had lost her husband and had somehow found peace. And while I was doing my best to try to search for light, today would be about staying busy. Part of me wanted to invite Gabriel, but I knew that wasn't an option. Even in a place far away from celebrities and that life, we couldn't go out together.

No wonder I didn't know who we were to one another, since we couldn't even go on a proper date.

"Do you want me to ask Ridge to send someone with you guys?" he asked. He moved forward, running his finger over Maisie's cheek, and then the top of my breast.

"I wasn't planning on it. I never had to when I was just Mal's sister, but if you think I should..."

He froze just then, as he stared at me. And that's when it clicked. The date had finally hit him.

"Are you sure you should go out today?" he asked, his voice devoid of emotion.

"I'm trying to figure out how to live my life. Today of all days."

"Yeah. I get that."

Again, no emotion.

I would give him grace today. Because I needed it for myself. And then I would have to think about what I wanted. What Maisie needed. The anniversary would be in the news and the world would be waiting for Wilder. For the band. For a glimpse of who they were now. But if I were out without Gabriel, there was a higher chance no one would bother me. I might write the music, I might be the mother of Gabriel's child, the sister of Mal Ashford...but I was still the unknown—exactly where I wanted to be.

"While you're out, I'll go through that box of mail Max sent over. It's taking over the cabin and I guess...I guess I should finally deal. I'll go through it eventually. It's weird that I almost resent some of it."

I stood up and moved forward so I could rest my hand on Maisie as Gabriel rocked back and forth. "I know. But so many people love you, Gabriel."

Me among them.

But I didn't say that.

He met my gaze, and the pleading in them nearly broke me. I wanted him to love me, but first, he needed to love himself. And even thinking that confused me. "I need to do better. I know that. I know I locked myself away. And I'm grateful that everybody gave me all that space. But I don't know what I'm supposed to say or do."

"Maybe just start there. That you're grateful."

Gabriel looked over my head, his face gray. "Do you think Max is going to want the band to say anything today?"

I froze, aware that he was talking about today's moment. That had to be some kind of type of growth. "You have to ask him. I'm not saying anything. It's not like I have social media anymore."

He grimaced, but I didn't elaborate. I'd had to delete my Instagram and a few other accounts when the news of Maisie had broken. My comments had been flooded with either congratulations, demands, or outright cruelty because I had dared to take their beloved rockstar. Maybe that was one reason that I was hiding out here with the Wilders, and again in Austin. *Because nobody knew who I was out here.*

I wasn't even sure I knew who I was.

He reached out and pushed my hair from my face. "I'm sorry. About all of this crap thrown at you. I can't even take you out for dinner or walk Maisie in the damn park. I'm sorry about the people who make this harder."

Hope mixed with the despair in the way as he spoke. "About your fans? You don't have to be sorry for them. But I could do without the women who hate me on sight."

He grimaced. "I'll never understand that."

"What? That people are jealous that I've touched you? Kissed you? Even though it is a parasocial relationship."

"I'd be jealous as fuck if somebody was touching you, so I get that."

I swallowed hard, trying to ignore the warmth sliding through me at that. There it was again, him dropping bombs of truth and emotion amongst the

267

devastation. I would never be able to understand this man. "We're not parasocial."

His lips curved into a slight smile. "No. We're not. But I am sorry. If they say anything to you, let me know."

I wasn't sure I'd ever do that to him. He had enough on his shoulders and, frankly, I was afraid of what would happen when I did.

"Would it help if I brought Ridge with me today?" I asked, knowing that I was leaning into his paranoia.

His shoulders immediately relaxed. "Yes. But you don't have to do it to placate me."

"It's totally placating you, but I will. I'll totally do it to keep Maisie safe. How's that?"

Gabriel leaned down and pressed his lips to mine. "Thank you. And totally not parasocial. I'll see you soon."

His phone buzzed, and I took Maisie from him as he went to answer. He was so good at that, changing the name of the game in the middle of us trying not to say the important things.

So we weren't parasocial, so what exactly were we?

I shook my head and went to get Maisie and me ready. When I texted Ridge that I was going out and Gabriel thought it would be good if I had someone with me, he said he would come along.

Ridge drove us all the way across town to the indie

bookshop that Callum had mentioned. There was truly no reason for me to do this today, but I needed to get out of the house and just let the sunlight hit my face. Aurora was also in a client meeting near here, so lunch with a friend would be the perfect way to pretend I was okay. I wrapped Maisie around my chest, loving the gift from Ava that let my hands stay free.

With Maisie safely tucked against my chest, and my purse on my shoulder, we walked the two blocks to the bookstore with Ridge keeping his eyes on every point around us.

"You know, I feel like Lark or Bethany right now. I just need bigger sunglasses and a hat." As both women were in the news constantly with their success, their lives were far different from mine. Only Gabriel truly understood how they lived day to day.

"I do have an extra ball cap if you need it."

My lips twitched, surprising me that I could laugh today of all days. "We're just picking up a book."

"And then lunch around the corner. And there's always donuts on the way home."

"I wonder how long we'd have to stand in line for that?" I asked, my stomach suddenly rumbling.

"I bet you if we drop either one of the famous people's names in our family, we can get in quickly."

I turned to Gabriel's brother, intrigued. "Do you ever do that?"

"Hell no."

I grinned as I went inside to pick up my pre-order. Yes, I had scheduled this today for a reason. I'd wanted to stay busy. If I could have scheduled doctor's appointments, hair appointments, and everything else today, I would have. As long as I didn't have to think about Mal, it would be fine.

But I knew that wasn't going to happen.

Thankfully, there wasn't a line, and I immediately picked up my book and walked side by side with Ridge to go meet up with Aurora.

We turned the corner, and a flash hit my gaze. I hadn't even realized that somebody was coming up until Ridge moved in front of me and I nearly tripped.

"Is that Gabriel's lovechild?" somebody called, and I lowered my head, cursing myself.

Ridge blocked the way for the two photographers, as I turned into the restaurant, covering the top of Maisie's head. She had been completely underneath the wrap throughout the walk but had slowly meandered her way out just to nuzzle against my chest, and I wasn't sure if they got a photo of her. I had no idea what I had been thinking, other than I hadn't been thinking, trying to live my life and taking my baby out in public.

So many reassurances to Gabriel, and I had fucked up.

"Are you okay?" Ridge asked.

"I'm fine," I lied.

"What's wrong?" Aurora said as she came forward, frowning. "Are you okay?"

"Can we just go home?" I said in place of an answer.

Aurora ran her hands over my hair and then looked down at a sleeping Maisie on my chest. "Of course. You look pale. Do you want to sit down?"

"I just want to get Maisie home."

I didn't even realize tears were sliding down my cheeks until Aurora wiped them away. Of course this was going to be the moment that I broke. Where everybody was watching. Aurora held me close as I covered Maisie completely, and then Ridge got us to the SUV quickly.

Ridge drove quickly through the tight streets until we got to the highway. "Aurora, Trace is going to come pick up your car later."

"I don't mind. I'm glad that we're all together."

I let out a breath, my hand shaking as I touched my daughter's cheek. "I'm sorry about this."

"Don't be. It's not your fault," Aurora reassured.

The other woman sat up front with Ridge as I sat in the back next to Maisie, knowing that I had done this to try to not think about the real world, and the real world hit back anyway. I held Maisie's little hand as she looked up at me, such innocence in her gaze.

"I'm sorry, Baby Girl."

"The photographer said he didn't get a photo of Maisie," Ridge growled.

"Do you believe him?"

"Hell no, at least I hadn't until he showed me his entire memory card. My arm's blocking her completely. But you're in the photos."

Relief hit me hard, even though I didn't like the idea of my own photo being taken. "That's fine. They can splash me all over the tabloids. It's my fault for being out."

"Don't blame yourself," Ridge bit out. I had a feeling he was blaming himself instead.

I shook my head. "I should have left Maisie with one of the Wilders or with the nanny we spent weeks trying to find."

Aurora leaned over the center console to frown at me. "You're breastfeeding. And you're allowed to walk around with your daughter. I hate people."

I sighed. "Same. But there's nothing I can do now. Gabriel's going to hate this."

"He's not going to blame you," Ridge countered. "If anything, he's going to blame himself."

"Which doesn't help the situation," I muttered.

They didn't say anything at that, as I just let the tears fall. Aurora twisted slightly so she could put her hand between the seats. I gripped it, needing a lifeline.

Of all the people around me, these two would understand what I was going through the most. Yes, it should have been Gabriel, but it wasn't. It was the two people in the front seats who had lost everything once and were crawling back to their futures. When we pulled into the resort thirty minutes later, my tears were dry, and Maisie was crying for lunch.

"Do you want me to bring over something?" Aurora asked.

I shook my head. "I'm just going to head back. Thank you for today. I'm sorry everything went off the rails."

Ridge leaned forward to give me a one harmed hug. "I'm sorry I didn't see them in time. Or at least knock them over."

I tried to smile, but there was nothing in me. He handed over Callum's book, and I nodded in thanks before heading inside.

Gabriel was nowhere to be found, but that was a good thing. I needed a moment.

I looked down at my phone and realized I had missed the group chat with my siblings. We were all hurting in different ways, and yet I was the one running away, just as Gabriel had at the start. I added my own texts to the chat but couldn't bring up the energy to feel anything more than the hollow ache ebbing within.

Maisie kept crying, and I knew she didn't want me.

She wanted her daddy. I wanted to resent myself for that, to kick at the world. But the one thing I could do was make Maisie happy. And that was by giving her to her daddy. Not myself.

I pulled out my phone and texted Gabriel.

ME:

> Maisie wants you. Are you on the property?

GABRIEL:

> We're at Lark's studio. The whole band. You want me to come over?

I swallowed hard, grateful that he was with the band. Because they needed him, too. Everybody was heartbroken and was doing so good about not talking about it. And that was the worst thing to do.

ME:

> I'll come right over.

GABRIEL:

> I'll see you soon.

I slid my phone into my back pocket, grabbed a few things for Maisie, and made the walk toward the studio. I needed the air on my face, as Maisie continued to cry. I hoped I wasn't ruining anyone's day with a little girl's tears, but I was crying right along with her.

Why did I think I could just be busy enough so I wouldn't have to think about Mal?

My brother was dead. He would no longer smile and laugh. No longer sit behind his kit and make jokes with the band.

He would no longer play and live his life to the fullest.

So many others had died that day, and I had done my best not to think about any of it.

Not until it was too late.

Gabriel met me halfway, a frown on his face. "I didn't know you were walking. Here, let me take her."

I immediately handed over Maisie, who quieted down as soon as he touched her. "I really want to yell at you for the way she responds to your touch."

He shook his head before leaning forward to kiss my temple. "She's just being temperamental. We know that when she's a teenager, she's going to hate me the most."

Images of Maisie as a teenager hit my mind, and it felt so far-fetched that I wasn't sure what to say. Because was Gabriel going to really be by my side at that moment?

The fact that I didn't know made everything hurt worse.

"What are you and the band doing?"

Gabriel rocked Maisie in his arms and frowned. "Talking about Mal."

I froze, hope sliding through me. "Good. Any stories I know?" I tried to keep my voice lighthearted, but I knew I'd failed by the way he stiffened ever so slightly.

"They're talking about how Mal skinny-dipped with Lacey once and ended up getting caught by the other band we were headlining with."

I cringed. "I don't know that story."

"Well, it ended with the band joining them, and I really don't want to tell the rest of it."

I shuddered. "Were you part of that?" I held up my hand. "No, I don't want to know."

Gabriel laughed. "No, I was out with you. Remember? It was when we snuck into that new superhero movie that we really wanted to see. But I never had time while on tour and hiding from cameras isn't always easy."

I smiled at the memory, the ice around me slowly beginning to melt. "I remember that. And we didn't get caught somehow."

"Sometimes it works." He paused. "Ridge told me what happened."

"I'm glad that you made me bring him. I feel so stupid."

"It's my fault."

"It's not. It's the people who want photos. Like those who send fan mail just for Maisie." Max had shown me those letters before giving them to Gabriel and I still felt weird about it. Gabriel and I had joked about parasocial relationships, but the admiration for my infant daughter terrified me. I was scared that they would want a piece of her just as they begged for Gabriel.

"I don't understand people. I just want to play music. And it took me a while to realize that's what I want to do. To still play."

"And I just want to write. And yet it's never that easy."

"No, it's not." We had moved, so we stood side by side, watching the wind breeze through the trees. He had one arm holding Maisie, the other around my shoulders. I hadn't even realized I was leaning on him, both of us not talking about the big things and yet talking about everything at once.

"Are you going to come to LA with us?"

Surprised at the change in subject, I took a moment to answer. "I would do it for Mal, but I also want to be there with you. For Maisie."

He relaxed against me, and I hadn't realized how tense he'd been. "We'll bring the new nanny and try to figure this out. Because I don't know what I'm doing, Briar."

"I never know what I'm doing. But I miss my brother, Gabriel."

He didn't say anything, just squeezed my shoulder. "We'll do LA. We'll play music, write some more. And show Maisie that this world isn't all about people taking things from us."

I didn't say anything to that, just leaned into him.

"I see him, you know," Gabriel whispered.

I looked up at him, frowning. "Who?"

His face gray, he looked down at Maisie in his arms. "Mal. I see him in the distance. Staring at me. Judging. Smiling. Everything. And I blame myself. I know it doesn't make sense. So no, I can't talk about it right now. Not today. But this thing between me and you? It feels real. And part of me really hates that it does."

When he didn't let me go and just held me, I tried to breathe, tried to think through the ache, as my heart shattered into a million pieces.

CHAPTER NINETEEN
GABRIEL

Rain falls down.
The tears slide through memory.
Heartbreak cuts deep.
Yet the world stands by while I fall.

The crowd sang along, the sound of the drums echoing in my ears. Kiera did her thing, and it felt right. Part of me wondered if I were being dishonest even thinking that, but somehow, we clicked as a band.

Joshua stood back, reveling in the noise, as Rocky stood silently by me, staring at the crowd. Tears slid down her cheeks, and I reached for her hand, squeezing.

Camera flashes lit up the concert hall, but I didn't

care what the news would say about us. Frankly, they were so busy worrying about how we would fail and falter. They didn't focus on our internal relationships.

They only seemed to focus on Briar. And the fact that we weren't feeding the media only seemed to enhance their needs.

"Thanks for coming out tonight," David called out, and I pulled myself from my thoughts. I was supposed to be the one who had spoken first in the past. It was *always* me. Only David had been forced to step forward —a spotlight he didn't like considering his past.

And I realized in that moment, I *could* do this.

I looked around the concert hall, trying to see if I could find Mal's ghost. What an odd thing to think. I knew it wasn't his *actual* ghost, just a figment of my imagination, but I didn't see him there. Would he still haunt me? Maybe. But as music flowed through my veins, and the crowd shouted our names, it felt like coming home.

I'd run away from my problems before, fell deep into my own despair and selfishness, and I wasn't okay. But music finally seemed like an antidote, rather than the drug itself.

"I know this is a smaller setting than we usually have," I began, and the crowds cheered for a moment before quieting down. They all seemed to want to know what I had to say. The problem was I didn't have an answer for them. Not yet. But as I looked around at my band, and then over into the side of the stage where Briar stood with Max and the rest of our team, I let out a deep breath.

"When we first started Wilder, the name was just a joke," I began, and Rocky reached out and squeezed my hand once again before moving toward the side so she could stand near Kiera.

"We couldn't think about a name, so Mal joked that we should just call it Wilder. Because it was all about me. And I had a kick-ass name."

People cheered, and Kiera let out a soft drumbeat, with Joshua laughing into the mic.

"He was right. I do have a kick-ass name."

Another round of shouts and applause, a few tears in the crowd.

"Although Ashford was pretty damn good, if I do say so myself." I turned to Briar, tears sliding down her cheeks as well.

I had to pull my gaze from her because if I didn't, people would know. And I wasn't even sure what I felt in that moment.

But I couldn't hide anymore. I knew that. I had to go forward. For Maisie. The daughter I never knew I wanted. And for Briar, the woman I told myself I could never have.

"We used to play in dive bars, at county fairs, and

people joked that we were decent, but they were ready to move on."

"Never! We love you, Angel!" someone called from the crowd, and people cheered and laughed, and I swallowed hard.

"Throughout it all, you guys were there." Another deep breath. "You found yourselves in our music, and let us do the same. Over a year ago now, everything changed."

I didn't know what I was doing, why I was speaking, but I realized that the others had come up behind me. David, broad-shouldered and stoic. Joshua leaned into Kiera as she held his hand and squeezed. Rocky on my other side, giving me strength.

"A year ago we lost Mal, Lacey, Hendrix, Orion, Chad, Marnie, Michael, and Sean." I paused, clearing my throat. "We lost our crew, who had been with us since the beginning. Those people made sure that we were healthy and didn't fly off the edge. They made sure that we were here for you. And they're gone. And I don't even have the words to convey how much I fucking miss them."

People were openly crying now, and yet the large concert hall was so silent I could hear their breaths coming in slight pants.

"Lacey kicked ass in her band. And I know that they're going through the same hell that we went through trying to find someone to replace her. Because no one's going to replace Lacey. She had such talent and made all of us laugh. They were our opening act, but they are going to continue to rise."

I looked over to the side at Briar again, who just gave me a soft smile, and I took in whatever strength I could.

"We lost Mal and—" I paused, and realized I didn't have any more words to say. I didn't want to speak about Mal. I *couldn't*. Because if I did, it would be over. And I'd have to find a way to move on. Only I didn't know if there was no moving on.

"And we miss him every single day," David said softly in my silence. I didn't have any more words, and the fact that I had spoken at all was too much as it was. "Every song that we play brings the memories of those who came before us, and those that we lost. As well as what comes after. So thank you for showing us love and grace as we figure out this new venture."

I turned to Kiera then and swallowed hard. "And everybody welcome Kiera Foley. She's a Wilder now, and I can't wait to figure out what new music we can make."

People cheered then, chanting Kiera's name, and she looked at me wide-eyed. I tilted the mic stand toward her, and she shook her head.

"Tell them hi. Come on, you can do it," I teased.

She glared at me, before leaning into the mic. "I'm much better behind my drums. But thank you for the warm welcome. I'm going to make you proud. And if you think I don't, I'll just keep beating things until I make music. How's that sound?"

People cheered, and I let out a hollow laugh, each of us going back to our positions. We moved into the next song, and the next, and as we ended our set, music still ran through my veins.

I ran off the stage, handing over my guitar to a new crew member. We were still trying to figure out the best way for things to work, but we were finding our rhythm. Then I moved to the side, my gaze on the one person who'd caught mine throughout the set. Without thinking, I cupped Briar's face in my hands and crushed my mouth to hers. She wrapped her arms around my waist, and I groaned into her.

"You did okay," Briar said, and I wiped her tears away with my thumbs.

"Only okay?"

"Yeah. I guess you can play guitar. Though you're going to have to do better if you want my songs."

I rolled my eyes and kissed her again.

"It's about damn time," Rocky teased.

I glared at her and her wife. "What?"

"You two have been making moon eyes at each other for a decade."

I froze, a deer in headlights.

Rocky's wife thankfully pulled her back. "Ignore us. Enjoy your night off."

My bassist rolled her eyes. "What? We all thought it. Mal would've been okay with it eventually."

My chest tightened, and then Kiera and Rocky's wife were tugging her away, as I looked over at Briar. Bulbs flashed and the sound of phone cameras clicked as they pointed toward the two of us. People shouted our names, bellowed questions, and I realized I still had my arms around her.

"Let's go get something to eat."

She blinked. "In the hotel room? Room service sounds great."

I shook my head and squeezed her hand again. I was tired of hiding and if the cameras were here, then maybe we could find a place without them. They'd already gotten their photos, after all. "No. Let's go out."

She raised her brows. "Like on a date? I don't think we've ever done that."

Guilt swamped me, and I pulled her away from the frenzy. "That's a problem I need to rectify."

"Gabriel. There are going to be cameras everywhere. It's LA."

The more she tried to warn me, the more I wanted to prove her wrong. She was perfection outside of the spotlight, but my life grew underneath it. There had to be a middle ground. If I were going to leap over the edge of a cliff against my best friend's wishes, I was going to do it full out. "Maisie's safe with Hilarie, and we should at least try."

"Is this because of what Rocky said?" she asked softly.

"Let's forget what Rocky said," I pushed. Something flashed over her eyes, and I couldn't read it. But I didn't want to think about what Mal would've said in this moment. Because if I did, I wasn't sure what I would feel.

"Come on, I'm a rockstar. Let me treat you to at least one fun night."

"Okay, but I'm not drinking champagne out of your belly button."

I threw back my head and laughed, as phone cameras continued to click. "Let's go."

The band dispersed, everybody going about their business, as one of the new crew members came up to me. "Hey, some person gave me this for you. Was I supposed to give it to you?"

Without thinking, I took it from him and frowned. "What is it?"

"It looks like a letter. Anyway, I have to go pack up."

I let out a sigh as Briar took it, a frown on her face. "He doesn't know that he's not supposed to do that. There's protocol."

I nodded, my mind going in a million directions. "Yeah. But they'll learn. I really miss our crew."

"I miss them too." She looked down at the note and paled.

Uneasy, I leaned toward her. "What is it?"

"It's not to you. It's to me and Maisie."

I tore the note from her hand and growled. "What the fuck?"

Maisie, you're so beautiful.
You must get it from your daddy.
We're so glad that you're making our angels happy.
And Briar? Don't worry.
We'll take care of Maisie too.
The fans love her.

It wasn't signed, and chills crept over my skin. "I'm going to give this to Max."

"I told you, Gabriel. People are just weird about things like that. But yes, I'm going to text Hilarie and check on Maisie."

While part of me wanted that, I knew if we gave in, we'd never go to anything that resembled a kind of life. "You're not leaving my sight. And I'm still taking you out on this fucking date. Let's just be normal for once?

Because nothing feels normal." He let out a breath. "We'll go see our girl and check in, then I'm taking you out."

She studied my face, worry in her gaze. "Okay. We can do that." She kissed my jaw, and someone else took a photo. I ignored them like I always did, and handed the note over to Max.

"What the fuck?" the other man snapped.

Max met my gaze, and I saw the flash of worry before it slid into pure determination. "I don't know who it was, but we need to make sure the crew knows not to give us this shit, okay?"

"You've got it. I'll work on it. You two be safe. I don't like this."

"I know we get a lot of mail like this, but I don't like the fact that they were here."

"We'll handle it. Take security out tonight for your date."

I nodded. "Only because Briar's with me."

He gave me a long-suffering look. "You need it for yourself, too. You're getting out there again. And people want a piece of you. They always did."

I shook my head, and then tugged on Briar's hand as we made our way out. Jeff, one of Trace and Ridge's men, smiled at me, and we made our way to the car.

"Where will it be?" he asked and tipped his invisible hat.

"Chauffeur, are we?" Briar asked with a laugh.

"What? I really do need one of those hats."

"First, to the hotel to see Maisie. Then let's head to Taste," I said, speaking of an off-the-beaten-path restaurant that I liked. Celebrities didn't really hang out there for photos, and there were enough hidden places that we would be able to actually enjoy ourselves.

Phone in hand, Briar looked up at me. "Oh, I love that place."

"I'll put it in the GPS and have Connor call ahead."

Connor was the other member of the team who was back at the hotel since we rotated them out. As Hilarie was in her hotel room with Maisie, it was a safer bet. We were still figuring out this traveling as a family thing.

My thoughts skidded to a halt at that.

Family. Were we family?

That was an odd thought.

Most of the crowd dispersed as we got to the hotel and checked in on a sleeping Maisie. Briar pumped so our girl would be set when she woke up and we left her with Hilarie and more security. Part of me wanted to stay there and hide, but I knew we needed to get out and at least *try*.

Once we got to Taste, I tried my best not to think about any thoughts that would lead down a path that would be a little too much. We ordered an array of appetizers, as well as enough cheese to supply the entire band and crew.

"I'm starving," I said as I filled up my plate.

"I noticed," she said with a laugh. "I don't think I've really seen you eat that much."

"Not recently. I haven't really been hungry." I shrugged. I had lost about twenty pounds when I'd been hiding. I needed to get back to lifting and taking care of my body so I could handle a grueling tour. While Briar had thought I'd filled out over the months, it hadn't been that true. I'd gained breadth in my shoulders thanks to working with Brooks and East, but I'd lost weight everywhere else.

"Well, I'm sure the cheese will help," she added dryly.

"What? I like cheese."

"So do I." She paused. "Although not as much as Mal. We used to go to this cheese place in London that had a conveyor belt."

I had frozen ever so slightly when she had said his name and told myself not to be an idiot. Mal was her brother. Of course she was going to mention him. But then again, the fact that they were brother and sister was how we got into this situation in the first place.

I cleared my throat. "He took me there a couple of times when we were over in London. I tried to get the fish and chips. He just wanted cheese."

"So, are you a vinegar or tartar sauce person?" she asked, and nothing felt awkward. Yes, speaking of her brother did, but this moment right here? It was what we had always done. Why hadn't I seen that?

"I like both," I finally answered.

Her head tilted as she studied me. "That's what I thought. Because I've seen you eat both, and now I was worried that I had forgotten."

"What about you?"

"I like tartar sauce. Which probably makes me lose some points."

My lips quirked into a smile at the look on her face. "All I know is that now I want fish and chips."

She met my gaze, her eyes bright. "Same. Maybe next time then."

I looked down at her, and we each swallowed hard. "Yeah, maybe next time."

By the time we finished our date, people had started to crowd the sidewalk out in the front. "I'm sorry. I didn't think they'd find us here."

"You just had an amazing show and kissed me in public. They were always going to find us. Let's get back to Maisie. I miss her." She put her hands over her breasts.

I raised a brow, and she laughed. "Yeah, we should probably take care of those."

"Why does that sound dirty?" she asked, though I still saw tension in her gaze.

I looked over her head and toward our security. "Hey Jeff? You ready to go?"

"I'm getting you out the back. Don't worry."

"I'm always going to worry," I grumbled.

Even though it was dark out, I slid my sunglasses on and took Briar's hand as we made our way out the back. Paparazzi were still there, cameras flashing, but I did my best to ignore them, pulling her into the back seat. She had her head down, her sunglasses on as well, and we didn't frown or look as if we didn't want to be there. I just needed to figure out how to make this work.

We settled into the back seat as Jeff drove on, and I squeezed Briar's hand.

"I'm sorry."

"It's okay. I'm just not going to be used to that. Ever. And I don't want Maisie to be part of it."

"Same. They don't get photos of our kid." I softly bumped into her shoulder. "And I've never been with a woman for long enough for them to want to take so many photos. Yeah, hanging out every once in a while, especially if the label wanted it, but I don't know, it's different."

We looked at each other then, and I had so much to say and yet I had no idea how to begin.

"No matter what happens, we're always going to be in each other's lives. And not just because of Maisie."

"I know. I know."

We were silent on the way back, and thankfully avoided the press as we made our way into the hotel room. Hilarie smiled brightly at us, as she handed over Maisie. "She was amazing. And you both checked in with me about a hundred times on text."

I met Briar's gaze, and we each gave each other a guilty look.

"Okay, so we are a little overprotective."

"You have a right to be. This little munchkin's adorable." She leaned forward and tapped Maisie's hands.

"I'll see you later, Baby Girl."

"Have a good night."

She waved on her way out, leaving Briar and me alone with our daughter.

"Okay. I should feed her, and then I don't know. I just feel awkward."

I swallowed hard and handed Maisie over. "Same. I'm not good at this."

"I have a feeling you used to be," she teased, and I shook my head. I turned on the TV so there wasn't an uncomfortable silence between us, and knew it was a mistake as soon as I had.

"The band Wilder played a sold-out show tonight, with

ticket prices soaring on second sales. It seems that they did a tremendous job with their new drummer, Kiera, filling the place of the late Mal Ashford. The band spoke about those they lost, and the recent anniversary of the bus crash that took so many lives."

"Yes," another reporter began. "They seemed to finally find their footing, though it was only the first main show. They do have a tour coming up, and an album to release. Rumor has it that they're going to try to find another way to get around other than tour buses. With what happened, I don't blame them."

I hadn't realized my hands had fisted at my sides, until I looked down at them, realizing that they were turning white. I forced myself to relax as the anchors continued.

"Another hot item tonight was the fact that it seems the lead singer Gabriel Wilder has cemented his relationship with the late Mal Ashford's sister, Briar. Briar Ashford is a multi-Grammy-winning songwriter who largely keeps in the shadows. However, it was reported that she gave birth to Gabriel Wilder's lovechild while the band was in reclusion. No word yet on if the relationship has achieved any more status other than there are engagement rumors swirling."

"Well, I wonder what Mal would have to say about his favorite sister and the notorious playboy Gabriel Wilder?"

I flipped off the TV as they continued and turned to see Briar staring at me wide-eyed.

"They sure do just put everything out plainly, don't they?" she asked, her voice soft.

"Don't listen to them. They're fucking idiots."

"Most of what they said was true, though."

I scowled. "It doesn't matter. They don't know us."

"Sometimes *I* don't know us. And I hate the fact that the last thing that I said to my brother was in anger. I would like to think that he'd be okay with this. Whatever this is. But it's always going to be between us. And I hate that."

"I don't want to talk about him."

"Gabriel. We *have* to. If we don't, he'll always be the ghost between us."

"I don't want to talk about him," I snapped, my voice rising. I let out a breath, trying to calm myself because Briar didn't deserve my anger. I wasn't angry at her. Maybe not even myself.

Maisie let out a wail, the sound echoing off the hotel walls.

"Shit. I'm sorry."

She shook her head as she rocked our child in her arms. "No. Let's have this out. Because we need to talk about my brother. You don't *ever*, Gabriel. You didn't even finish your thoughts while on stage about him. And I'm worried. Because I love Mal. But I can't talk to you if I don't know what you're thinking."

"I can't." I paced, running my hands over my face.

"Because if I talk about him, then he's gone. And I know that doesn't make any sense." I tilted my head as she opened her mouth to say something. "I'm trying here, Briar."

Briar looked down at Maisie in her arms, who was still sniffling, and shook her head. "I need you to try harder. Because this right here? This feeling as if we're playing house and not real? It scares me. And I don't want to break, Gabriel."

My heart raced and my hands fisted at my sides. "I don't want to break either. But I don't know what I'm doing."

"We're running out of time to figure that out."

"I know."

And I stepped forward and held her in my arms—Maisie between us.

It was true, there were only going to be so many moments like this, where we could pretend the real world wasn't out there. But for now I held Briar, and looked down at our daughter, and knew that I was in love.

And for the man with all the words for his songs, I surely had none of them now.

CHAPTER TWENTY
BRIAR

In the three days since our first date, things had fallen into a routine. One where we were so careful about what we were saying that we weren't saying anything at all.

And yet, we were truly acting like a family. We hadn't gone on another date, mostly because the press surrounded us, and it was hard for Gabriel and me to leave together. So he would go to the studio, working on his album with the band, and I would go to the other side of town and head to a friend's house to work on my music, or just get out of the hotel life. Thankfully, Lark, one of Gabriel's cousins-in-law, had a house out here that she shared with her husband, Everett. While they had offered for us to stay at their place, it was a little far from the main studio. I didn't mind it though, because it gave me time to just get out of the limelight.

I was heading over there today, and I was excited to see Lark since she was in town, as well as Rory. I had gotten to know Rory decently well when I had been spending most of my time on the Wilder Retreat, but she was out here for work, having come for a book signing and a meeting with her publisher.

We wouldn't meet for a few hours, though, and that meant I could have a lazy morning. Which was odd because I felt like I didn't have enough of those. I had woken up early to feed and change Maisie, and now she was sleeping again, leaving me to my own devices. I lay in bed, the fluffy comforter so warm that I snuggled into it.

"You look far too comfortable right now," Gabriel said as he walked back into the bedroom, a towel wrapped around his waist.

I swallowed hard as I watched a droplet of water roll down his chest and over his six-pack.

For a man who said that he needed to work out more to gain back the muscle he'd lost, he was still all muscle. Yes, he probably needed to gain a few more pounds back, but as I had licked nearly every inch of that body, I just liked him, no matter how he came.

"If you keep looking at me like that, you're going to make me drop this towel."

I licked my lips and let my gaze lower. His cock pressed against the towel, slightly peeking through, and I grinned.

"I'm pretty sure your dick has a mind of its own right now."

He looked down at himself, and then slowly ran his gaze over my comforter-covered body.

"Well. It seems he does." He checked his wrist that did not have a watch on it and beamed. "And it looks like we have a couple of hours just to ourselves. Oh no. What shall we do?"

He sounded far more lighthearted than I had ever heard him, and maybe it was because we were living in this bubble. I knew things would burst soon, but I didn't care. Instead, I let the comforter fall, and his eyes went straight to my breasts.

"Are you really naked under there?"

"I'm wearing panties. I had to change my shirt, and realized I didn't have one close. So I just got back in bed. It's very comfortable under here. I think I need this set for my own house."

"Whatever the brand is, we'll get it for whatever house I buy. Because, dammit, I really need to pick a place to live."

"Are you really going to find a place near your brothers?" I asked.

"Yeah. And probably a place out here, too. Us

staying at hotels really isn't conducive to raising Maisie, you know?"

"Yes, totally." I couldn't believe I was having this conversation topless, but it had to mean something. Right?

"I know I am saying important words and everything, but I can't really think right now."

A laugh burst from me as he tackled me onto the bed, and then his towel was off, and we were rolling around on the king-size bed.

"You're ridiculous."

"So says the woman that is just showing off her breasts to me. What did you expect me to do." He cupped my breasts, pinching my nipples between his fingers.

I gasped, arching in his hold. "Gabriel."

"You're still so sensitive. You fed her and pumped, right?" he asked, his voice soft.

"Yes. But still be careful."

We had had a milk incident the day prior, and while it hadn't changed anything between us, it had startled us for sure. I was still getting used to this whole having sex with a man that I loved and who happened to be the father of my child thing. My life had surely taken a turn since the night I had finally given in, and I was just coming to terms with that.

I pushed those thoughts from my mind, knowing I

wouldn't be able to keep doing this soon. Instead, I leaned back into the down pillows as Gabriel explored my body with his mouth. I lazily ran my hands through his hair as he sucked on my neck, his hands so gentle on my breasts.

"I still can't get over the way you feel below me," he rumbled against my skin.

"So says the man who's hovering above me," I whispered.

"Oh yeah? You like what you see?"

I looked down between us, at the rock-hard erection pressing against my belly. "It's okay."

He growled and leaned forward to bite my lip.

"Ouch!"

"Be nice. Say you're sorry."

"I'm sorry," I teased.

"Not to me, to him." He pointed at his dick, and I snorted. "Don't laugh at my dick. That wasn't very nice."

With a roll of my eyes, I wiggled beneath him and pushed at his hips, so he rolled on his back. "I'm very sorry, Gabriel Wilder's Dick. Is there anything I do that can make it up to you?"

As I was kneeling between his legs, he slid his hands behind his head and wiggled his eyebrows. "There are a few things you can do."

I gripped the base of his shaft, and he sucked in a

breath, and I just kept going. He was so thick around the base that I couldn't touch my middle finger to my thumb, so I used my other hand to pump him once, twice.

He groaned, as I leaned down to kiss his tattoo-covered thigh, and then his other. I shifted slightly, licking at the base of him, and then cupped his balls.

"You sure are taking your sweet time to apologize."

"Shush, I'm busy." And then I licked up his length, leaving soft kisses along the vein.

"Jesus Christ," he growled, before arching his hips up.

I squeezed harder, knowing that he liked it like this, and relishing the fact that I did know that. That we had memories of each other. When he slid his hand over mine and pressed down softly, I looked up at him, mouth parting.

"Just like that. You know exactly what I like."

I licked my lips, and then moved a bit higher.

His eyes rolled slightly as I sucked the tip of his cock into my mouth, letting my tongue slide at the top slit. The salty moisture at the end coated my tongue, and I gently lowered my head, taking more of him in. He groaned again; his hand sliding through my hair.

"That's it. Just like that."

I hummed against him, taking him deeper. He was far too big for me to swallow him whole, but as I gripped the base of his shaft with both hands, and relaxed my throat, I was able to cover all of him. The tip of his cock touched the back of my throat, and I swallowed.

"Holy hell." He lifted his hips slightly, and he went a little bit further, gagging me. When he pulled back, his eyes widening, I lowered my head again, taking him deeper. "That's it. That's my Briar," he growled, tightening his hand in my hair into a fist. And then I moved my head again, while he lifted his hips up and down. He fucked my face, that groan of his nearly too much. And when his balls tightened in my hand, and he tugged at my hair, I kept my mouth on him, knowing what would happen next.

"Briar!" he called out, and then he was coming down my throat. Hot and wet, I lapped every single morsel of him up. I licked up his shaft, and then blew cool breaths along him, as he breathed out harshly through his nose.

Before I could even say a word, though, he flipped me over and tore my panties off.

"Hey! I don't have many of those."

"I don't care."

And then he buried himself between my legs. I closed my eyes, rocking my hips up to his face as he spread my folds and sucked on my clit.

When he pierced me with two fingers, I nearly came off the bed, but he used his other arm to pin me down.

And then he explored me, kissing my thighs, and every inch of me. He pressed his face closer to my pussy, one long lick and then two short ones, before adding a third finger and twisting.

I came then, my eyes closing as stars shattered beneath the lids. I couldn't think, couldn't breathe. It was all I could do not to fall into a puddle in his arms.

"You're so fucking beautiful when you come."

I opened my eyes lazily, trying to focus, and realized he was hard again. "How on earth?" I whispered, and he just grinned.

"You do things to me." He moved us then, so he was on his back, and I slid over him. "That's it, sit on me."

"Next time I'll sit on your face," I teased, and his eyes darkened.

"I love it when you talk dirty."

And then I sank down on him, his length stretching me in all the best ways. I pressed the palms of my hands to his shoulders as I leaned over him, riding him slowly. We usually went hard and fast, both of us needing each other, but in that moment, I took my time, building the pleasure up.

He leaned forward, taking my nipple into his mouth. When he tightened his hold, I moved even slower, rocking my hips against him. And then he laved attention on my other breast, before moving one hand to wrap around the back of my neck.

"Eyes on me, Briar. Eyes on me."

And when I met his gaze, I almost said it. I almost told him everything. That I loved him. That I always had.

But before I could say anything, his mouth was on mine, and both of us were coming. Falling into each other as we dug our fingers into each other's arms. Thoughts and function left my body, the ability to do anything but be in this moment gone. I just held him, not knowing what else to say.

By the time we cleaned up and fed Maisie again, Gabriel was running late for his meeting with the label. He pressed a quick kiss to my lips, and then kissed Maisie's cheek before running out. He had security with him, as people called out his name downstairs. Women smiled at him, begging him to sign their skin or any part of them that they could give him.

Jealousy was an angry monster, and I wanted to tell them to stop. That he was mine. That we were both thinking about futures and homes and raising Maisie. I didn't know what happened after this weekend. We were living one day at a time, but I needed more.

I finished getting ready and was grateful when Jeff said he'd drive me out to visit Lark and Rory. While I wanted to bring Maisie with me, after the press had found us the first night, I hadn't traveled with my daughter yet. As soon as we got back to Texas, things would change. But for now, I felt like a terrible mom taking time away from my baby just to visit with my friends.

The multi-Grammy award-winning world-famous singer was hiding in the back of a restaurant, with Rory by her side. The two had become friends when Ava had married Wyatt. As Rory and Ava had known each other for years, it was nice to have more connections out there. Honestly, it was nice to have these women in my life to call them friends. I felt like I didn't have enough of those.

"I'm so glad you're here." Lark hugged me tightly, and then Rory did the same.

"How was your signing?" I asked. "I'm sorry that I wasn't able to come."

Rory waved me off. "It was wonderful. The author did most of the work. I just drew."

"Your illustrations are fantastic. I can't wait to start reading them to Maisie when she's older."

"I'll make sure she gets a signed copy." Rory winked. "And I know why you couldn't come. You guys are a hot ticket in the news right now. And the bookstore wouldn't have been able to handle it all."

"It's why I couldn't come too. But this restaurant is good at keeping my secrets. So we should be fine."

"It's always that 'should', isn't it?" I asked, honestly a bit nervous.

"Yes, but there's nothing we can do, really. Unless we hide on the Wilder compound forever. And while part of me wants to do that, I have to live my life."

I smiled at Lark, and knew she was right. While I was nowhere close to being in that stratosphere, Gabriel was getting there. And frankly, whatever Gabriel touched also seemed to be out in the media. Wilder getting back together and finding their footing had just catapulted them into the stratosphere. They had already been on that route before losing Mal, before the accident. And now it just seemed to steamroll.

Everybody wanted a piece of him.

And I was one of them.

"I'm just glad we're here."

"Same. It's hard to find people who get it."

"And I'm neither one of you," Rory said with a laugh. "So thank you for helping out the children's book illustrator who really can't afford these prices," she said with a laugh.

My eyes bugged out of my head as I looked at the menu.

"Lark."

"I know, I know. But it's the price you pay in order to hide. There're a lot more mom-and-pop shops outside of LA."

"Okay, but if I'm going to eat a burger for this price, it better come with gold."

"They do have gold foil on some of them," Lark said, and Rory and I met gazes before bursting out laughing.

Rory and I shared a burger, without the gold, and a plate of onion rings. Lark went with this chicken wrap thing that we each took a bite of, and it was honestly a perfect lunch.

We didn't talk about important things, but we did talk.

"Maisie's getting so big," Lark said. "And it really makes me want one of my own."

"Oh really?" I asked.

"Yes. But East and I want to plan a bit more."

"Well, I really didn't plan this."

Lark winced. "I'm sorry. I know you didn't. But it's all working out, right?"

My smile turned slightly brittle, and the woman noticed.

"Oh. I'm sorry. I just thought..." Lark's voice trailed off as she shook her head.

"As someone with a complicated relationships of her own, you don't need to talk about it if you don't want to," Rory said.

"I almost want to ask you what you mean by that, but since I don't want to talk about mine, I won't ask about yours."

"Deal." Rory held out her hand, and I shook it, both of us laughing.

"And now that I have eaten this entire wrap and some of my own foot, we should head out."

"Yes, though I am sad that I didn't get the gold foil," I teased.

We packed up our things, and I continued to text Hilarie throughout the lunch. She had sent countless photos of Maisie, and while I knew that me taking an afternoon with the girls was good for me, I really wish I could have been able to take her.

However, without us having a home of our own, it was difficult to figure out how to keep Maisie safe and out of the press. We would get the hang of it, but for now, I was forced to leave my baby back in loving and safe arms at the hotel.

"Is Jeff waiting for you outside?" Rory asked, and I nodded.

"Yes, I texted him. Do you need a ride?"

"My team and I have her," Lark said with a smile. "They know the drill."

We headed through the back, but I nearly tripped over my feet as Lark cursed. "I'm sorry. This isn't working out the way that I wanted."

Cameras flashed as people shouted for Lark and me, and before I could figure out what to say, or what facial expression I could have, Jeff was there, leading me to the car. Thankfully Rory ran with Lark toward hers, but everybody crowded in, photographers knocking into me.

"Is it true that you and Gabriel are getting married?"

"How do you feel about the rumor that Gabriel's actually in a relationship with his bandmates Rocky and Kiera?"

"Do you think it's true that Kiera orchestrated the accident so she could take Mal's place?"

"How would your dead brother feel about your love child with his best friend?"

"Is it true that you got pregnant on purpose so you could get close to Gabriel since Mal wouldn't let you?"

My gaze shot up at that one, my mouth dropping as I looked at the woman who said it. She sneered, as more photos flashed.

Jeff nearly shoved me into the car, and then we were skidding out of the parking lot.

"I can't..." I whispered, my hands shaking.

"Ignore them. It's worse out front, and unless we were going to stay there for the next five hours, getting you out of there right now is the best. I don't know what the hell that they're doing there, but they loved the fact that you were with Lark."

"What else are they saying?" I asked.

"Don't look," Jeff grumbled.

I did so anyway, scrolling through the feed on social media. "They think I'm using them for my own career?

I don't even work only with them. I don't want to be a pop star. I don't even know what I want."

"It'll die down. There'll be a new story soon. Everybody's just in a frenzy because of the anniversary. And Gabriel Wilder finally settling down."

I shot Jeff a look. "He's not settling down. We're not even...I don't want to talk about it."

"I misspoke. Or frankly, overstepped. But I'll get you back. Make sure you text Hilarie so they know we're on our way."

Heart in my throat, I did as he said.

Hilarie texted me back immediately and added a picture of Maisie in her arms.

Guilt swamped me because I was out here, having a girls' lunch when my baby girl was back at the hotel. I should have stayed there. Hell, I should be back in Austin or even in Ashford Creek. Anywhere but here.

My chest tightened, and I tried to calm my breathing. The drive back to the hotel went quickly, and I had a feeling Jeff sped to get us there. He got us through the back gates so nobody noticed we were in, and then I practically ran through the hotel to get to my room.

"Here's Mommy," Hilarie said as she handed over Maisie.

"Thank you so much."

"It's no problem. I saw the news. Those assholes."

She winced. "I should probably not curse in front of her."

"I think Gabriel and I do it more. But thank you."

"I'm going to give you guys some space. I wrote out everything that we did so you know where we're at on the schedule. But everything's going to be okay." Hilarie squeezed my arm, and I took in her strength since I clearly didn't have it.

"Thank you, Hilarie."

"I'm glad you took time for yourself. You never do."

"And look how well that turned out."

"Ignore them. They don't matter. Only you, Gabriel, and this baby do."

Hilarie left then, and I just rocked Maisie, who babbled in my arms. She was getting so big, and yet, everything felt as if it was going far too fast around me.

A man with broad shoulders walked into the adjoining living room of our suite, and I whirled to see Brooks standing there. His eyes widened as I nearly fell, and he ran toward me. "Are you okay?"

"What are you doing here?" I asked, confused that Gabriel's brother would be here.

"I'm here to see the next show. Not all the Wilders can get out often to see him. And we wanted to make sure you guys weren't alone."

"You saw the news then?"

He winced. "Some of it. They're way out of line."

I continued to rock Maisie, frustrated.

"Do you want me to hold her? That way you can continue your pacing?"

I scowled at him but handed over his niece. My child gripped at Brooks's shirt and looked happy as could be.

She really was a Wilder girl.

"Do you want to talk about it?"

My hands were shaking, and I knew this wasn't a good time. "No. Because I need to talk about this with Gabriel, but God forbid he ever lets me."

His eyes widened, but I didn't stop.

"And no, to answer your question before, I'm not okay. I don't know what any of this means. I fell into this. And it's not like he and I talk. I don't even know who he is anymore. And that's so idiotic to say because I'm sleeping with him, and I'm raising Maisie with him. I'm here for him. And yet all I do is go from one thing to another without thinking. Because I want to be with him, and I'm not letting myself even feel that. So part of me feels like I'm not here. And now I'm lashing out at you, even though I should be talking to Gabriel."

"Yes, I guess you should."

I turned and the floor nearly fell out from beneath my feet. Gabriel stood there, his long hair pushed back from his face, and his eyes vacant.

"I didn't know you were here."

"Clearly."

Brooks looked between us and cleared his throat. "I'm going to go take Maisie with me."

Throat dry, I looked over at Gabriel's brother. "Hilarie is in the next room if you want to see her."

Brooks gave me a look, and I thought I saw pity there, before he walked out with my daughter.

I stood there, staring at Gabe, and while tears threatened, I wouldn't let them fall.

"So, I guess we should talk?" he asked, and I raised my chin.

"I've been trying to talk for weeks. So yes. Please. Just say something. *Please.*"

And I stood there, waiting for him to say something, knowing I needed to do it first. Because this was the moment I had dreaded. The moment I would have to walk away if I wasn't strong enough.

But one of us had to take the next step.

CHAPTER TWENTY-ONE
GABRIEL

I knew that nothing good ever came from eavesdropping, but I had listened anyway. I had been the idiot who had constantly tried to ignore my feelings when it came to Briar. It was easier to live in a fantasy world, than let reality crash down around us.

"Can we talk about that night? Can we talk about anything? We keep dancing around it, making plans, and yet not doing anything, and it's killing me. Please."

I ran my hands over my face and knew that it was time. It was long past time. "What do you want me to say? The fact that every time I look at you, I think of the vitriol your brother and I lobbed at each other? That the last words we had for each other were cruel?"

"He was my brother too!"

I staggered back, watching the emotions pass over her face. Rage, pain, guilt, sorrow. Everything all at once. Everything I had been feeling and trying to ignore.

She lifted her chin, tears in her eyes. "Do you know why I slept with you?"

"What?" That hadn't been what I'd been expecting her to say at all.

She moved forward and put her hands on my chest. "Do you know why I slept with you that first night? Because it wasn't alcohol. We might have lied to ourselves, but it wasn't alcohol."

Hope and judgment warred within me because she was right. Damn it. She was right. "Briar."

"No. I slept with you because I wanted to. Because every time that we were around each other, I felt *safe*. Even though you went out and partied with everyone else, and did your thing, you were my safe space. And I wanted to be with *you*. Yes, the alcohol took off the nerves, but I was there. And so were you. Don't lie to yourself anymore. Don't lie to me. Maisie may have been unplanned, but she wasn't a drunken mistake."

I stiffened. "I've never said that."

"No, but one day she's going to grow up, and she's going to want to know the story of how she came about."

"Briar—"

"The media's already made their own story. They call her a *lovechild*. But lovechild in their mind doesn't mean she was created in love. No, they mean in secret, behind my brother's back. And maybe that was the case, but only because we never had a chance to tell him."

"Exactly." I threw my hands in the air. "He left us on that bus, and I never got to say I was sorry."

"For sleeping with me? Or for not telling Mal? Because he never owned me. Yes, you and I sleeping together would probably rock the boat when it came to Mal, and it *did*. And we would have all figured it out. My brother was a hothead, but he *loved* you. He loved me, too. He would've been okay with it. The rest of my family's okay with it."

"I wasn't best friends with the rest of your family," I said, knowing that was lame as hell.

"The only time that they ever wanted to beat the shit out of you was when they thought you walked away from me."

"They're the ones that dragged you away from me before I could talk to you at the graveside."

"And neither one of us would have been ready to talk then. We were both in soft casts and covered in bruises. Some of the bruises my brother had put on you."

"And I deserved it."

"Why on earth is sleeping with me deserving of you getting punched in the face? Tell me, on what planet is that okay?"

"You don't understand. You're his sister."

"That was the worst thing to say," she spat. "My brother didn't own me. I hated the way he reacted. It was out of line. But he's gone. And we don't get to fix that. I don't get to be mad at him anymore for the way he reacted."

"But I still get to be mad at myself," I said into the silence, and her eyes widened. "I tried to bury myself into oblivion, tried to hurt my hands by working with East and building things and not caring if I got hit with a hammer or scraped my knuckles. I didn't pick up a guitar until right when you came to the property. I wanted to forget everything because all I could do was see him beside me."

"Gabriel."

"I thought it was just me being drunk at first. And I kept drinking. And then I stopped drinking, and he would still be there so I would pick up the bottle again. I don't need to drink now. That was never the real issue. The issue was every time I looked in a different direction, Mal would be sitting there, judging me. Hating me for what I did."

"But what did you do? We were adults who made our own choices."

"Because I loved you," I shouted.

Her eyes widened, and I ran my hands over my face. "I was falling for you even before I kissed you that first time. Because of your smile, and the way that you laugh. I loved your talent. I loved that you never backed down with all of us, and we're a lot. As a band, as a group with the crew, and everyone. We're a lot. But you always stood toe-to-toe with us. And I was so fucking guilty for wanting you."

"You never said—"

I cut her off. "Of course I didn't. Because when Mal was alive, I fucked up. I didn't know how to tell you, and I wasn't even sure if it was real or not. You know the world we live in. Nothing feels real. I mean, look at the narrative they're painting right now."

She shook her head. "And you said it's all lies."

"*It is.* Because Maisie isn't a lovechild. She's *our* child. And you're right. I wanted you, and it didn't matter if we had one or fifteen drinks…I wanted you that night and I had you. Just like you had me."

"Well, that's something we can agree on finally."

"But I never get to go back and tell Mal this. My best friend's dead, Briar."

She moved forward then, and wiped the tears I hadn't realized had fallen onto my cheeks.

"I know. He's gone, and I miss my brother so much. Maisie's not ever going to know her uncle. He's not going to be able to figure out a new nickname. He's not going to call her Bug like he called me. I'm not going to hear him laugh and tell me I'm an idiot for falling for you. He's not going to sing really bad karaoke to the Spice Girls when he gets drunk just to make me smile. We don't get that anymore. And I hate it. I hate that the crew died, that Lacey died. I hate the fact that I don't think I could ever get on a bus again."

"I don't think I can either," I rasped. "I don't know what we're going to do on tour. We're going to find something. At least I can get on a fucking plane, in a car. But every time I see a bus, I just imagine you falling backwards, and me throwing myself on top of you. And you still got hurt, Briar. Even though I tried to protect you, you still got hurt."

I hadn't even realized that was on my conscience until the words were out, and Briar shook her head, tears streaming down her cheeks.

"You couldn't stop what happened. And you did protect me. Everyone said it would have been worse if you hadn't covered me with your body. You got hurt to protect me."

"But Mal is still gone."

"Yes. And we're standing here, shouting at each other, and I don't know what I feel anymore. Because I don't know what I'm supposed to do when we walk out of here. The media will always be there, and that means they're always going to wonder if I'm getting ahead in my career because I fucked you. And because I'm friends with Lark now."

I growled. "Why would they think that?"

"Because it's what they do. You see the hate mail that I get just by being with you. We can't even leave this hotel together because we're afraid that they're going to get photos of Maisie. Where are we supposed to raise her? Are we even going to do it together? We keep ignoring these questions because they're too hard, and I can't do it anymore."

"What does that mean?"

"If this is too much, it was always going to be too much."

"So you're saying that you can't take my lifestyle?" I didn't know why I was saying the words, but I was so damn scared that it was easier to yell rather than think.

"I don't know why I'm here. But I love you, and I don't know what I'm supposed to do with that."

The words should have been a balm to soothe my soul, but it just lashed out at me, scaring me to death. I couldn't protect her on that bus, just like I couldn't protect Mal. How the hell was I supposed to do that with the media, and people scrambling to get more of the band and Maisie? How was I supposed to keep her safe?

"Then go home," I said, wanting to take the words back as I even said them. "Be safe there."

"You want me to go home? And what, take Maisie and you can see her whenever you're not on tour? Is that what you want? I just told you that I love you, and you're telling me to go home."

"Because I can't keep you safe." I tugged on my hair, my breaths coming in pants. "The cameras are always going to be there. The questions are going to be there. But this is my life. I don't know what else I could do."

"I don't know either. But I'll leave. And if I leave, I'm not coming back."

"I don't know what to do because I fucking want you. I love you, Briar. I've always loved you. And that's the problem. Because I don't know what to do about it. I don't know how to live this life with you by my side without fucking it all up. Because I fucked it up with Mal, and I'm going to do the same to you. And the same with Maisie. And I'm so scared that my life is going to ruin that little girl's life, just like it's hurting you. I don't know what I'm supposed to do."

"Gabriel..." she began, but before she could say anything, Brooks slammed into the room.

I turned to my brother, dread pooling in my gut.

"Maisie's gone."

My knees shook as Briar moved forward, leaning into me.

"What?" Briar and I said at the same time.

"I don't fucking know." Brooks slid his hands through his hair. "I took Maisie to Hilarie, and I figured we would just chill there while we waited for you guys to get it out of your systems, but then my phone rang with a work call, so I left the two of them. When I went back, they were gone. I can't fucking find them."

My heart leaped into my throat, and I pushed past my brother, running down the hall. "Maisie! Hilarie!"

Briar ran past me, and slammed into our nanny's room, but nobody was there. It looked like someone had ransacked the room, and I pulled Briar back to me.

"Let me go. I need to find her."

"No, we can't touch anything. Right? If someone took her, the cops need to see this."

"We already called them," Jeff said from behind me, and I whirled, Briar in my arms. "You're going to need to see this."

He held out a note in a plastic bag, and bile rose in my throat.

"What does it say?" Briar asked, her voice so fucking strong. So strong that I knew that I would be the one to break here.

"It's in Hilarie's handwriting," Brooks said softly as he looked over Jeff's shoulder, my brother's strong shoulders tightening, his face going gray.

Leave her.
Take me, Gabriel, my angel.
And we can raise our baby together.

"The cops are on their way. We'll find her," Jeff promised, but I wasn't listening to him.

It was all I could do not to panic, throw up, do something.

I had done this. My job had done this.

Someone had taken our child, and it was all my fault.

I looked down at Briar, waiting for her to yell at me, to push at me, but instead her knees buckled, and I held her close as the world stood still. I knew the choices that I had made had led to this. Maisie, gone. The woman I loved in my arms, breaking down, ready to leave.

And I knew it was all my fault. Just like Mal.

My best friend had been right. I did fuck up everything I touched. I fell to the floor with Briar in my arms, as my brother moved forward, and then I couldn't think of anything else.

CHAPTER TWENTY-TWO
BRIAR

"How did we miss this?" Gabriel asked once again as he paced in front of me. He would move his hands from his hips to run through his hair and then repeat the process. It was almost a constant for me, the way he would move. From one side of the room to the other, trying to get a hold of what exactly had happened.

Yet I knew there were no answers for what had happened.

Because the person we had trusted with our daughter had taken her.

"Do you think she's the one who sent fan mail before?" I asked. I hadn't even realized I was speaking until my voice echoed through the hotel room.

Brooks, Lark, and Rory turned toward me, eyes wide.

"What mail?" Brooks asked, the gravel in his voice sounding as if he had screamed for hours on end. Maybe he had, and I just hadn't heard it.

After Brooks and Jeff had run into the room, I had nearly blacked out for a good ten minutes. Maybe longer. I hadn't been able to hear anything other than the sound of Gabriel's heartbeat beneath my ear. He had steadied me until I knew I had to be the one with the backbone of steel. Gabriel had found his own, and I needed to stand tall near him. If I wasn't strong, I would break. And I had already been on the verge of breaking before. When we had been fighting over wanting the same thing.

How idiotic our fight had been. If we had just sat down and listened to each other weeks ago, we wouldn't have been at that. And we wouldn't have left our daughter with someone we thought we could trust.

"There were letters. Weird ones about how I wasn't good enough. How they wanted to take my place with Maisie and Gabriel."

The man that I loved turned to me, his pale face going ashen.

"Let's see if Max or Jeff still have everything. They collect it all just in case—" He swallowed hard, before running his hands over his face. "Just in case something like this happens. But I didn't think anything like this would ever happen."

I stood up and moved toward him, hands outstretched. He immediately pulled me into his arms, crushing me against him. "We have to find her. Why can't we be out there looking for her?"

"Ma'am," the officer said from the doorway. "It's best if you all stay here. The media have already caught wind of this, and they've circled the building. We have everyone out there searching for your daughter. Is there anything else you can tell us about this Hilarie Sawyer?"

"You have all the information we have from the background checks. They were thorough. She has a degree in child education and references."

"Not only did my brother's security team go through her, but we also had an additional agency do it. Just to make sure we didn't miss anything. How the hell did this slip through the cracks?"

I clung to Gabriel as he did the same to me, and our friends and family stood by, feeling just as helpless as we did.

The detective nodded. "If she doesn't have this sort of experience or pattern in her past, something might have triggered it. We won't know until we find her."

"And you're going to find her," I warned, my voice so

steady it should have worried me. And though I had no action in front of me that I could attain, time passing through my fingertips, I couldn't break down again.

I needed to be here.

"Let's go through everything again," another officer said, and while frustration slammed into me, I answered all of their questions.

Yes, Hilarie stayed on whatever property we were at.

Yes, she had days off.

Yes, she had her own home.

Yes, we left her alone with our daughter.

No, we had no idea she would do this.

No, we hadn't met Hilarie's family.

Yes, we had as many background checks as possible for her.

No, it hadn't been enough.

"Okay, we'll be here if you think of anything else," the officer said, but another one stood at the door, and I wasn't sure if they were keeping people out, or keeping us in.

Because I knew every single person in this room wanted to run out and search through the streets of LA for my daughter.

"He was right about the media out there," Rory whispered as she looked through a tiny crack in the drapes.

"Stay away from the windows," Brooks barked.

Rory just raised an eyebrow at him.

"I'm the only one here that the world doesn't know. And they didn't see my eye as I looked through the window."

"You can't know that," Brooks warned.

Rory held up both hands before moving forward. She put her hand on his arm, and he stiffened.

"They're going to find her. I'm not going to take any other answer as an option."

Brooks just glared at Rory, and I wanted to believe her. With every ounce in me, I needed to believe her. But every single scenario running through my mind didn't have a happy ending. And I wanted to throw up.

"I'm so damn sorry. This is all my fault."

I looked up at Gabriel and shook my head. "I don't blame you. You did everything you could to keep her safe. I blame Hilarie. I blame whatever weird cult-like fanatical thing some fans fall into. You've never once gone out on stage and demand people adore you. And you were always careful with the fans that got too close. I know that. I saw that. You and Mal were the same. So I can't blame you. Because if I blame you, then everything inside me would break. And I can't do that."

"We'll give you some privacy," Lark whispered as she pulled the others into the adjoining living room.

Gabriel held me, as we stood there swaying back and

forth. "I'm sorry for yelling. I'm sorry for being such an asshole for the past what, year?"

"I'm sorry for not speaking my mind when I should have. We were both so scared that we put our own barriers in the way. It's just so stupid."

"We're going to find her. And then we're going to put tracking on all of us."

I wanted to laugh at that, but I realized that Gabriel wasn't joking. "I think that might be illegal," I whispered.

"Maybe not. We'll find a way. And I'm never letting you or Maisie out of my sight again."

"Same. Because Hilarie wants you. She wants Maisie, but she wants *you*."

"You think I don't know that? I'm so damn scared about what's going to happen to you or Maisie if she doesn't get me. Because she was ready to throw you away. What if she hurts you?"

"She'd have to get through all of the Wilders and Ashfords first. And she would have to survive me killing her."

"You probably shouldn't threaten murder when cops are listening."

"I really don't care right now. She has my baby."

And so we stood there, before we paced, and Rory forced us to eat something. I wanted to scream and shout and throw the food, but that would be ridiculous. Maisie needed us to be strong.

And when my breasts fell heavy, tears finally slid down my cheeks because I needed to pump.

The others gave me privacy, but it was Gabriel who held my hand, and I pumped so my daughter would have food when we found her.

"She took the diaper bag, and a couple of bottles, but is it enough? I want my baby to be okay."

"We're going to find Maisie. And then we're going to find a home that we can keep her safe in that's just ours. And we're going to be a family."

I stared up at him, not knowing what to feel.

"Gabriel," I began.

"No. I'm tired of pushing you away because I'm scared. We've always been a family, you and me. And not just because of Mal. And I was too blind to see it for too long. So we're going to find our child, and we're going to make sure Hilarie's in jail for a long fucking time. And we're never going to let this happen again. Because we're going to find a way to be steady. To cement what we have. Because I'm never letting you go again."

"I love you," I whispered.

"I love you so fucking much. I'm sorry. So sorry for everything."

"We need to find Maisie," I whispered.

Another hour passed, and then a second. I had to pump one more time, and I felt like we were losing hope. Someone had turned on the news, and people were scrambling to figure out what had happened to our daughter. But there were no answers.

It wasn't as if I could go door to door.

When Rory stood in the doorway, I looked up at her.

"What is it?"

"I know you don't use social media often anymore, but you should see this."

I stood up quickly, Gabriel behind me.

"What is it?"

Rory handed the phone to me and pointed at one of the trending stories. "Both sets of your fans are searching. They're pleading for Hilarie to give Maisie back. The people that love you, that love your work, who loved Mal, are doing all that they can to make sure that Maisie gets back to you. I know that there aren't any right answers now, and everything that I say is just going to hurt. But people out there love you. Just like people in here do. And we're going to find her."

Rory was crying then, and I held her phone in my hand, clutching it like a lifeline. There were so many posts, so many pleads. There might've been hate in some of the comments, but I didn't see them. Only love, and worry. Because they wanted our happy ending.

And every thread of my soul desperately needed it.

When one of the officers walked back into the room, his face slightly ruddy, I stood up, Gabriel with me.

"Did you find her?" Gabriel asked, his voice a rasp.

"We did."

My knees nearly gave out, and Gabriel held me steady. "Is she okay? Where is she? I need to see my baby."

"She's safe. The paramedics are with her, and we have Hilarie Sawyer in custody. We'll go through it all in detail, but let's get you there. It's going to be a circus with the media soon, but we're going to get you to your child."

Everything moved in a blur at that moment, and I wasn't sure exactly how I made it into the car, or how quickly we drove to the motel where Hilarie had stashed our daughter.

I was glad that they had already dragged her away. Because I wasn't sure what I would have done if I saw her. I was afraid I would own up to the promise I had made to Gabriel, and then Maisie's mother would be a murderer.

The media and fans hadn't shown up yet, but they would be there soon. I knew that we would have to move to another location, but for now, I just needed to see Maisie. We leaped out of the car as soon as it stopped with our group behind us.

And as Maisie's cries hit my ears, my heart sped up.

I ran as quickly as I could. Gabriel beat me, his long legs taking wide strides. And then Maisie was in his arms, and I flung myself into both of them, tears streaming down my cheeks.

"Baby Girl. Baby Girl."

"We're going to have her checked out at the hospital, but your baby girl's just fine. Fed and bathed and changed. I know that this isn't going to give you any sense of relief, but she was taken care of."

But not by me. Maisie hadn't been taken care of by me. And as Gabriel held onto me, Maisie between us, I just looked up into the eyes of the man that I loved and let myself feel for the first time since Maisie had been taken.

"I love you."

"I love you too. We're going to make this work. And I'm never letting you go."

And then he kissed me, and Maisie nuzzled between us.

We were a family, the three of us.

Because Mal had loved Gabriel for a reason, and I loved him. I loved the man holding me with every thread of my being that I had tried to ignore for so long.

And after we went to the hospital and found ourselves on the private jet that Lark shared with another artist, we made our way home to the Wilders. There were interviews to be made and police reports to be sifted through. I knew the bureaucracy of the trauma that had nearly broken us would need to occur.

But for now, Maisie smiled up at us from her carrier, and I held Gabriel's hand.

I had loved Gabriel Wilder for far longer than I had cared to admit.

I had loved the friend, the rockstar, the broken man. The father.

I loved every piece of him, even though I hadn't let myself believe.

And as we headed back toward the Wilders, with my family on another plane to meet us there, I knew that this was only a new beginning. There would be no going back.

I had to hope that if we had been given a chance, Mal would have approved of the two of us. In a hope of hopes, I knew it was true. Because Mal loved both of us. And if he had been thinking clearly, he would have calmed down, and we would have had that time to breathe.

But time had taken him from us far too soon. And had nearly done the same to Maisie.

And I was tired of making mistakes because I was scared.

So I would fight for Gabriel. I would fight for me.

I would fight for us.

Because we were a family.

The Wilders, the Ashfords, the band. All of us. We were never alone, even though sometimes we had lost our way.

I had my Wilder. *Both of them.* And I would never let go again.

CHAPTER TWENTY-THREE
GABRIEL

Like I always did on mornings where the fog drifted in and a sense of reflection washed over me, I searched for that familiar ghost. It was odd to think that while I didn't believe in ghosts, a part of my mind desperately craved it.

But Mal was nowhere to be seen. He didn't need to watch over me as I made countless mistakes after mistakes. Because I was no longer drowning myself in pity or hiding from life. Instead, I watched as my niece ran around the backyard with my other nephews and nieces and looked down at the little girl in my arms.

"Your family is a little loud," I teased. Maisie put her hands on my mouth, and I blew raspberries. "But you know, I still think you look like a princess in the dress."

She smiled up at me, those dimples peeking out that reminded me of Mal.

This little girl was an Ashford and a Wilder through and through. It depended on the time of day for which family she really looked like. At least, that's what people told me. I just saw my little Maisie.

"We should probably change her before she gets her smash cake," Briar said with a laugh as she came forward. She slid underneath my free arm, and tickled Maisie's belly over her poofy princess dress.

"You're right. But seeing her with pink frosting all over that dress? It sounds like a good photo."

"Then you get to wash that dress, Mister," she warned, and I leaned forward and kissed my wife softly on the lips.

In the months since the kidnapping, things had gone full force. Rather than frozen in amber as we had been for nearly a year, Briar and I did the one thing that we had never been good at.

Talked to one another.

We had released a statement thanking the authorities and the public for searching for Maisie and doing all that they could. We even asked them to donate in Mal's and Maisie's names to local charities because people had wanted to do something. They had felt just as helpless as we had.

They had come out in full force, and the attention

that we had tried to avoid came back in full force. But instead, it was no longer about the lovechild and secrets. Now it was about the family we had made, and the connections we wanted more than anything.

People knew who Briar was, and not just because of my name or Mal's. But because of her talent. And soon we would be heading toward the Grammys where I was pretty sure that she was about to win at least two more. She would probably beat me in one of the categories, but I was ready to be a gracious loser. Mostly because afterwards she would take pity on me, and we'd have a great night.

We stood now on the land that I had bought near my brother's property. It wasn't huge, but it was private enough with security precautions that we felt safe. My family stood on our back lawn, laughing and talking with one another as we celebrated Maisie's first birthday.

We still needed to finish decorating some of the rooms, and do a few updates for this older home, but it was nice to have projects in mind. A future where it didn't seem so dim.

And in the next month, the new Wilder album would release, and the hype around it was already monumental to the point it was a little worrying. We were releasing in an off time for awards, and that was on purpose. We hadn't wanted the extra pressure.

Although, we could still be contenders for the following year.

But the album was finally what we needed it to be. Mal's voice would be on some tracks, ones that we had made before everything had changed. And Kiera's voice was on the others. Because somehow, we had found a way to meld our band into who we were now. We were still Wilder, but we were new, different.

And my band stood on our property, laughing and joking with their families and mine.

There were enough Ashfords and Wilders here that I was sure that they probably needed name tags for those who didn't know them.

Callum, Briar's older brother, was over on the other side of the yard surrounded by friends and speaking with Rory. The two of them had bonded when Callum and the other Ashfords had come rushing in to check on their sister. Although I wasn't quite sure what was going on there.

Bodhi and Teagan were hanging out with the band, talking about Mal and sharing stories. And it was good to see so many of Briar's family members here and not wanting to murder me.

I still had to grovel to them every once in a while, but I didn't mind. I had done my groveling to Briar, and I would do it again every once in a while just to take it home.

Soon we would be working on the next phase of our lives; we were finally taking on an overseas tour. Briar and Maisie would be with me for part of it, but not all of it. And I knew the separation was going to be difficult. But we would find a way.

With the help of the three nannies that we rotated in and out who had had so many background checks that I was surprised they hadn't balked. But all three of them wanted to erase Hilarie's name from the memory of anything having to do with our family.

If I would've looked into the future that moment when I had walked away from the gravesite and thought that I hadn't had a home, I would never have been able to imagine this moment. Standing on property that I owned, holding my little girl and the woman that I loved, and excited to see what happened next. We had a tour line up that people would kill for, Briar was making music she loved, and our family finally felt right.

We even had a cabin up in Ashford Creek so we could be near Briar's family. I wasn't quite sure how that was going to go, but we were going to do it for Mal. Because that's where he had grown up, so Maisie needed to see parts of it.

Though there were histories there that I knew weren't going to be easy.

"You're lost in thought. Are you okay?"

I smiled down at my wife, as we had married in

secret a month after the kidnapping. Our families had known about it, of course, and while Brooks had stood for me and Teagan for Briar, we hadn't wanted anyone else there. Not that we didn't love them. In fact, the Wilders were in the wedding business after all. But trying to find a way to make it happen without the noise of the rest of the world meant we had to keep it a secret.

Briar wore my wedding ring, and my name, and I wore hers.

We were all Wilder Ashfords. And my brothers gave me so much shit for having Ashford as a second name. But since Maisie had already been named that way, we followed suit.

I had a feeling Mal would be over the moon by that —and would continue to give me shit. "I was just thinking about how everything has changed."

"Same here. Although if you do get overwhelmed again, let's not pass out, shall we?"

I growled and kissed my wife hard on the lips. Maisie pushed me away from her and patted my mouth.

"Okay. A little possessive," I said as I blew raspberries on her cheek. "And I only passed out once."

"You almost passed out a second time at our wedding."

I glared at her. "I thought we weren't going to talk about that ever again."

"You asked. I did not agree."

I pinched her side, and she laughed, and I knew that this was it. This is what I had wanted all this time. And I hadn't realized it. No number of parties, going out late at night, and being with anyone at any time could stand close to where I was now.

I might still be a rockstar, a title that made me laugh. But somehow I'd become a family man—who still played at sold out stadiums. But my priorities had shifted.

Aurora tapped my shoulder, her sundress billowing around her.

I smiled down at my sister-in-law. "Is it cake time?"

"You know it. I made the cutest little smash cake for her, and two other cakes for the rest of the group."

"You spoil us," Briar whispered.

"I try. Come on, let's go get this little girl covered in pink frosting."

"Let's change her dress!" Briar called out, and then we were all moving, and I pulled out my phone to record my daughter inhaling her cake. She shoved her face into the side, and I laughed, wondering how many photos and videos I was going to have of this kid before I needed to upgrade my phone.

"Mal, you would've loved this," I whispered.

I didn't see his ghost again. And that was fine with

me. Because he was still here, in that little girl, and in the family that I knew still mourned. Just like I did.

As I watched my wife wipe cake from our daughter's cheeks, I knew another song was in me. And then another, and then another. Because I would never stop what I did. Never again.

I wouldn't go back to the man who hid in the shadows and tried to drown himself. I had everything to live for.

And the scariest thing was that I had had it in my hands all along. So I would never let them go.

I was a Wilder, an Ashford, a father, and a husband.

And for a man who hated titles, I wanted to latch on to every single one.

Because I was finally home. After all this time.

CHAPTER TWENTY-FOUR
BROOKS

BEFORE.

"Brooks, sit down with me."

"I can't," I said as I leaned forward and brushed at the little amount of peach fuzz on the top of her head.

Amara smiled up at me, that smile just as beautiful as the first time I had seen her all those years ago. We had been sixteen, the both of us waiting at the DMV for our driver's licenses. We might have gone to the same high school, but it wasn't as if I had known every single person on our campus.

And so, while waiting next to the girl with gorgeous blue eyes, blonde hair, and a retainer that she kept playing with, I knew that I was in love.

I just hadn't realized it was a love that was unending and broken until it was nearly too late.

"You should sit."

"I need to go get you some water. I'll be right back."

I didn't know why this panic kept gripping my chest. It wasn't as if this was a new feeling. A new state.

My beautiful wife, the woman that I had loved for over a decade, was dying in front of my eyes and I could not stop it. I used my hands to build things for a living. I constructed things. I made them sturdy. My goal in life was to make sure that what I built could withstand the test of time.

And yet, I could not keep my wife safe. She was fading before my eyes, and I could not just sit here and watch it happen. I needed to be doing something.

But there was nothing I could do.

"I have water. Come and sit down. We need to finish our show. And I want to ask you something."

And because I honestly could never say no to Amara, I sat down next to her, my hip against hers as I held her hand and ran my finger along her jaw.

"Let me get you your scarf. Your head must be getting cold."

She continued to smile up at me, and I did not like the look in her eyes. The resignation. The knowing.

Stage IV breast cancer wasn't always a death sentence. That's what they kept telling me. But her cancer was aggressive and had spread to multiple areas of her body. That's what Stage IV was, after all. She had done multiple rounds of chemo and had lost her hair more than once. Now it was growing back because she was on radiation. The radiation that left burns along her body around her ports. The allergy she had developed to the adhesive having ripped off chunks of skin that were now being burned by the same medicine that was supposed to keep her alive.

I had no idea how Amara could do this. How she could keep so strong in the face of what was to come.

I was weak. Breaking inside, and yet my wife could withstand anything. That's what she kept telling me.

My wife smiled at me, the dark circles under her eyes deepening. "Before we start the show, I want to ask you something."

Again, I couldn't say no to her. I never could before. And sure as hell not now. "What is it, Baby? What can I do for you?"

"You always ask that. And you always say anything. But I'm going to ask something very scary. Can you do that for me?"

I froze, the lump in my throat making it difficult to breathe. "What is it? I'll do it. Anything you want." As long as it kept her here with me, I would do anything.

"I really need you to think about this. I need you to

promise me that you'll think about what I'm saying and then promise me you'll do it."

"Just tell me, Amara. I promise, I'll do whatever you say."

"Don't regret those words." She squeezed my hand, and the energy sparked back into her eyes, the energy that I had been missing all these years.

Clawing panic squeezed my throat, but I tried not to let it show. I needed to be the strong one, because Amara was allowed to break down. She didn't at the hospital, didn't in front of her friends, but she was allowed to in front of me.

So I had to be the strong one.

"When I'm gone—"

"No," I cut her off. "No, we're not going to say those words."

"Brooks. I love you with all of my heart. But you know that it's not going to be much longer."

Another crevice opened up in my heart and I raged against whatever god would listen. "Amara. I'm going to yell. And you know I don't yell at you." My voice cracked, but she ran her fingers over my hand in answer.

"When I'm gone, I want you to clean out this house. Don't look at the boxes of bandages and scarves. Don't look at the house that has become my comfort and your horror."

"Amara."

I wasn't sure what I was supposed to say, though, and she squeezed my hand even harder. But there wasn't enough strength in that hand. Everything was breaking inside me, and I hated myself. It should be me in that bed. It should be me wasting away, but it wasn't. It was the sweetest girl I had ever met instead.

"I need you to promise me that you'll try."

"Amara," I said again, this time the tears freely flowing.

"Find love again. It's not fair. *Life isn't fair*. I don't know what's coming next, and I am being so mean to you right now. But I need you to move on."

"Don't you make me promise that. I'm not going to. You can't fucking ask me to do that." Every ounce of rage at her cancer coursed through me in that moment, and I couldn't catch my breath.

"But I can. It's the cancer prerogative." She smiled, but I couldn't reciprocate. That had been our running joke between us. Because when she needed ice cream or needed me to do something that I really didn't want to do, we mentioned the cancer prerogative. It was ridiculous, but sometimes we needed to find the humor in the hell. There would be nothing left if we didn't.

"No. Not this time."

"Brooks. My love. My best friend. Please. Try. Go out

on dates. Find another woman. We both know that it's just been the two of us."

I swallowed that lump in my throat, nodding. We had both been sixteen-year-old virgins when we had gotten together, meaning the two of us had only slept with each other. And in my mind, that was how it was going to be. My one and only.

"You can't ask this of me."

Amara wasn't crying, but I was. I wasn't sure if she'd practiced this speech, or she was so dehydrated she couldn't cry anymore. "But I can. Don't die with me, Brooks. I need you to find that happy ever after."

"You're my happy ever after, Amara. That's what we promised."

"And I'm going to break that promise. I'm going to love you for the rest of my life. And I hate that I know it's not long enough. Love me, Brooks. Love me for all your years. But I also need you to do something else. Live. Find someone that loves you just as much as I do."

"That's not going to happen."

"It might. Your heart is so big, Brooks. You take care of your brothers. You take care of me. You have so much in you. Let someone take care of you for once. Don't give up on life because life is giving up on me."

Damn this woman. She'd always been good with

words when I got lost in my head. And now every word cut like a knife.

"I hate you right now," I growled.

"No you don't." Her smile softened, her shoulders relaxing.

I leaned over and brushed my knuckle along her too thin cheek. "You're right. Because I could never hate you. But I love you so much. You can't make me promise that."

"But I'm going to make you anyway."

Tears streamed down my cheeks, and I leaned forward, pressing my lips to her chapped ones. "I promise," I lied.

And then I laid down next to my wife, and held her as we watched a movie, and I tried not to think of that promise.

Amara died three weeks later. And as I stood in my backyard, her ashes on the mantle inside, I swore that while I loved my wife, and would always do so, I was going to break our final promise.

Because I would never love anyone like I loved my wife. I didn't have it in me.

ONE YEAR LATER.

I was drunk. The amount of whiskey in my system was probably an issue. But I needed all of the alcohol. Every ounce in this bar if I had to. I couldn't be at home for this, and I didn't want to. I had already ignored the countless phone calls. The sad looks from our neighbors.

We all knew what today was.

I lost my wife one year ago today, and drinking wasn't going to bring her back.

But maybe I could pretend for this moment.

I was at an airport hotel bar of all places, having driven hours just to get out of my neighborhood, get out of the places that reminded me of the woman that I loved.

Somehow I had ended up near a major airport, and figured I would get on a plane and go somewhere. I didn't know where. I had a bag, and I'd fly somewhere. Do something spontaneous and uncaring. Anything that wasn't Brooks Wilder. For now, I would spend the night in this airport bar and think of something to do next. And get drunk.

"Another," I said into the din, and the bartender nodded, filling up my glass. Someone sat next to me, but I didn't bother to look over. The place was busy, people milling about, waiting for the hours to pass before they could go to sleep, and then hitch a ride onto the shuttle.

I knew that I wasn't making any sense. I was just going wherever the wind blew me. Only I didn't want to stand still. Because standing still would mean I would have to think of Amara.

"A glass of rosé please," a soft voice said from beside me, and I saw a woman out of the corner of my eye lower her shoulders in a deep sigh.

The bartender shook his head. "Sorry, we don't have any of that. White or red."

"Then how about whatever he's having," she said, using her thumb to point toward me.

The bartender immediately poured her two fingers of whiskey, and she nodded, before tilting her glass toward mine.

"Cheers."

I didn't feel like adding to that, but before I could say so or move my glass, she knocked back the entire glass in one sip and didn't even shudder.

Well, damn.

"Another please," she said, and the bartender gave us a look, before shrugging and pouring us some more. "You really don't have good taste in whiskey, but thanks," the woman muttered next to me, and I didn't really know why she was talking to me, but I continued to drink.

And again.

And again.

NOW.

I sat on a wooden bench that I had built with my own hands, staring off into the land that my family now owned. I was born a Wilder, but now I was a Wilder with my brothers and cousins, building something that meant something.

The sun was starting to set, and it was about damn time since it was nearly nine o'clock. I never really realized how close to the equator South Texas was. Well, it wasn't that close, but far closer than up north.

Someone sat next to me on the bench, breaking me out of my geography reverie, and by the vanilla scent hitting my nose, I knew exactly who it was.

"I don't really want to talk," I growled, annoyed with myself for speaking first.

"I know you don't." Rory didn't say anything else, and the two of us stared off into the distance, the sun taking its damn time to set beyond the horizon.

"Why are you here?" I asked, not speaking of this bench. But this town, this retreat.

"Because I have nowhere else to go."

And with that kind of answer, I didn't have much to say, so I sat next to the first woman that I had slept with after my wife had died, and didn't say a damn word.

And I swore I could hear Amara whisper in the wind, *Try. For me.*

And I cursed under my breath and ignored that vanilla scent.

I had been drunk and had slept with someone who wasn't my wife. It didn't matter that Amara had been gone.

I'd broken something inside, broken everything.

And I still wouldn't keep my promise.

NEXT IN THE WILDER BROTHERS SERIES:
Brooks and Rory fix a mistake in Endlessly Yours.

IF YOU'D LIKE TO READ A BONUS SCENE:
CHECK OUT THIS SPECIAL EPILOGUE!

BONUS EPILOGUE
GABRIEL

The crowd chanted our names, their voices reverberating throughout the stadium. I closed my eyes as the shouts of the crowd washed over me, and I let myself sway to the beat of the drums.

Kiera increased the tempo, and I swayed a little bit more, before opening my eyes, guitar in hand.

I looked over at Joshua, his grin wide, then over at Rocky, who continued to sway, her face glowing.

"What if I were to run?" I began, and the crowd went wild.

We began the first few chords of *Echoes of Goodbye*, and I looked up to the rafters, knowing that Mal wasn't there, he had never been, yet I still allowed the warmth of what could have been wash over me.

And then I sang.

People shouted, singing along with every single word that Briar and I had written together.

My Briar. The woman that I loved. My wife.

I was never going to get over saying *my wife*.

We let the song continue, as David went in for backup vocals, Joshua adding his. And then Rocky and Kiera sang along as well, each of us blending our voices for the person who wasn't here with us.

And the crowd *indeed* went wild.

Everything felt right, as if this was where I was meant to be. I looked over to the side stage, and smiled, even as I sang.

Briar stood there in jeans that hugged her curves, a cropped top, a long flowing shirt, and had Maisie on her hip. Maisie waved her little chubby hand at me, and I waved back.

I had no idea how we had ended up with a toddler. Time did indeed move far too quickly.

The crowd noticed my wave, and they cheered even louder. Some of them might have thought I was waving to them, but others knew that my family was here tonight. The Wilders were here to watch Wilder. Of course, everything felt as if I were exactly where I needed to be because I was with the people who meant the most to me.

As we finished the final chord, and everyone screamed, I began to make my way over to the side of the stage as Rocky ramped up the crowd. I moved forward and pushed my guitar to my back as I wrapped my arm around Briar's waist and took her mouth with mine.

She laughed, before kissing me back, and Maisie tapped both of our cheeks with her hands.

"My turn. My turn."

I kissed Maisie on the cheek, then the other cheek, and then blew raspberries on her belly.

She laughed, clapping her hands.

"How's my little girl doing?"

She couldn't quite hear me with her ear protection on, but she still smiled and leaned to kiss my cheek. Then she rubbed the stubble and grimaced.

I rolled my eyes and looked at Briar. "Everyone's a critic."

"I think you look hot with a beard. Just saying."

"I think you look edible right now," I muttered, grateful that Maisie couldn't hear us.

Even though the band was waiting for me, I took a few more seconds to place my hand over Briar's stomach.

Her eyes went wide. "Gabriel," she snapped, even though a smile played on her face.

"I can't help it. I'm all caveman with my woman and shit."

"Shit!" Maisie shouted, and Briar narrowed her gaze

at me. Apparently our daughter had learned how to take off her ear protection. Damn kid.

"Do not let this baby have their first word be a curse word like Maisie's was."

Maisie's first word had indeed been shit. It could have been worse. Much worse. And I was pretty sure that it was my brother's fault that Maisie cursed, not mine.

And that was what I was going to stick with.

"Come on, you know what you have to do."

Briar's face drained of color, before she swallowed hard. "Only for you, Gabriel Wilder."

We weren't ready to announce the pregnancy yet, and with the outfit that she was wearing, it hid it quite well. Our family knew, of course, as well as the band, but the world didn't need to know yet.

Every day was another way of finding balance when it came to our lives with the media, the fans, and the world.

We didn't always do it right. Sometimes we did indeed have to run from paparazzi. Or hide Maisie's face from photographers who didn't understand the meaning of no. But usually we had a decent balance. A lot of the usual photographers did their best not to get photos of our daughter. They knew the rules, and if they wanted to stay anywhere near us without a restraining order, they were going to respect our privacy. So, they didn't snap pics of our kid, and we let them take photos of us as we left a restaurant in New York.

It was an odd way to live, but we were making it work.

And I wouldn't have it any other way, honestly. Because this was the way that we had paved for ourselves. Parents, musicians, rock gods, and Wilders.

Brooks came over, a shit-eating grin on his face as he held out his hands. "Okay, give me my niece. You guys have work to do."

Maisie immediately jumped into his arms without a care for her safety. Of course, Uncle Brooks would always be there to catch her. He lifted her up into the air, tossed her once more as Briar let out a shocked gasp. Then my brother pushed me toward the stage.

"They're waiting on you both. Go."

"Maybe we should change our minds and do something else," Briar said, and I scowled at her.

"Oh no you don't. It's time. You promised yourself."

"I hate you and love you right now."

"Oh Gabriel, your cult is waiting," Kiera called out, and the fans screamed even louder, stomping their feet.

"Wilder! Wilder!"

"Okay, my Wilder, let's go."

"Ashford. I'm an Ashford."

"Well so am I, Babe. We're both. But you've promised yourself you'd do this. Now let's go."

And as I strummed the first note of the song, everyone squealed impossibly louder. And I made my way onto the stage, Briar at my side.

I wasn't sure I could even hear my thoughts over the sounds of the crowd. The band grinned, each of them taking their positions, as I went up to the mic.

"As you know, my lovely wife here writes some of the best songs out there. Don't you think?"

The crowd cheered.

"And because she lost a bet, I'm forcing her to sing our song."

Again, people shrieked, and it felt as though the rafters vibrated.

We had won the Grammy together the last year because of the song we had written together, *Echoes of Goodbye*. But we'd won another Grammy for *Stay for Me*.

And Briar and I had never sung it together. She wasn't on the album as a singer, but songwriter, and had sung it outside of our studio, but now she was singing in front of the world.

Because she indeed had lost a bet. A naked one.

And yet I knew she was blushing from head to toe, and I couldn't wait to find out for myself later.

"Okay, wife of mine."

Another cheer.

"You sure do like claiming me," Briar teased.

The crowd had gone insane at this point.

"He's a menace," Kiera called out.

"Ridiculous," Rocky agreed.

"I'm a little jealous. I guess I should go find a wife," Joshua added.

"I'll be your wife!" somebody called from the front row, and others added in their offers.

"Well, you're in it now," David said with a laugh, as he began to play a soft melody.

"Are you ready, Baby?" I asked, and Briar nodded. "Always."

"Staying is only easy if you have nowhere else to run," I began, and she leaned forward, her beautiful alto voice joining mine, and the crowd went wild.

And I once again fell in love with my best friend's sister, my wife, the mother of my child, and the last piece I'd been missing—even though she'd been there all along.

NEXT IN THE WILDER BROTHERS SERIES:
Brooks and Rory fix a mistake in Endlessly Yours.

A NOTE FROM CARRIE ANN RYAN

Thank you so much for reading **Pieces of Me!**

Want to know what's next? I'm not leaving Brooks and Rory out in the cold for long. Endlessly Yours will bring their romance to the fold and bring the Wilder Brothers to a close.

But that's not the last of the brothers! That's right, Briar's family is getting their own story in the ASHFORD CREEK SERIES. The first book, Legacy, is Callum's romance and things are about to get...growly. I am so excited to let the Wilders keep their HEAs in their small town and visit the new small town up north in Colorado - Ashford Creek.

If you've loved the Wilder Brothers, Ashford Creek will be right up your alley.

The Wilder Brothers Series:

Book 1: One Way Back to Me (Eli & Alexis)

Book 2: Always the One for Me (Evan & Kendall)

Book 3: The Path to You (Everett & Bethany)

Book 4: Coming Home for Us (Elijah & Maddie)

Book 5: Stay Here With Me (East & Lark)

Book 6: Finding the Road to Us (Elliot, Trace, and Sidney)

Book 7: Moments for You (Ridge & Aurora)

Book 7.5: A Wilder Wedding (Amos & Naomi)

Book 8: Forever For Us (Wyatt & Ava)

Book 9: Pieces of Me (Gabriel & Briar)

Book 10: Endlessly Yours (Brooks & Rory)

NEXT IN THE WILDER BROTHERS SERIES:
Brooks and Rory fix a mistake in Endlessly Yours.

IF YOU'D LIKE TO READ A BONUS SCENE:
CHECK OUT THIS SPECIAL EPILOGUE!

If you want to make sure you know what's coming next from me, you can sign up for my newsletter at www. CarrieAnnRyan.com; follow me on twitter at @CarrieAnnRyan, or like my Facebook page. I also have a Facebook Fan Club where we have trivia, chats, and other goodies. You guys are the reason I get to do what I do and I thank you.

Make sure you're signed up for my MAILING LIST so you can know when the next releases are available as well as find giveaways and FREE READS.

Happy Reading!

ACKNOWLEDGMENTS

The number of times I nearly rewrote the book in its entirety makes me laugh. In order to write Gabriel and Briar's story, I had to open up a few wounds I wasn't ready for and frankly, the characters weren't ready for. But I'm so so happy with their final HEA.

And I couldn't have done it without so many people!

Thank you to Amy, Brandi, and Fedora for your edits, comments, and ears as I ranted about these two characters haha.

Thank you one more time to Brandi for reading my random texts about certain aspects of this book neither one of wanted until we realized it NEEDED to happen haha.

Milk & Honey - Lauren, Ann, Ashley, Classy, and all of Team Carrie Ann. THANK YOU for bringing joy back into my world. I know I am cared for and able to focus on writing because of you.

Mom — I love you and thank you for joining Team Carrie Ann. Our chats while working at the house are some of my favorite points of writing a book.

Thank you to Emma Wilder for being the true Wilder of this group. You know my characters more than me sometimes and finding the right voices is so important.

And on that note, thank you Samantha Cook and Aiden Snow for bringing Gabriel and Briar to life. Your voices were meant for these two and I am so happy with how it turned out!

Thank you Jaycee for this amazing covers and Wander for your image. Y'all bring the Wilders out in force and I am in love with them!

Thank you R, S, and K for doing what you do and reminding me that I'm not alone in this endeavor.

Thank you to the Belles Besties—Tina, Kelli, Harlene, and Faith! Our text chat is nearing two years right now and it brings me life and book love!

Emily and Tina - our chat group is a little intense and I am sorry for talking so much but OMG I love us. Though we should probably nap at some point. Y'all helped bring this book to life and I am so happy to know you.

Alecia, darling, thank you for your push and drive and for introducing me to Bradley. I mean...I couldn't focus without you and our bike rides.

And thank you to so many more on Team Carrie Ann. This book is shaped by all of you.

And Dear Reader: This book is for you. Always.
~Carrie Ann

ALSO FROM CARRIE
ANN RYAN

The Wilder Brothers Series:

Book 1: One Way Back to Me (Eli & Alexis)

Book 2: Always the One for Me (Evan & Kendall)

Book 3: The Path to You (Everett & Bethany)

Book 4: Coming Home for Us (Elijah & Maddie)

Book 5: Stay Here With Me (East & Lark)

Book 6: Finding the Road to Us (Elliot, Trace, and Sidney)

Book 7: Moments for You (Ridge & Aurora)

Book 7.5: A Wilder Wedding (Amos & Naomi)

Book 8: Forever For Us (Wyatt & Ava)

Book 9: Pieces of Me (Gabriel & Briar)

Book 10: Endlessly Yours (Brooks & Rory)

The Cage Family

Book 1: The Forever Rule (Aston & Blakely)

Book 2: An Unexpected Everything (Isabella & Weston)

Book 3: If You Were Mine (Dorian & Harper)

The First Time Series:

Book 1: Good Time Boyfriend (Heath & Devney)

Book 2: Last Minute Fiancé (Luca & Addison)

Book 3: Second Chance Husband (August & Paisley)

Montgomery Ink Denver:

Book 0.5: Ink Inspired (Shep & Shea)

Book 0.6: <u>Ink Reunited</u> (Sassy, Rare, and Ian)

Book 1: <u>Delicate Ink</u> (Austin & Sierra)

Book 1.5: <u>Forever Ink</u> (Callie & Morgan)

Book 2: <u>Tempting Boundaries</u> (Decker and Miranda)

Book 3: <u>Harder than Words</u> (Meghan & Luc)

Book 3.5: <u>Finally Found You</u> (Mason & Presley)

Book 4: <u>Written in Ink</u> (Griffin & Autumn)

Book 4.5: <u>Hidden Ink</u> (Hailey & Sloane)

Book 5: <u>Ink Enduring</u> (Maya, Jake, and Border)

Book 6: <u>Ink Exposed</u> (Alex & Tabby)

Book 6.5: <u>Adoring Ink</u> (Holly & Brody)

Book 6.6: <u>Love, Honor, & Ink</u> (Arianna & Harper)

Book 7: <u>Inked Expressions</u> (Storm & Everly)

Book 7.3: <u>Dropout</u> (Grayson & Kate)

Book 7.5: <u>Executive Ink</u> (Jax & Ashlynn)

Book 8: <u>Inked Memories</u> (Wes & Jillian)

Book 8.5: <u>Inked Nights</u> (Derek & Olivia)

Book 8.7: <u>Second Chance Ink</u> (Brandon & Lauren)

Book 8.5: Montgomery Midnight Kisses (Alex & Tabby Bonus(

Bonus: Inked Kingdom (Stone & Sarina)

Montgomery Ink: Colorado Springs

Book 1: Fallen Ink (Adrienne & Mace)

Book 2: Restless Ink (Thea & Dimitri)

Book 2.5: Ashes to Ink (Abby & Ryan)

Book 3: Jagged Ink (Roxie & Carter)

Book 3.5: Ink by Numbers (Landon & Kaylee)

The Montgomery Ink: Boulder Series:
Book 1: Wrapped in Ink (Liam & Arden)
Book 2: Sated in Ink (Ethan, Lincoln, and Holland)
Book 3: Embraced in Ink (Bristol & Marcus)
Book 3: Moments in Ink (Zia & Meredith)
Book 4: Seduced in Ink (Aaron & Madison)
Book 4.5: Captured in Ink (Julia, Ronin, & Kincaid)
Book 4.7: Inked Fantasy (Secret ??)
Book 4.8: A Very Montgomery Christmas (The Entire Boulder Family)

The Montgomery Ink: Fort Collins Series:
Book 1: Inked Persuasion (Jacob & Annabelle)
Book 2: Inked Obsession (Beckett & Eliza)
Book 3: Inked Devotion (Benjamin & Brenna)
Book 3.5: Nothing But Ink (Clay & Riggs)
Book 4: Inked Craving (Lee & Paige)
Book 5: Inked Temptation (Archer & Killian)

The Promise Me Series:
Book 1: Forever Only Once (Cross & Hazel)
Book 2: From That Moment (Prior & Paris)
Book 3: Far From Destined (Macon & Dakota)
Book 4: From Our First (Nate & Myra)

The Whiskey and Lies Series:

Book 1: <u>Whiskey Secrets</u> (Dare & Kenzie)

Book 2: <u>Whiskey Reveals</u> (Fox & Melody)

Book 3: <u>Whiskey Undone</u> (Loch & Ainsley)

The Gallagher Brothers Series:

Book 1: <u>Love Restored</u> (Graham & Blake)

Book 2: <u>Passion Restored</u> (Owen & Liz)

Book 3: <u>Hope Restored</u> (Murphy & Tessa)

The Less Than Series:

Book 1: Breathless With Her (Devin & Erin)

Book 2: Reckless With You (Tucker & Amelia)

Book 3: Shameless With Him (Caleb & Zoey)

The Fractured Connections Series:

Book 1: Breaking Without You (Cameron & Violet)

Book 2: Shouldn't Have You (Brendon & Harmony)

Book 3: Falling With You (Aiden & Sienna)

Book 4: Taken With You (Beckham & Meadow)

The On My Own Series:

Book 0.5: My First Glance

Book 1: My One Night (Dillon & Elise)

Book 2: My Rebound (Pacey & Mackenzie)

Book 3: My Next Play (Miles & Nessa)

Book 4: My Bad Decisions (Tanner & Natalie)

The Ravenwood Coven Series:
Book 1: Dawn Unearthed

Book 2: Dusk Unveiled

Book 3: Evernight Unleashed

The Aspen Pack Series:
Book 1: Etched in Honor

Book 2: Hunted in Darkness

Book 3: Mated in Chaos

Book 4: Harbored in Silence

Book 5: Marked in Flames

The Talon Pack:
Book 1: Tattered Loyalties

Book 2: An Alpha's Choice

Book 3: Mated in Mist

Book 4: Wolf Betrayed

Book 5: Fractured Silence

Book 6: Destiny Disgraced

Book 7: Eternal Mourning

Book 8: Strength Enduring

Book 9: Forever Broken

Book 10: Mated in Darkness

Book 11: Fated in Winter

Redwood Pack Series:
Book 1: An Alpha's Path

Book 2: <u>A Taste for a Mate</u>

Book 3: <u>Trinity Bound</u>

Book 3.5: <u>A Night Away</u>

Book 4: <u>Enforcer's Redemption</u>

Book 4.5: <u>Blurred Expectations</u>

Book 4.7: <u>Forgiveness</u>

Book 5: <u>Shattered Emotions</u>

Book 6: <u>Hidden Destiny</u>

Book 6.5: <u>A Beta's Haven</u>

Book 7: <u>Fighting Fate</u>

Book 7.5: <u>Loving the Omega</u>

Book 7.7: <u>The Hunted Heart</u>

Book 8: <u>Wicked Wolf</u>

The Elements of Five Series:

Book 1: From Breath and Ruin

Book 2: From Flame and Ash

Book 3: From Spirit and Binding

Book 4: From Shadow and Silence

Dante's Circle Series:

Book 1: <u>Dust of My Wings</u>

Book 2: <u>Her Warriors' Three Wishes</u>

Book 3: <u>An Unlucky Moon</u>

Book 3.5: <u>His Choice</u>

Book 4: <u>Tangled Innocence</u>

Book 5: <u>Fierce Enchantment</u>

Book 6: <u>An Immortal's Song</u>

Book 7: <u>Prowled Darkness</u>

Book 8: Dante's Circle Reborn

Holiday, Montana Series:

Book 1: <u>Charmed Spirits</u>

Book 2: <u>Santa's Executive</u>

Book 3: <u>Finding Abigail</u>

Book 4: <u>Her Lucky Love</u>

Book 5: Dreams of Ivory

The Branded Pack Series:

(Written with Alexandra Ivy)

Book 1: <u>Stolen and Forgiven</u>

Book 2: <u>Abandoned and Unseen</u>

Book 3: <u>Buried and Shadowed</u>

ABOUT THE AUTHOR

Carrie Ann Ryan is the New York Times and USA Today bestselling author of contemporary, paranormal, and young adult romance. Her works include the Montgomery Ink, Redwood Pack, Fractured Connections, and Elements of Five series, which have sold over 3.0 million books worldwide. She started writing while in graduate school for her advanced degree in chemistry and hasn't stopped since. Carrie Ann has written over seventy-five novels and novellas with more in the works. When she's not losing herself in her emotional and action-packed worlds, she's reading as much as she can while wrangling her clowder of cats who have more followers than she does.

www.CarrieAnnRyan.com